SEASICK

SEASICK

KRISTIN CAST
& PINTIP DUNN

DELACORTE PRESS

Text copyright © 2023 by Kristin Cast and Pintip Dunn
Jacket photos used under license from Shutterstock

All rights reserved. Published in the United States by Delacorte Press, an imprint of Random House Children's Books, a division of Penguin Random House LLC, New York.

Delacorte Press is a registered trademark and the colophon is a trademark of Penguin Random House LLC.

Visit us on the Web! GetUnderlined.com

Educators and librarians, for a variety of teaching tools, visit us at RHTeachersLibrarians.com

Library of Congress Cataloging-in-Publication Data is available upon request.
ISBN 978-0-593-64930-5 (trade) — ISBN 978-0-593-64931-2 (lib. bdg.) — ISBN 978-0-593-64932-9 (ebook)

The text of this book is set in 12-point Adobe Caslon.
Interior design by Ken Crossland

Printed in the United States of America
10 9 8 7 6 5 4 3 2 1
First Edition

To Steven: I finally listened to you.

—K.C.

To my good luck charm: Adisai,
a boy of many nicknames.

—P.D.

PROLOGUE

PROLOGUE

The ax skewered the man's chest, its heavy, sharp metal blade buried in his blood-soaked T-shirt. Even from across the deck, with the steady rain plastering her hair against her cheeks, the girl smelled the coppery scent mixed with a putrid stench that made her stomach clench.

The bodies.

She pressed the back of her hand to her mouth and bit down hard. The smell came from the murdered corpses on nearly every level of the megayacht.

And blood. There was so much blood. From the handle of the ax to the splatter across the once-pristine chaise longues. From the girl's bloody palms to the pool of crimson that stained the deck.

The girl swayed as if the *Seraphina* were tipping, sinking, drowning them. Black patches dotted her vision and acid surged up her throat, burning the back of her tongue.

She didn't want to do this. She'd rather free dive with the sharks that lurked in the deep Atlantic waters, lured by the stink of death.

But it had to be done.

Shakily, she lowered herself to the deck and began to crawl toward the body. The night sky rumbled, and the wood dug into her palms. She took a tiny sip of air—and immediately gagged. The sour rot of flesh was now *inside* her.

Get it together, she ordered herself, swiping the punishing raindrops from her eyes. *This is your new reality.*

She arrived at the body. She wouldn't—*couldn't*—call it by name, by anything that was once alive. Clenching her teeth, she wrapped her hands around the wooden ax handle, slick with rain and blood. Her arms flexed. Her muscles bunched. And then she yanked with every last cell in her being.

The ax dislodged with a final gush of blood, and she fell back against the teakwood deck, banging her head. Lightning flashed just as bursts of pain exploded in her eyes—but she was okay. In fact, she was more than okay.

As the body count grew, so did her need for a weapon. The ax was essential. Or she would be next.

EIGHTEEN HOURS
EARLIER . . .

ONE

NAYA

8:46 A.M.

Naya Morgan was going to make everything fit into her suitcase if it was the last thing she did. She dropped to her knees, pinning down the top of the overflowing bag. Whoever wrote the email saying she could only bring one carry-on bag clearly did not understand how many outfits were needed for a weeklong trip to Bermuda. Besides the scheduled meals and team-building activities, who knew what they were going to do? The one thing she did know for sure was that each of her friends, the trendsetters of Yatesville, would be dressed to kill.

Her mom and stepdad's tax bracket meant she would never actually be able to compete with the off-the-runway fashions of her peers, but she had to try. She had no plans to continue to be friends with her haughty group beyond this trip, but she didn't want to be judged or ridiculed while on the boat, either.

So Naya had packed an ensemble (and a backup) for every possible situation, along with a copy of *Sailing in Style*—the guide she'd found in the ninety-nine-cent bin of her favorite indie bookstore—two family-sized boxes of cereal, and enough beef jerky to feed a small army. Some would call it *overprepared*. She called it *necessary*. After all, being "overprepared" was one of the reasons she'd received a coveted Yates Society scholarship and a place on the megayacht that would take her on the celebratory cruise of a lifetime. Not only had each of this year's inductees graduated high school—though some lacked Naya's academic achievement awards—but they'd also made it through the arduous, months-long selection process and were being rewarded with this amazing adventure.

Naya's forehead creased and a wash of embarrassment and anger heated her cheeks as she remembered the *Rumor Has It* article that had clearly been aimed at her acceptance into the society.

"Diversity inductee," she grumbled.

Well, this diversity inductee had maintained a high GPA throughout high school, volunteered with different disaster relief programs, had been the president of the Pre-Med Club, and was a few months away from attending Johns Hopkins with the goal of one day becoming the chief of ER with a career longer than the existence of *Grey's Anatomy*.

Naya threw her weight against her suitcase and zipped it closed before collapsing onto her back and stretching her arms overhead in triumph.

A wet nose nudged her elbow, and she rolled onto her stomach, smiling as Smoochie's long tail shook his even longer

Twinkie-shaped body. He rubbed against her like a cat, his wiry, terrier-mix fur tickling her arm.

She kissed the golden-white scruff on the top of his head, ignoring his cranky growl of protest.

"I'll be back soon, Smoochie." She continued to scratch behind his ears, refusing to tell him that she would be off to college and gone for good by the end of the summer.

Naya's phone trilled and she reached up, grabbing it from her floral duvet.

Taylor.

Naya jumped to her feet and ran to her vanity. She had to do a once-over before answering the video call from her best friend. She would sooner die than look a complete mess. Her friends were perfect. So she had to be, too.

Flecks of pink paint drifted to the floor as she dropped into the chair and swiped her flat iron off the plate she used to keep from further scorching the garage-sale vanity she'd painted to match her floral wallpaper. The final video call ring sounded while she smoothed the flat iron through the baby hairs curling around her temples. Satisfied every last whorl had been straightened and she had no petal-pink gloss on her teeth, Naya took a breath and redialed.

Taylor answered on the first ring. "Hey, slut!" she chimed, leaning back against a blue-and-white-striped chaise, its attached umbrella shading her from the bright Miami sun, the steady whoosh of ocean waves crashing in the distance.

Naya combed her fingers through her brown locks, wincing when they caught in her damaged ends. She needed a trim. "I thought we weren't saying that anymore."

Taylor frowned, her perfectly contoured lips tilting into a

disapproving glower. "Slut-shaming requires actual insertion, and you haven't graduated past cunnilingus."

Naya's cheeks flamed at the word choice, two red spots burning against her light-brown skin.

"That reminds me!" Taylor sat up a little straighter. "You know what I just read?"

Naya's eyes widened, and she pulled up her browser. She knew exactly what Taylor was talking about. Even though they'd left high school behind, it was still all anyone talked about online, but she'd been so preoccupied packing she hadn't even checked the site.

Rumor Has It . . . appeared on the screen in a perfect hand-lettered cursive font fit for the royalty Everly Fuller thought she belonged to. Before Naya could scan the latest entry in her classmate's gossip rag, Taylor cleared her throat and began reading:

"Guess who scored five TDs last Friday? Don't blame you if you're confused. The former 'star'"—she held up a hand and put air quotes around the word—"quarterback was never very good at hitting his mark. Guess he's prepping himself for college by scoring . . . lying down. But what will his high school sweetheart do when she finds out he's playing her? Well, if she needs a shoulder to cry on, you know where to find me. Ever yours, Everly."

Naya blinked and skimmed the post. "Gemma . . . ," she whispered. "This is about Gemma Hasting. She's going to be heartbroken." Naya brought Taylor's face back to full screen. "She and Cole are going to Stanford together in the fall. They're road-tripping there and everything."

Taylor shrugged. "One of the many reasons high school

flings should be left behind along with the rest of high school."

"They're in love," Naya countered.

"Oh, dear, sweet, naive Naya . . ." Taylor sighed and left the shade of the umbrella, her phone bobbing slightly as she headed away from the palm trees and toward the water.

With her peachy skin and long blond hair, Taylor looked like most of the people in their hometown of Yatesville, Oklahoma, a wealthy suburb of Tulsa that had gushed from the earth like the oil that ran through each family's blood. Unlike Naya, whose light-brown skin and decidedly non–old money origins made her a beacon of *otherness,* Taylor belonged.

Naya frowned. Believing in love didn't make her naive. Her glance fell on the framed photo Étienne had given her for their sixth-month anniversary—prom night, and it had been perfect. *He* had been perfect. And then he'd left.

She shook her head.

No more crying.

"So." Naya cleared her throat and swallowed her sadness. "How does Everly get her hands on these *rumors?*" She emphasized the last word, knowing full well every rumor had proved to be fact.

"Doubt we'll ever know." Taylor lifted one sun-kissed shoulder. "A good reporter never reveals her source."

And in Naya's opinion, Everly Fuller was the best. She'd been running her gossipy Lady Whistledown–style online column long before anyone watched *Bridgerton.*

Smoochie's collar jingled as he jumped onto the bed and burrowed under the unmade covers.

"When do you get here?" Taylor asked, a seagull's cry echoing from her end of the call.

Naya unplugged her flat iron and sighed at her luggage. There was no possible way she could stuff another thing into her bag. "I land in Miami around one, then I'll head straight to the marina. I'm super excited to see the boat."

"I think you mean mega*yacht*." A gust of wind twirled Taylor's hair, giving it an even beachier wave. "And this is what *I'm* super excited for you to see." She flipped the screen, and Naya was greeted by an expanse of glittering ocean that blended into a cornflower-blue sky.

Naya's cheeks plumped with a smile. "I cannot wait to see the ocean in person."

Taylor zoomed in on the whitecaps as they rolled onto shore in glimmering lines of foam. "It's gorgeous. I have no idea why our parents insist on living in a landlocked state."

Money.

Naya bit her bottom lip. Not having any was something Taylor and her group of friends would never understand. It was the reason she was currently admiring the sea from miles away instead of beside her best friend, who could afford to fly to Miami two days before their yacht was due to leave. It was the reason the Yates scholarship and its accompanying celebratory trip would change Naya's life forever.

Naya set her flat iron on top of her bulging bag and dropped down onto her bed next to Smoochie and his pile of covers. "Is everyone else there?"

The image bobbed and Taylor's shoes made a soft *flip-flop* in the sand as she headed closer to the group and their row of chaise longues, empty except for one, set up a few feet from the water.

"Wave to Naya!" she cheered, thrusting the phone at her uninterested peers.

Amelia turned, her smooth, flipped chestnut-brown bob unmoving, her Forbidden Love lilac-colored lips lifting in a smile. "On your way yet?" Before Naya could answer, a football crashed into the open cooler beside Amelia. She squealed as ice water sprayed her lavender sundress.

"Serves her right," Taylor mumbled. "She's dressed like someone's grandma."

Gabe charged into view, his bare shoulders streaked with sunscreen. "Shit. Sorry, Amelia." He brushed a hand through his dark curls as he bent and picked up the wet football. "Hey, Naya." He offered a quick wave before running back to Brett and Finn, who stood waiting in the distance, ankle deep in the lapping waters of the ocean.

"Finn!" Taylor shouted. "Say hi to Naya!"

The tall blond offered a quick wave before jumping into the air to make a catch.

"Speaking of Finn . . . ," Naya began, returning the gesture. "Weren't you just saying that high school flings need to stay in high school?"

Taylor panned from one end of their section of beach to the other. "Finn isn't a fling, Naya," she said, annoyance barbing her voice. "He's, like, completely obsessed with me."

Naya pursed her lips. Leave it to Taylor to downplay her own feelings.

"Where's Everly?" Naya asked, digging her toes into the tight weave of her carpet.

"Who knows? Probably off pouting because she's not getting enough attention." Taylor bent over to pull a drink from the cooler. "Hurry up and get here." She pooched her bottom lip and slid the silver-and-red can into a koozie. "You know I hate being alone."

"You're not alone so . . ." Naya motioned as best she could to Amelia, Gabe, Finn, and Brett, each getting smaller as Taylor headed back to her umbrella.

The Coke can let out a sharp *hiss* when Taylor cracked the top. "It's not the same without you." She took a sip, and her lipstick didn't smudge. "Last night I suggested we skinny-dip. Something you would have totally been up for."

Naya's stomach squeezed. Taylor was fearless and bold and spontaneous. She was a speedboat, hurtling toward a future of promise, and Naya was just trying to hold on.

"Amelia turned bright red, like, complete tomato. I mean, you'd think I'd just shit out a goat instead of showing my round ass." Taylor rolled her green eyes. "Besides, it was just the pool at the rental house. I mean, there's literally no one else there but us." She cocked her pointed chin. "Derek hasn't even shown up yet. Thank god."

Again, Naya's stomach clenched. "What is Amelia even thinking? I know she's eighteen, but he's so . . . teachery."

"And he cannot dress." Taylor shook her head and took another drink of her pop. "Someone should burn those hideous khaki cargo shorts."

Naya tilted her head. In her mental list of reasons their friend should definitely not be with their former math teaching assistant, Mr. Cunningham, ehm, *Derek,* his clothes hadn't even made the top ten.

"Daddy issues." Everly's voice floated to Naya before she saw her lithe, swanlike figure appear behind Taylor, her pearl-white cover-up blending with her skin, making her look like a rich Victorian ghost.

Naya winced but kept quiet as Taylor settled the back of her head against the lounger and stared up at the girl nobody liked but everyone wanted to be friends with.

Taylor's brow furrowed. "Love that you're gracing us with your presence, Ev."

"A tad late, but someone has to be responsible for making sure the truth's being told." Everly leaned down, examining her on-screen reflection. "And don't act like you have no idea what I'm talking about." She brushed her ash-blond hair from her thin shoulders, lobster red from the harsh rays of the Miami sun, and gathered it into the kind of sleek ponytail Naya had to spend hours to achieve. "You know some girls are always trying to replace Daddy."

Naya stiffened, her stomach dropping. Amelia's father was always traveling for "work," but she and Taylor shared a sorrow no one else in their class understood. The loss of their fathers had come quickly and at the exact same time.

Naya held her breath.

Whenever she thought about her father's death, she couldn't help but picture the helicopter as the twisted, smoking ball of steel they'd shown on every news channel throughout the Midwest. Her father had been in that mound of broken parts. He didn't have money like the majority of their town, but he'd indulged one time—taking a flying lesson from Taylor's dad—and it had killed them both.

There was a moral to the story in there somewhere, but Naya could never get past that harrowing image to figure out what it was.

At least she'd had Taylor's friendship. More than that, she'd had her sympathy, which didn't feel forced or patronizing.

The friends had helped stitch each other's wounds. They were bound forever, and Naya wouldn't have it any other way.

Taylor glanced at her best friend, her sharp gaze nearly burning a hole through the phone. "My father isn't off somewhere with his mistress, Everly," she said without glancing up. "He's fucking dead."

Everly thrust one thin, praying mantis arm into her woven Loewe tote and pulled out a bottle of sunscreen. "I'm talking about science. Like, real, actual facts, Tay."

"I'm sure there are zero actual facts to back up that claim," Naya said, her throat tight with emotion.

"Both of you need to calm down with the histrionics." Everly's cool smile was punctuated by the splurt of sunscreen as she squeezed the tube.

Naya's eyes burned. Everly was prodding a wound, hoping to get a juicy bit of gossip she could post in her column. *Rumor has it someone lost it on a Miami beach . . .*

"Okay, fine." Everly held up her sunscreen-streaked hands. "You're not ready for a psychology lesson."

"From you? Never. Thanks, though." Taylor got up, syrupy brown Coke sloshing from her can. "Oh, Ev, almost forgot to mention that your journalism nemesis is coming on our little trip."

"Yana?" Everly asked.

Naya had done an excellent job of avoiding a face to face with Yana Bunpraserit throughout high school and was hoping to get out of Yatesville with her streak intact. After all these years, she'd gotten good at keeping her guilt packed away. Well, unless it was February 17—Yana's birthday—or she caught a glimpse of her in the hall or read one of her articles in the *Yatesville Sun* or thought about her for even a moment.

Like now . . .

"Winner of the coveted *Yatesville Sun*'s summer internship herself." Taylor nodded, her green eyes gleaming as she stared at Everly. "Didn't you apply for the same position?"

"And I would have gotten it if it hadn't been for the shady shit Yana was willing to do," Everly snapped.

Ironic coming directly from the creator of *Rumor Has It*.

Naya cocked her chin. "What shady dealings could Yana possibly get up to?"

"Guess you'll have to wait and see." Everly patted her tote, which no doubt held her trusty laptop. She never left home without it. "Now if you'll excuse me, I have to finish my latest column. Lots of secrets flying around with this group. Luckily, I—and only I—know exactly where to find them." She flashed her straight, veneered smile and sauntered away.

"She's horrible," Naya whispered, not completely convinced Everly was out of earshot.

"Such a dick." Taylor took a long swig, downing the rest of the pop. "Being her friend is almost impossible sometimes."

This time, Naya stayed quiet. She'd had the *why are you friends with her* conversation, mixed with the *if everyone stopped talking to her, her column would stop, too* reasoning, with Taylor so many times that it was officially a dead horse.

"Oh!" Taylor's thick brows raised, and Naya could envision her excitement lifting her onto her toes. "Speaking of friends—and the fact that I am the absolute best one in the whole entire world—I have a couple surprises for you!"

Naya's cheeks heated. Gifts from Taylor were great, extraordinary even. They were items Naya's mom and stepdad could never afford, like electric water sledding and scuba diving lessons (even though they'd received their certifications in a lake instead of the ocean), but the presents were also another neon arrow pointing to Naya's otherness. She didn't look like the rest of them *or* have her own limitless credit card.

"You shouldn't have gotten me anything."

"I should, I could, and so I did." Taylor nodded defiantly. "Plus, this trip is a huge deal. We're Yates Society inductees, Naya! Our futures are now set. There's no going back." Her lips quirked. "You'll thank me for your first surprise when you see it this afternoon."

A wave of vanilla drifted into Naya's room as her mom knocked on the open door.

"Hey, I have to go, Taylor. I'll see you soon."

"Bye, Mrs. Morgan!" Taylor shouted. "I'll take care of Naya! Promise."

Naya angled the screen in her mom's direction, and they waved their goodbyes, before she ended the call and dropped her phone onto her bed. Smoochie yipped when it landed on him.

"Sorry, Smoochie," Naya said, pulling the pastel-pink duvet back to reveal his scruffy, copper-colored fur, long nose, and hazel eyes.

Rose sat on the edge of the bed and pulled the blanket-wrapped Smoochie onto her lap. "He is very good at burrowing." She kissed the top of his head, leaving a dark-plum lipstick print on his fur. "Ready to go?" she asked, her amber gaze lifting to meet Naya's. "I want to make sure you're there in time to check your bag."

"Almost." Naya slid off the bed and plucked her flat iron from her swollen luggage.

"Life will be easier if you leave it behind," Rose said with a laugh as Naya tried to cram the tool into the bag. "Your curls are beautiful."

Naya jammed the flat iron into the suitcase and grunted as she sat on top to rezip it. "I like my hair better straight."

Rose's smile didn't quite reach her eyes as she touched the ends of her own tight curls.

A lump hardened in the back of Naya's throat. Her mom was beautiful. She'd given Naya her heart-shaped face, round chin, and thick eyelashes, but her soft slopes, full curves, and the golden irises that blazed like stars against her deep-brown skin were completely Rose Morgan.

"Mom—"

Rose shook her head, and another warm gust of vanilla swirled past Naya. "Baby, explore different looks with your hair, your makeup. Just promise me you won't get a tattoo until you're grown."

"Only four days and"—Naya checked her phone—"seven hours and thirteen minutes until I'm legal."

Smoochie yawned and fixed his heavy-lidded gaze on Rose as she scratched the scruffy fur between his ears. "I mean *grown* grown—a *real* adult."

Naya pinned one hand to her hip. "And how old is a *real adult*?"

Keys jingled as her stepdad leaned against the doorframe, spinning them around his pointer finger. "Thirty."

Rose punctuated his quip with a laugh.

Naya sighed and rolled her eyes, completely aware of the way the gesture highlighted her seventeen-year-oldness, before grabbing the handle of her bag and righting its wheels.

"I got it," Marcus said, dropping the keys into the pocket of his basketball shorts.

"I know neither of you are super excited about me going on this trip, but—"

Rose took Naya's free hand in hers. "It's not that I'm not excited for you. I'm happy you have this opportunity. Your dad and I have always only wanted what's best for you. Marcus, too." She squeezed her daughter's hand, the creasing corners of her round eyes the only sign of her forty-four years.

Marcus draped his arm over Naya's shoulder and pulled her against him. "We are so proud of you."

Another squeeze of Naya's hand from Mom. "You know that, right?"

Naya returned her mother's grin, understanding what was going unsaid. Rose didn't want her to get caught up in the privileges that the Yates and countless other well-to-do families in Yatesville were afforded because of their wealth and skin color. Even though Naya wasn't rich, there was a part of her, a significant part, a fifty percent part, that belonged to people like the Yates whose white ancestors had sailed boats across the sea. But those boats had been filled with slaves— African people whose pain had built this country and whose strength and hope lit her mother's and Marcus's dark skin from within.

"I love you guys." Naya closed her eyes and said a silent *I love you* to the memory of her father, who had been nothing like the other elitist white families in town.

Rose slid Smoochie off her lap and stood, wrapping one arm around her daughter and the other around Marcus.

"We love you, too," they said in unison.

Her mom kissed her cheek and pressed her curls against Naya's straightened hair. "I cannot wait for your adventure to begin."

Rumor Has It . . .

This is it. *The* day. The one circled on my calendar next to a big red kissy mark. (Lipstick courtesy of Killer Lips. See discount code below!)

This year's Yates Society inductees have been announced! Drumroll, please . . .

Of course, yours truly is at the top of the list.

Keeping me company are some of Yatesville High's best, brightest, most bee-you-tiful students.

That is, except for one . . .

She's sorta pretty.

Friends with the right people.

Yet she comes from a more or less underprivileged background.

You might be wondering *how* she ever got invited to join such a prestigious, exclusive society.

The answer is simple: diversity inductee.

Times are changing.

Readers, I'd say I'll miss ya while I'm cruisin' the deep blue sea to pink sandy beaches—but I never lie.

Ever yours,
Everly

Code: **dyingforyou20**

TWO

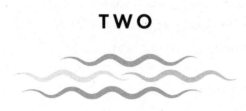

YANA

8:52 A.M.

Puke was so gross.

There was nothing sexy about it. Nothing beneficial or even remotely convenient. For Yana Bunpraserit, however, it was an ordinary facet of life. And that meant she dealt with vomit the way she dealt with everything else—calmly, efficiently, and with as little drama as possible.

"Just don't go," her little brother, Adisorn, called through the closed bathroom door. "You already have a full ride to Northwestern. What's the point of you joining this society?"

Yana flushed the toilet, which got rid of the sick with a single push. Too bad the upcoming debacle of a cruise couldn't be handled as easily.

"We've been over this." She swished bright-green liquid around her mouth, the antiseptic burning her tongue. And then she spat it out and gargled again. "I'm going. The scoop of the year might be on that yacht."

The text message had arrived from an unknown number a week ago. It flashed through her mind now, like it had been doing, oh, every ten minutes or so.

> **Unknown:** Only you can expose the cheating ring. Ever Yours won't report this rumor for one simple reason: it involves her.

The text obviously referred to Everly Fuller, the spoiled princess who bizarrely believed that her gossip column could somehow compete with their school newspaper, where Yana had just finished her reign as editor-in-chief. *Rumor Has It* had more readers, sure. (Tenfold more, if Yana was being honest.) But Everly only posted salacious gossip and unsubstantiated rumors, nothing like the hard-hitting news of the *Viking Shield*, which delved into real topics such as book censorship in libraries, hate crimes in the halls, and the need for gender-neutral bathrooms.

Clearly, the publisher of the local newspaper, the *Yatesville Sun*, agreed. It was Yana who was given an internship as a junior reporter at this local arm of an award-winning national news conglomerate, not Everly. Yana, who was on her way to becoming a top-notch journalist via Northwestern. Yana, who would wow her publisher and rock her whole town with an exposé on Yatesville's most elite teenagers.

She just had to embark on this cruise from hell to get it.

"You're throwing up," her brother pointed out. "Is an article really worth it?"

Yana paused with her hand on the doorknob. Was it? She puked when she was stressed. It used to be a serious problem. Her classmates in middle school had bullied her mercilessly.

But years of therapy had helped her control the unfortunate habit, and it had been ages since anyone had witnessed her regurgitating.

This story—and these people—pushed her buttons. But that only made her more determined.

"Yes," she said firmly as she walked into her bedroom. "It is."

Adisorn was lying on her twin bed, his socked feet propped against the wall. Good thing their Thai family didn't wear shoes in the house, or Yana would have muddy prints tracking across the cheerful yellow stripes of her wallpaper.

Twin feelings of annoyance and tenderness rushed through her. She loved her brother, two years younger at sixteen but many inches taller. Sometimes, it felt like he was the only one who got her, who could see through her crisp, sensible exterior to the uncertain girl underneath. Oh, she had a handful of friends, similarly studious types from the school paper. But she hadn't had a true confidant since Naya. So, she and Ady it was. The two of them against the rest of the world, she often felt but never said out loud.

Instead, she crossed the room and rubbed his buzzed head.

He knocked her hand away. "Stop. I'm not a little kid anymore."

"Really?" she teased. "You mean, you no longer ask the barber to give you fuzzy hair?" He had been twelve and had no idea how to ask for a buzz cut.

He sat up, his ridiculously large feet thunking onto the ratty rug. "Lots of guys find my haircut plenty attractive."

"Probably because it reminds them of a bristle pad. It's like a car accident—grotesque but you can't look away."

Ady grabbed Yana's favorite teal sarong out of her open duffel bag and tossed it across the room. Shrieking, she tried—and failed—to catch it.

But she wasn't mad. Not really. She was just happy to see her brother smiling again.

Last year, Ady had come out to their parents, to his friends. Everyone was . . . trying? Yana guessed that was the best word.

In an attempt to relate, Papa had bought enough books on sexuality to line an entire shelf, while Mama was on a quest to implement a gender-neutral term of respect in Thai, to be used in addition to the masculine *krub* and feminine *ka*. Their parents' relationship with her brother often felt forced as they adjusted.

Meanwhile, his friends had responded to his revelation with "cool" and "I'd cook you, one-on-one." And yet more than one of his basketball buddies had drifted away. All in all, it had been a crap sophomore year for him.

It was difficult enough to navigate their small Oklahoma town, being part of the only Thai family. Yana couldn't imagine how it would feel to be both a person of color *and* gay.

She did know, however, the heartbreak of losing a friend.

"Sorry I called your hair a bristle pad," she said lightly. "I'm just grumpy because I'm going to be stuck on a yacht with seven of my least favorite people."

"It won't be that bad," Ady ventured. "Naya will be there, right?"

Yana plastered on a smile, one as plastic as the rose and jasmine garlands they used when praying to the Buddha. "Naya and I haven't been friends for a long time. You know that."

"But she still cares about you. Why else would she drop

off those homemade snickerdoodles for your birthday every year?"

"Maybe 'cause her mom makes her?" Yana arched an eyebrow. "Or, I don't know, maybe she puts laxatives in them?" Just for Yana to experience torture from both ends.

Ady snorted. "I rescue them from the trash every year, and I haven't gotten sick once."

"Yeah, but you're a human garbage disposal."

"Better that than a rabbit obsessed with greens," he shot back.

"Oh, I *do* adore green food." Yana bobbed her head sarcastically. "Green M&M's. Green Popsicles. Green tea Pocky sticks."

"Next time it's my turn to cook dinner, I'll put Thai green chiles in your fried rice."

Yana hid a smile. If anyone could distract her from the lingering pain of losing her best friend, albeit years ago, it was her goofy brother.

So, Naya dropped off cookies every year. Judging from the way Ady scarfed them down, they probably even tasted decent. Her old friend had come a long way from the girl who had baked a coffee cake with Yana in the third grade by sticking the batter into the oven, mixing bowl and all. But who cared? Naya did nothing to stop the snide comments and microaggressions of the popular kids in her circle, who not so surprisingly were the other inductees of the exclusive Yates Society.

Yana swore, if Taylor Stewart mixed up Taiwan and Thailand one more time, she was going to throw a drink in the blond's face. How Naya could replace her—someone thoughtful, someone kind—with such a mean girl, Yana would never understand.

No wonder Yana acted so tough. Like nothing bothered her. She'd had to in order to survive.

"It's not just the guest list that gives me the ick, though," she said slowly. "Something about the society just feels off. . . ."

The Yates Society had been around for generations, and in addition to a full-ride scholarship to the college of your choice, it promised prestige, friendship, and connections for life. Of course, that was easy to do when the scholarship always went to the same type of students at Yatesville High, the founder's alma mater. The in crowd. President of the student council, captain of the swim team. Never to students like Yana.

She got good grades, granted, and she had been in charge of the school paper, but she didn't fit in with the bulk of her peers. She never had. Not when she made a spectacle of herself throwing up in the middle of the cafeteria. Not when she was teased for her full name, Yanaporn. (The other kids couldn't care less that the Thai pronunciation was "Yana*pawn*.") And not now, a high school graduate on the brink of moving on to her real life, instead of peaking at eighteen.

Stranger still was that her invitation to join the society had arrived a little over a week ago, just days before the anonymous text. As far as Yana knew, the rest of the inductees had been announced last month. No explanation was given for the late invite. Did one of the inductees drop out, to be filled by a candidate off the waitlist? Or was the society under some sort of pressure to diversify its membership beyond Naya? Or . . . was there some nefarious connection between her invitation and the text?

These questions sent her journalistic brain into overdrive. But that wasn't the only mystery that shrouded the society.

"We know almost nothing about the benefactor, Seraphina Yates. Since the society only picks inductees from Yatesville High, the logistics, itinerary, and invitation came from the school." Yana placed the sarong carefully back into her duffel bag, where it joined her trusty composition notebook and six of her favorite YA fantasy novels. She would need a multitude of worlds in which to escape if she was going to survive this trip. "Urban legend has it that Seraphina's this eccentric billionaire who never let her spouse or their children or their children's children take her last name. So no one outside of her family has any idea who this woman is. She never did interviews. And yet I'm supposed to go on an all-expenses-paid cruise on a yacht in order to 'celebrate' my achievements, knowing practically nothing about the hostess? Who does that?"

"Rich people." Ady smirked. "Besides, *my* parents don't seem worried."

"Well, *my* mama is thrilled, 'cause she thinks it means they've finally accepted us in this snobby-ass town." The use of the personal pronoun was a long-standing joke, since in fact they had the same parents.

"*My* papa would probably send us to an isolated log cabin in Murdertown, USA, if it meant people no longer looked down on us," he responded.

"I volunteer *my* brother to venture into the middle of nowhere." Yana could've kept the joke going, as they often did, but Ady's expression turned solemn.

"Ce Ce." That was his name for her when they were

kids. "Sister" had become "Sissy," which easily morphed into "Ce Ce."

"Tell me again." Her brother came to stand in front of her, giving her a direct view of his Adam's apple. He was so close that she got a whiff of his Irish Spring soap. "Did you accept this scholarship only because of the article? Or was it also because of . . . me?"

His voice cracked on the last word, and all of a sudden, she thought of the boy she'd held on her lap during circle time on his first day of preschool. Yana's heart both melted and hardened, if such a thing were possible.

"Nah." She did her best to scoff. "I won't even let you wash your dirty socks with my laundry. You think I'd give up an entire week for you?"

Lie. She'd do anything for Ady. She went to every single one of his basketball games without fail, even though she hated sports. She always let him have the last sakoo sai moo— tapioca dumplings filled with minced pork and peanuts— although they were her favorite, too. She even purchased an extra birthday or Mother's or Father's Day present every year for him to give to their parents, knowing he would forget.

His shoulders relaxed, however, as he bought her explanation. "I just thought maybe you heard me talking to my mama. . . ."

She gave a fake laugh. "Okay, *nong chai*." Little brother. That was her nickname for him, 'cause she liked to rub in the fact that she spoke better Thai. Thank you, hundreds upon hundreds of Thai dramas. "I've got more important things to do than eavesdrop on your conversations."

"Good to know." Adisorn shot her his slow, easy grin,

confident once more. He ambled to the door. "I have to get to basketball practice. Later, nerd."

"See you," she said, but her smile dropped as soon as he was gone.

Truth was, Yana had considered declining the invitation to join the society. Months ago, before she received the full ride to Northwestern, she'd applied on a whim; now, she no longer needed the scholarship. She had no desire to be another poster child for the society's "progressiveness." Having graduated high school, she was getting the hell out of Yatesville at the end of the summer—and never looking back.

Turning down the invitation would've been the proverbial middle finger she had always been too polite to raise, a final screw you to the people who had always made her feel less than, to the not-so-subtle comments that definitively placed her as other.

Then, the anonymous text about the cheating ring had arrived.

What was more, she'd been in the kitchen later that day, pouring herself a glass of iced tea made with condensed milk, when she'd overheard Ady and Mama's murmured conversation in the hallway.

"If Yana turns them down, will it ruin my chances?" her brother had asked.

Their family-run restaurant, Siam Garden, wasn't a roaring success. To drum up enough business, they had to serve not just Thai cuisine but also Chinese, Vietnamese, Japanese, and Korean (not that their clientele could tell the difference). Their parents could barely afford proper-fitting clothes for their children (especially at the rate that Ady grew), much less college tuition.

Ady wasn't academically inclined like Yana, but he was generally well-liked and a solid addition to the basketball team. He was popular enough that the selection committee, made up of members from Yatesville's most elite families, might just consider him worthy to receive an invitation in a couple of years, especially if Everly was right and *diversity inductee* was actually a thing now.

But not if his older sister snubbed the society. Not if she did what no one in the history of their town had ever done and turned down the coveted invitation.

Yana had had her brother's back from the moment he was born; she had cradled him on a pillow and lisped "Rock-a-Bye Baby." She wasn't about to stop now. So yeah, Adisorn was one of the reasons that Yana had accepted the society's invitation.

The people of Yatesville had taken so much from her, from her family. This cruise, for more than one reason, would give her the opportunity to take some power back.

Yana was going to get on that yacht and glide across a treacherous ocean with the very group of people from which she yearned to escape.

Even if it killed her.

May 3

Rumor Has It . . .

It's the eve of senior prom, and you know what's got me more excited than my slinky black dress, with the slit cut up to *here* and the back dipped down to *there?*

The look on one girl's face when she learns that a certain tall, dark, and handsome varsity athlete asked her to prom for one reason—and one reason alone.

Can I get a *bow chicka wow wow?*

I abhor toxic masculinity as much as the next gal, but he is *fathoms* out of her league, and she should've known it.

Especially 'cause I told her. And as you know, I never lie.

Ever yours,
Everly

THREE

YANA

2:45 P.M.

The *Seraphina* stretched white and gleaming along the turquoise blue water. At least three levels of dark tinted windows and sleek, curved edges rose above the sea. A steel-blue mermaid figurehead graced the prow. Her hair fluttered in metal waves against the sides of the ship, and her spiky crown just cleared the top of the railing.

Swallowing hard, Yana dropped her duffel bag to her feet as she paused to get her bearings. A couple stood at the prow, his-and-hers blond hair whipping in the wind.

Hair like that—a thousand different shades not from the sun—could only belong to two people. The girl turned, nestling her cheek against her boyfriend's clean-shaven face. Yep, Yatesville High School's favorite couple had arrived. Taylor Stewart and Finn Kelley. Wild laughter and a fair amount of acid clawed up Yana's throat. What would they do with their matching hair if they broke up? Chop it off?

She could see the headline now. *Yatesville High's It Girl Mourns Breakup—and Her Long Blond Locks.*

Deliberately, Yana breathed in for four counts and then out for four. She'd made it this far. Flown halfway across the country by herself 'cause her parents couldn't afford an extra ticket to drop her off in Miami. Got a rideshare to take her to the port. And she hadn't thrown up once. (If you didn't count the retching in the airplane's tiny toilet closet. Which she didn't. That was just motion sickness. Had to be.) She stood up for what was right, even if—*especially* if—the stance was unpopular. Her life's ambition was to make sure that the voices of the marginalized were heard. She wouldn't let this view—of the yacht or of her bullies—intimidate her now.

Yana half turned, trying to convince herself that she believed her own words, when a male voice—a real one—spoke over her shoulder. "Yana? What are you doing here?"

She looked up into Gabe Williams's playful brown eyes. His long, curly hair flopped onto his forehead, and he was grinning as though they shared an inside joke. As though a *they* existed.

She'd been fooled by that smile before, and she wasn't about to be fooled again.

"Same as you, I suppose," she said coolly, not an ounce of emotion betrayed. "I'm a Yates inductee."

"That's amazing!" Gabe exclaimed. "I had no idea, but I'm so glad." His voice was warm, engaging. One might think it genuine if one didn't know any better. "No one deserves the scholarship more."

Yana stiffened. Seriously? He had some nerve talking to her like this. Two months ago, they'd had a few whirlwind weeks of flirtation, culminating in a series of searing late-night kisses. For the first time in years, she'd let down her guard, just a little bit.

He'd invited her to prom. She had little use for flowers—all they did was die—but Gabe had been thoughtful enough to get her a wrist corsage, its petals made from the pages of her favorite book, *Pride and Prejudice*. ("No books were harmed in the process!" he'd hastened to reassure her.) Yet this kindness was negated by the dance itself, where he had proceeded to ignore Yana once she made it clear she wasn't going to sleep with him. To make matters worse, he'd spent the rest of the evening hanging out with her archnemesis, Everly.

This was why she had built her walls. Because people couldn't be trusted.

"Can you believe this boat?" Gabe continued. "It's more luxe than the yachts on *Below Deck*."

She blinked. "You watch *Below Deck*?"

"And the spin-offs." He lowered his voice conspiratorially. "You see, there was this cool girl I used to hang out with. And she was obsessed with reality shows. I guess you could say, she turned me onto their appeal."

Yana willed her face not to react. He was talking about her. She adored reality TV, especially if there was an element of competition. Her supersecret dream was to appear on *The Amazing Race*, not because she particularly wanted to be on-screen, but because it seemed like the most fun a person could have. Travel. Adventure. Different foods and cultures.

She was only sorry that she had confided this dream to Gabe.

Annoyed at herself for feeling anything, Yana focused on the salty sea air, the concrete beneath her tennis shoes, the sputter of engines. Anything but her roiling emotions.

Gabe was a jerk, unworthy of her time. Just because he was unfortunately attending the same college this coming September didn't change anything. Northwestern had a huge campus. With any luck, she wouldn't cross paths with him for four entire years.

A whistle blew and two people walked down the gangplank—sorry, the passerelle.

She recognized Mr. "Call Me Derek" Cunningham, the young student teacher in math who was also the advisor of the student council. By his side—surprise—was Amelia Brown, the former student council president. Those two were *tight*; Yana had often seen them roaming the school corridors together. The rumors had run rampant, especially after Everly's thinly veiled post about the couple in *Rumor Has It*.

Yana, however, refused to fuel the gossip by speculating about their relationship, even in her own head. Amelia had always been nice to her—the only girl in the popular crowd who never made fun of Yana. What was more, she was eighteen, and they had graduated, so Yana figured Amelia could date whomever she wanted. Derek wasn't even that old. Around twenty or twenty-one, Yana guessed, since he'd just finished his junior year in college.

She leaned over to pick up her duffel bag just as Gabe blurted, "Let me get that!"

They reached for the strap at the same time, their fingers colliding. Electricity zapped between them, and Yana yanked back her hand. Too late. Her skin tingled. She could still feel the warmth of his hand, the press of his flesh.

"Sorry," she said to cover up the flush of her cheeks.

But Gabe's grin only widened. "I'm not," he said softly.

He took a step closer, his black tennis shoes kissing her white ones.

His chest was *right* at eye level, hugged by a black cotton T-shirt. That was the only reason she looked. The only reason she remembered the last time they'd touched. His steady heartbeat, vibrating through her like tiny shock waves. His soft lips caressing hers, with just the right amount of tongue. Just the right amount of bite. Her hands curled against his hard, solid pecs, wanting but not daring to move. To wander.

No. *No.* She took two deliberate steps back. It didn't matter how appealing he was or how much she *had* liked him, past tense. He'd made his intentions patently clear. He'd embarrassed her. He didn't deserve another chance.

"How's Sandy?" Gabe blurted, before she could make up an excuse to get away.

Her hermit crab. The only pet she'd ever had, due to her brother's allergies. The one that the pet store owner had estimated would live six months. Well, Sandy was six years and counting, probably due to the spacious habitat that Yana had built from an aquarium, sand, and saltwater and freshwater pools, with plenty of humidity.

"The same," Yana said wryly. "He only comes out when no humans are present. The only sign of life is the scratching I sometimes hear in the middle of the night. So basically, I'm taking care of an invisible pet."

"Aloof pet owners unite!" Gabe said. "Nine times out of ten, Tangerine sticks her nose in the air and walks away when I try to cuddle her."

Not that his fluffy white cat's attitude made him love her any less. *"Who's a pretty girl?"* Yana had heard him coo to the cat more than once. *"Tangerine, that's who! The prettiest girl in the entire world!"*

It was adorable, Yana had to admit. But you want to know what wasn't adorable? Gabe acting aloof on prom night.

"I have to check in," she said, if not nicely, then at least civilly. "I'll catch you later." Hopefully not, though.

She marched away before he could respond, proud of herself for not getting sucked back into his charm. She'd rebuilt her walls, so thick that they were now impenetrable, and she wouldn't let them—any of them—hurt her again.

Yana approached the passerelle, but neither Derek nor Amelia noticed. Judging from the slump of Derek's shoulders and the stiffness of Amelia's spine, this was not the start of an epic vacation.

"*You* said we had to wait until after graduation." Derek's low voice was carried by the breeze. "Well, it's been six days. When are we—"

He broke off when Amelia nudged his shoulder, and they both turned to Yana, practiced smiles on their faces.

Yana forced her feet forward. Holy crap. Was Everly actually right? Were these two in a full-blown relationship? "Hello. Am I . . . er . . . interrupting?"

"Not at all," Derek said. With his sandy hair and nondescript glasses, he looked exactly like what he was: a bland teacher's assistant. Fairly strict, very boring. Yana wondered what Amelia saw in him, as a confidant or otherwise.

"We were just discussing the transition to next year's student council," Derek continued.

Amelia nodded, her sleek bob bouncing. Even her hair was perky. "Can't forget about Yatesville High simply because I graduated!"

"There's never been a student council president like her." Derek's tone warmed. "And there never will be again."

He placed his hand on Amelia's shoulder. She grimaced and moved away, covering up the expression with her ever-present smile.

Or had Yana just projected her own feelings onto Amelia?

The sun was glaring, and Yana remained a little woozy from the motion sickness she had suffered during the airplane ride. There was no telling how wild her imagination was running.

"Now, how can I help you, Yana?" Derek's brow creased. "You aren't coming on this trip, are you?" He riffled through the papers on his clipboard.

"Um, yeah, I am." Yana shifted her weight onto her other foot. How come no one knew she was supposed to be here? Had the invitation been sent by mistake? Had they overbooked like Spirit Airlines or something?

"Ah, here you are," Derek said as he reached the last piece of paper on his clipboard. "So weird that your info's not with the others'. This is for you." He handed her a black goody bag printed with the yacht's insignia. "Now, give me your phone."

Yana blinked. "My mother will worry if I don't text every few hours—"

"Hey, I don't like it, either," Derek said, jerking his head toward Amelia. "You should've heard this one whining about not being able to post to Insta. But I'm just following marching orders. The powers that be want you all to bond, and apparently they think electronic devices get in the way of that. So, I've been tasked with collecting the phones, and Mrs. Stewart, the society's liaison, will meet us in Bermuda with them."

"She says she's flying because she gets motion sickness." Amelia lowered her voice. "But between you and me, I think she can't be bothered with babysitting a bunch of teenagers."

Reluctantly, Yana handed over her cell in its glittery mint-green case. Thank goodness she had decided to bring physical books!

As Derek took the phone, the tattoo on the underside of his forearm flashed. Was that . . . a penguin? Chirping out the words *You Got This*?

She met Derek's gaze once more. He'd always been an NPC in her life, blending seamlessly with the classroom's blank walls. But maybe he, too, suffered with anxiety. Maybe he also dreamed of bigger and better.

Even as she puzzled over her new image of the teaching assistant, Amelia looped her arm through Yana's and hurried her up the passerelle.

"I'm thrilled you're here," the vivacious girl said. "Your calmness is exactly what we need to balance out the drama. We haven't left, and Everly and Taylor are already at each other's throats." She rolled her eyes. "Hey, want to be my roommate? Everly claimed the main cabin for herself, and Taylor and Naya are rooming together. So that leaves me. I promise I only take ten-minute showers, give or take an hour."

She grinned, and Yana couldn't help smiling back. "Sure," she said. Maybe not every inductee was as terrible as she thought. "By the way, congrats on Harvard. You must be so excited."

Amelia wrinkled her nose. "Maybe congratulate me when I don't flunk out?"

"Why would you flunk out?" Yana asked, mystified. In

addition to being student council president and founder of the robotics team, Amelia had been on the honor roll every semester since kindergarten.

Amelia sighed. "You won't believe how many tutors I've had. One for calculus, one for physics, two to help me run the robotics team. I've got a writing coach who basically wrote my application essays. Another expert to 'brand' me so that I'd be attractive to colleges. My parents won't give it a rest. They just won't accept that I'm naturally a B student." She shook her head. "I don't know how they see this working out long term. I mean, are they going to hire tutors for me when I'm a high-powered attorney? Maybe I'd be doing all of us a favor if I actually did fail."

Yana blinked. This was the first crack she'd ever seen in Amelia's polished facade.

"Enough about me. I tend to be an oversharer," Amelia rushed on. "You smell absolutely divine. What are you wearing? Jo Malone's Orange Blossom?"

Um. Yana didn't have a clue who Jo Malone was. Perfume might be the one and only extravagance to her no-frills self-care routine—T-shirts, denim shorts, and high ponytail for the win!—but she only indulged herself by picking up samples at the fragrance "counter" of the local superstore.

"Doesn't matter who it is," Amelia continued as they entered the lounge, which was outfitted with gold-trimmed armchairs, silk throw pillows, and a wet bar. "Fair warning: I'm totally stealing your scent this weekend. Not that I have anyone to impress."

"Oh, I thought you and—" Yana clamped her mouth shut, horrified at what she had been about to say.

"You were going to say Derek, right?" Amelia shuddered,

and it looked convincing. "I've heard the rumors. College guys only think about sex. No, thank you."

Yana's smile faltered. In the snippet of conversation she'd overheard, she didn't for one moment believe that Derek and Amelia had been discussing next year's student council. But if they weren't a couple, what if . . . was it possible . . . that they were part of the cheating ring? He was a teacher, albeit just an assistant. He would have access to exams and grades that students wouldn't have. What's more, Amelia had just admitted that she had a lot of help in maintaining her grades. The scenario seemed possible. Maybe even probable.

Yana hated that she was already having such suspicious thoughts about this kind girl, who was being so friendly to her. But she couldn't forget her reasons for being on this yacht. She had to keep her eyes open for every possible clue.

She left her duffel bag in the lounge, like Amelia instructed, and as they slowly made their way to the main deck for a safety briefing that started in fifteen minutes, Yana felt eyes on her. Not Derek's or even Gabe's. Something . . . bigger. More ominous.

Glancing around, Yana spotted sleek black cameras nestled into the corners of the ceilings. Security cameras, no doubt. Watching their every movement. Maybe even listening to their every word.

Yana shivered. She wasn't the only person with an agenda on this yacht. And those cameras could expose the truth of Amelia and Derek's relationship—and any other secrets hiding underneath this group's glossy surface.

FOUR

NAYA

2:47 P.M.

Naya leaned against the stern's railing and watched as a member of the crew adjusted the wrinkled corner of the printed backdrop that had been set up behind a literal red carpet laid out on the main deck. Although, she didn't have anything to take a photo with since her phone had been confiscated. . . .

The crew member tucked the end of her long braid into the collar of her polo before bending over to adjust the canvas banner emblazoned with the Yates Society's glittering gold logo. She could have used an extra set of hands to keep the frame steady as she reattached it.

Naya forced herself not to move, her toes digging into her sandals' hard insoles. She wouldn't go help. She wouldn't. There were people for that. Other people. People who were paid to fix red-carpet issues. She was a guest, an inductee.

A diversity inductee, the pesky voice inside her head offered.

No, not a diversity inductee, one of the elite. Just like everyone else.

She could get used to this—a life filled with luxury and occasional rudeness.

Naya took a deep breath and relaxed her shoulders. She *would* get used to it. Pre-vacation trips, megayachts that would transport her to exotic locales, looking out for herself and only herself—these were everyday experiences for the Yates Society inductees. And she was one of them now.

The crew member let out a frustrated groan, and Naya rushed from the railing and headed for the opposite side of the yacht.

Coward.

Again, she ignored the voice inside her head. After all, she wasn't a coward. She was a realist. She wouldn't give any of her peers the opportunity to nickname her "the help."

As she strolled by the dark windows that sprouted up from the main deck of the massive boat, Naya combed her fingers through her hair, frowning at how puffy her roots had gotten since she'd arrived in Miami.

Humidity seal, she thought, distracting herself with a mental inventory of the items she'd stuffed into her toiletry bag. *Straightening serum—*

A reflection in the tinted floor-to-ceiling windows caught her attention, and she whirled around to face the culprit. "Finn?"

With a grunt of exertion, he extended one arm overboard. Metal glinted as a pair of hedge trimmers spun end over end before splashing into the water just beyond the marina.

"What are you doing?" Naya craned her neck, trying to catch another glimpse of the tool, but it was already on its way to the sandy bottom.

"Naya!" Finn jumped and cast a furtive glance over his shoulder before dragging his hand through his hair, one corner of his mouth ticking up in a lopsided grin. "Just testing the whole message-in-a-bottle thing. Maybe it'll be waiting for the girl I love when we get to Bermuda."

"Oh yeah." Naya crossed her arms over her chest. "And which blond would that be?"

Finn's Adam's apple bobbed.

Sandals slapped against the shiny wood floor, saving Finn from having to lie to his girlfriend's best friend about hooking up with the only other blond female on the boat.

"My two favorite people!" Taylor cheered, and motioned for a crew member to follow as she rushed over to Naya and gave her a half-hug. Even with Taylor in flats, Naya only came up to her nose.

Finn dodged Naya's gaze as he took a coconut from the silver tray the crew member held out and planted a kiss on Taylor's cheek.

Naya used to give him points for confidently standing next to Taylor when she was in heels and a few inches taller than his five feet ten inches, especially since many of his peers were intimidated by a tall woman. But Naya had given Finn too much credit.

Her nostrils flared at the thought of Finn and Everly, but this was not the time, and a celebratory trip was definitely not the place to air dirty secrets.

"I'd love to say we could get this party started with some bubbly or at least some rum in these festive little drinks, but they must have the good stuff locked up with our phones," Taylor groaned, and snatched a coconut, completely oblivious to the tension swirling around her.

The crew member brushed a speck of lint from his pressed polo before wordlessly extending the tray to Naya. "Oh, no, thank you. I can't. I'm allergic—"

"To luxury?" Taylor asked with a mischievous smirk.

Naya rolled her eyes. "To coconuts."

"I'll add it to the list," Taylor said.

"You make it sound like I'm allergic to everything." Naya crossed her arms over her chest to keep from grabbing the pineapple, melon, and strawberry kebab sticking out of the coconut's white liquid. She wouldn't spend the first day of the trip itchy. Luckily, she wasn't so allergic to anything as to need an EpiPen, but gastrointestinal upset and hives sure ruined a party.

"Apparently not enough to keep you from coming," Finn grumbled.

Naya jutted her chin at the two remaining coconuts on the tray the crew member patiently held. "Everly joining us for a toast? I'm sure you'd love to spend more time with her, wouldn't you, Finn?"

Finn sputtered, nearly spitting the tropical drink all over his girlfriend.

"She wishes." Taylor lowered her Cartier sunglasses and leveled her piercing gaze at Naya. "Remember those surprises I mentioned?"

Naya's stomach clenched. She was grateful—would always be grateful—for everything Taylor did for her, but the last thing she wanted was a big show of their class differences. Whatever the surprises, they would no doubt serve as giant spotlights highlighting that Naya wasn't really like the rest of them, and she didn't want her fellow inductees to be reminded of that fact.

"Yeah . . ." Naya glanced at Finn for a clue, but he only shrugged and draped his arm around Taylor.

"Come out, come out, wherever you are!" Taylor cheered, turning to the open tinted-glass doors.

A chill climbed up Naya's spine, and she pressed her fingers into her biceps. There was something about this boat, about being so close to her goals and dreams, that set her on edge. A feeling that one wrong turn would send everything crashing down.

A tall, lanky figure popped out from behind the darkened glass, arms raised like the points of a star, blue-and-white-striped shirt and matching shorts gleaming in the afternoon sun.

Naya's fingers went slack, and she dropped her arms to her sides. "Oh my God!" She lifted onto her toes. "You're kidding!"

"Surprise!" Étienne yelled, charging toward her and scooping her into his arms. He lifted her off the ground and she wrapped her arms around his neck.

Étienne was *here*. Her ridiculously hot French boyfriend was in her arms. He was supposed to be gone, flying halfway around the world, her heart in his luggage.

Naya nuzzled his neck, inhaling his woodsy scent—the earth after a rainstorm, the wind blowing through lush green leaves. Spring in Oklahoma would always make her think of Étienne, and how senior year had ended far too soon.

"I can't believe you're here." The ends of his shaggy hair feathered against her lips as she spoke. "I thought I wouldn't see you in person until fall break."

He lowered her to the ground and brushed her hair from her cheeks, cupping her face in his strong hands. "Vous êtes mon coeur. Je ne peux pas vivre sans toi." *You are my heart. I can't live without you.* God, his accent made her want to melt. His mouth grazed hers, the words caressing her lips like silk.

Naya's fingers trailed down the buttons on his shirt as her heart beat against her ribs, in her ears, in the tips of her fingers. They were the only two people on the planet, floating above the sea.

His hands smoothed down her bare shoulders, over her back, along her hips. She shivered from his touch, and he pressed his body more firmly against hers.

The morning after graduation, they'd said their goodbyes and she'd entered the rest of her life without him by her side. Six months hadn't been enough time with him, and fall break was heartbreakingly far away. Every day without him had reminded Naya how foolish she'd been in the beginning of the year, ignoring the new exchange student.

When Étienne, Louis, and Remy, the three exchange students, had come over from France, Yatesville High had practically held a parade in their honor. Naya hadn't wanted to belong to the group of girls and guys who'd giggled and swooned at the trio's mere existence, regardless of the fact that she'd aced every French test she'd ever taken and was dying to speak French to someone from the actual country.

Hindsight being what it is, she should have thrown herself at Étienne the moment he walked through the classroom door.

"*Tu m'as manqué,*" he whispered against her ear.

"I missed you too."

"Now we get to be alone together in paradise."

Naya's entire body warmed as she imagined, not for the first time, what it would be like to truly *be with* Étienne.

At prom, he'd held her close and told her she was the most beautiful, most wonderful, most magical woman he'd ever met. He hadn't expected to be rewarded for conveying his feelings, and he never felt entitled to her body. And honestly, that only made her want to give it to him more, but she'd promised herself she'd wait until after high school. She didn't want to run the risk of messing up her future before it even started.

She lifted her chin, their lips a breath apart. He dusted a kiss on her mouth that sent a trail of fire straight to her core.

"Wait." Naya blinked up at Étienne, his eyes the same golden brown as summer wheat. "You weren't awarded a scholarship. How—"

"Taylor," he said, his hair falling into his eyes as he nodded over Naya's shoulder. "She's responsible. She wanted to make this trip special for you. So do I."

Taylor's sharp clap made Naya flinch.

"I did an amazing job keeping this quiet, right?" Taylor leaned against Finn. "They're so in love. Isn't it adorable?"

"Not as adorable as you, babe," Finn said before pressing a kiss to Taylor's cheek.

Taylor smiled and brushed back her hair. "Since my mom is the Yates Foundation's liaison and in charge of getting everyone situated, pulling a few strings was simple enough." Taylor fished in her pocket and took out the Louboutin lipstick that looked more like an antique pendant than a tube of makeup. "Like this yacht's not big enough for one more person?" she mumbled as she glided the silky red paint across her lips.

Finn, who had been in charge of holding his girlfriend's

drink while she reapplied her makeup, handed the coconut back to Taylor before lifting another and offering it to Étienne.

"No." He shook his head. "Naya is allergic. I don't want to give her hives."

"I'm sure she'll be fine as long as you don't go from sticking your tongue in the drink to sticking it in her mouth," Taylor said, hiding her grin behind a triangle of pineapple.

"Starting early, aren't we, Taylor?" Étienne eyed the beverage as if searching for poison. "After prom, I thought you would never drink again."

It was Finn's turn to hide his laugh as he turned to set the coconut back on the tray and dismissed the crew member with a nod.

"She wasn't *that* drunk." Naya cringed before the words had even left her mouth, the memory of a completely inebriated Taylor hiking up her puffy dress to pee in the middle of the street flashing in front of her eyes.

"Thanks, Naya." Taylor shoved her lipstick back into her pocket. "That was super convincing."

"You said so much that night," Étienne murmured, brushing his hand through his hair. "And what is the saying about drunk people and truth?"

"People say weird stuff when they're wasted, okay!" Taylor shouted, her brows practically reaching her hairline. "I mean . . ." She turned to Finn and traced a slow line down his chest. "Finn has said all sorts of things when he was plastered that I would *never* repeat."

Naya frowned. Unfortunately for her, Taylor had indeed repeated most of them. "And on that note . . ."

Taylor rolled her eyes. "Well, everyone does things they're

not proud of. Case in point, you two were about to rip off your clothes and devour each other right here in the middle of the day for God and everyone to see."

Étienne entwined his fingers with Naya's. "Sometimes I cannot get enough of her."

Naya's breath caught in her chest, and for the second time in ten minutes, her body heated.

Finn snorted into his coconut and Taylor gave him a playful jab in the ribs before asking, "Naya, one question: How the hell are you still a virgin?"

"Taylor!" Naya screeched, then bit her bottom lip, her gaze sliding down the lean muscles and sun-drenched olive skin that she knew were hiding beneath Étienne's striped shirt and matching shorts. Oh yeah. This trip would change *everything*.

Rumor Has It . . .

Don't know about you, but the only thing that might drag me out of my Giza 45 Egyptian cotton sheets on a Saturday morning is the spectacle of ridiculously muscled pecs, lats, and biceps powering through the water at our varsity boys' swim meets.

Okay, that's only half true.

I wouldn't get out of bed for your average bunch of high school boys.

But if one of those seniors allegedly took performance-enhancing drugs in an effort to follow in the swim strokes of his gold medal–winning Olympian father, risking expulsion and family scandal?

Well, then here I am, ever-reliable Ev, reporting for duty! Sir. Yes, sir!

Ever yours,
Everly

FIVE

YANA

3:18 P.M.

"Psst," someone said to the left of Yana. They weren't talking to her—clearly. All eight of the society inductees (plus Étienne? Was he a last-minute invite like her?) mingled on the main deck, waiting for the safety briefing to start. The delay, they were informed, was because Derek had insisted on a toast with the entire crew.

At least, the *other* kids mingled, in the hot tub a few steps down from the primary level, on the teak decking that surrounded it. Most of them had changed into swimwear already, while Yana sat on a white chaise longue in the shade, still in her airport clothes. The sky and the ocean were in a competition to see which could be bluer, but she wasn't in the mood to appreciate their beauty. Instead, she sucked in the salty breeze and attempted to look at anything but the truth: that she was alone.

"Yo, Yans."

Okay. So, that wasn't her nickname, but she supposed anything was better than "Porn."

She turned. Brett, the built, redheaded swim star, was sitting on the stemless end of the L-shaped couch. He wore slippers and a fluffy white robe with the yacht's insignia over his swim trunks. Yana had spied her own set in the cabin she shared with Amelia, but had been too intimidated to put them on. Brett, however, lounged as though such luxuries were an everyday occurrence, the cell phone cupped in his lap mostly hidden by the leg he had bent over his knee.

A cell phone. How had he managed that?

"You've got to see this." Brett waved her over.

She didn't know him. Had no reason to doubt him . . . except for the fact that he was Gabe's best friend.

And yet, other than Amelia, Brett was the *least* objectionable inductee. They weren't pals, not by a long shot, but at least they didn't have a past.

"So long as you don't ask me what I'm doing here, I'll look at anything," Yana warned as she sat next to him.

A crew member in khaki shorts and a polo shirt offered her a silver platter covered with various canapés. Yana ordered herself not to salivate. She easily identified the escargot, steak tartare, and caviar arranged on delicate toast triangles—the type of upscale food that she had never tried but that was commonly featured on one of her favorite shows, *Top Chef.*

Was it uncouth for her to take one of each? Nah. Besides, she wasn't likely to have this opportunity again. She carefully placed three pieces on a napkin on her lap, then popped the first one in her mouth. The snail practically melted, an explosion of butter, garlic, and parsley. Oh my God. The steak tartare and caviar were just as delicious. She closed her eyes in order to more thoroughly savor the flavors. This trip might be worth it for the culinary experience alone.

"Oh, I know all about why you're here," Brett said knowingly, pulling her back to the present. With no similar qualms, he had taken the entire tray from the waiter and was popping the canapés into his mouth like candy.

"And why's that?" Yana stared, fascinated, at the rapidly disappearing amuse-bouches. By her estimation, the swimmer had just gobbled up a couple hundred dollars' worth of food in under a minute.

He smirked. "Isn't it obvious? Someone wants you here. Manifested your appearance with a single thought."

She had no idea if he was serious, but chills crept up her arm. What did someone in the elite society want with her? Its members had never been interested before. Girls like Taylor and Everly knew they'd be accepted by the Yates. What did Brett know that she didn't?

"Check this out," he said, changing the subject.

Yana pushed aside her questions and peeked over his shoulder. He had reversed the camera on his cell phone, tilting it up so that it was recording the scene *behind* the couch.

Derek stood at the mahogany bar, pouring sparkling wine into a dozen glasses while Amelia fluttered by his elbow. An intricately carved ice sculpture of an anchor was displayed on the bar, drops of water sluicing down its edges. An ice sculpture in this heat? What would the rich think of next? It would probably last ten, twenty minutes tops.

"Our friendly chaperone's determined to prepare the toast himself," Brett muttered under his breath. "He's already sent away the chief stew. Now he's trying to get rid of Amelia."

As if on cue, Amelia said, "I'm just trying to help."

"You're underage," Derek snapped, more irritable than he had ever been in seventh-period calc. No matter that he was barely of age himself. "Besides, you know you're clumsy. I can't have you spilling this champagne everywhere. It's limited edition."

Hurt, Amelia retreated off camera, and Yana turned away from the screen, feeling guilty for spying.

"I didn't take you for a gossip," Yana said lightly.

"Moi?" Brett said innocently. "Nah, not a gossip. Not even a future investigative reporter like you. I'm just obsessed with true crime. I listen to no less than ten podcasts. Watched *Death on the Nile*, like, a dozen times. I've even read a thriller or two." His grin spread wide. "All of which practically makes me a detective, amirite? And I've deduced that something is afoot."

Yana's lips twitched; she appreciated his humor. Maybe she should be surprised that he knew about her future ambitions, but, well, Yatesville was a small town. Even if Brett had never actually read *The Viking Shield*—Yana wasn't exactly sure who did—everyone knew everything about everyone else, even nobodies like her. "So, what's the big mystery here?" She nodded toward the bar behind them, trying not to let on that she was digging for information.

"It's twofold," he said. "First, the Yates are a little creepy, don't you think? Supposedly, there are file cabinets on board this yacht, with thick folders on each of us. You have any dirty secrets, Yans?" He waggled his eyebrows. " 'Cause I guarantee, they're documented in those files."

"And second, what's the deal with those two?" He gestured to Derek and Amelia. "They've been whispering since we boarded. Trouble in paradise? Or maybe"—Brett lowered his voice—"they're not even lovers. Maybe they're partners . . . in crime."

"What crime would they have committed?" Yana asked, the back of her neck prickling.

"Any!" he said dramatically. "They could be planning a heist. This boat must have tons of valuables. Or they're blackmailing their fellow rich and shallow, rebuking privilege. Maybe they're even plotting a murder!"

Or orchestrating a cheating ring, Yana thought. She was tempted to chime in with details from her conversation with Amelia, but she refrained. For all she knew, Brett himself could be part of the very scandal she was investigating.

"You're a bad influence," she said instead.

"Flatter me some more!" Brett rolled his shoulders as though she had given him a particularly satisfying back rub.

"Five minutes in your company, and I'm already relishing rumors like Everly."

Brett rested his feet on the stylish coffee table, all metal and curved white lines, and interlocked his fingers behind his head. He had tossed the empty silver platter aside. "Then my work here is done."

Yana glanced over her shoulder. Derek was carefully handing out the champagne flutes to the captain, deck crew, stewards, even the engineering team. They moved into the shade, probably so they wouldn't melt like the ice sculpture. Derek began his long-awaited toast. She hoped the crew didn't fall asleep. His monotonous, droning voice knocked out most students.

She turned back to Brett. "Hey, how did you sneak in a phone?"

"Easy. I stuck it in my undies." He grinned. "It was touch

and go for a moment there. I ran into Mrs. Stewart, and the way she was eyeing me, I thought for sure she would get a little frisky." He waggled his eyebrows playfully again. "I barely escaped her cougar claws. Had to tell her that I don't date women, much less older ones."

"Reeeally?" Yana drawled. "That's a theory. Hate to break this to you, but you are *not* irresistible to every human with a heartbeat."

"Tuh. Have you *seen* the muscles on this body?" Standing up, Brett whipped off his robe and began to strut in front of the couch. Catcalls and whistles erupted across the deck from Amelia, Taylor, and Naya—as well as one of the male stews.

Yana couldn't blame them. Brett wasn't Yatesville High's star swimmer for nothing. He'd had a meteoric rise from district to state to regional champion over the last two years and received a full athletic scholarship to Berkeley. There was even talk about him joining the Olympic team. He certainly had the chiseled six-pack, rock-hard shoulders, and bulging biceps to back up his talent.

The model walk, and the ego inflation, continued. Yana laughed along with the rest of the group. She wasn't part of Brett's cheering squad—she was still sitting on the couch—but she could appreciate his antics. Maybe this was a baby step toward a change in their dynamic. Better late than never, she supposed.

The only person who didn't appreciate the show was Everly. "Now, now, kids." She crossed her arms over her tiny bikini top, obviously displeased that the attention wasn't on her. Yana wasn't concerned. Everly hadn't so much as acknowledged her since she came on board.

"Don't encourage him," Yana's nemesis continued. "It would be like applauding an alcoholic for drinking."

Their side of the deck fell quiet, with only the splash of the waves and the murmur of the adults' conversation disturbing the silence. As if synchronized, the teens' eyes bounced between Brett and Everly.

"What are you implying, Ev?" Brett asked tightly.

"You read my column. You know *exactly* what I'm saying." Her voice was cool, but her eyes were green fire. "Never seen an athlete improve so quickly. Never seen that kind of muscle without pharmaceutical help, either."

"You have no idea what you're talking about." Good humor gone, Brett stormed to the prow and rested his elbows on the railing, leaving the conversation and its ugly overtones.

Gabe hoisted himself out of the hot tub so he could stand by his friend, and the others returned awkwardly to their individual conversations.

Yana took a shaky breath. The atmosphere had turned nasty, quick. Which, frankly, seemed normal for any interaction that included Everly. As Yana looked at the swimmer's strong back, though, she had to wonder what her new friend was hiding.

"Once we cast off, we'll be cruising on autopilot at a low speed until we reach Bermuda at six in the morning!" Captain Andy waved around his champagne flute twenty minutes later, approaching the end of the safety briefing. He had flappy jowls and red cheeks, and his feet were planted shoulder-width apart at the side of the hot tub. One wrong move, and he'd tumble right in. "Either get off this yacht now or you'll be trapped here with me, the crew, and your fellow inductees for the next *fifteen* hours. *Dun dun dun dun duuun . . .*"

Yana shivered. His choice of words made her feel, well, trapped. She'd never been claustrophobic, but being stuck with these people made her visualize the yacht's walls closing in. *Relax,* she ordered herself. Captain Andy wasn't trying to be ominous. The guy was just over the top. Not to mention flushed. Even his *hands* looked red. Or was that just the sun reflecting off the pile of bright-orange life vests next to him?

"Is that a bad imitation of the *Jaws* theme song?" Finn called out.

"What's *Jaws*?" Everly asked, tilting her head and kinda petting her own hair. She would never twirl her stick-straight hair like the archetypal mean girl, of course, 'cause that would mess up the look she'd probably spent two hours perfecting.

Finn grabbed her by the waist, even though his girlfriend, Taylor, was standing only three feet away. "It's a movie about a shark who stalks people and sinks his jaws into them like this. . . ." He pretended to gnaw on Everly's long, elegant neck, and she shrieked delightedly.

Both Yana and Taylor narrowed their eyes—but for different reasons. Yana never thought she would have anything in common with the rich girl, but the obvious flirtation between Everly and Finn set off alarm bells in her head. Was this a clue? If the anonymous texter was correct about Everly, did her closeness to Finn mean that he was also involved in the cheating ring? Would she have pulled him into it as a way to one-up Taylor?

Yana would have to work on her glare, though. Taylor's

was a magnitude more murderous. Back in the fall, Taylor and her friends had taken an ax-throwing class—Yana had seen the evidence on social media—and the way the rich girl was clutching the water blaster, it looked like she was lining up her next target.

Captain Andy clapped his hands. "Okay. Pair up and practice putting on those life vests before we wrap up this meeting. There are plenty to go around, and you never know when we'll have to use the rescue tender—or in layman's terms, the speedboat—we're towing behind us."

Great. Yana hated the pairing-up part of literally any exercise. It wasn't any easier now than it had been in gym class years ago. There were nine of them, since Étienne had shown up and since Derek wasn't participating in this safety activity. One guess who the odd person out would be.

Apparently on a different wavelength from the others, Gabe made a beeline toward her, life vests in hand, a hopeful expression on his face. He seemed oblivious to the slender white arm Everly held out behind him.

"Don't even think about it," Yana warned. Would she be as annoyed if Everly hadn't been in the background, reminding her that on prom night, Gabe had made clear he preferred the gossip's company?

Didn't know. Didn't care.

"Yana, I—"

"I said no. Thank you," she added primly.

Gabe slunk away, joining Amelia and Brett to become a group of three. In spite of Yana's rejection, he had the wherewithal to ensure that she wouldn't be left without a partner.

In the meantime, Taylor marched over to Everly, probably to ensure she kept her rumor-spreading hands off her boyfriend. Suddenly without a partner, Finn clapped one hand onto Étienne's shoulders, and the two moved to the side to bro out.

That left Naya.

Yana watched as her former best friend glanced around, realizing who was left. Slowly, Naya picked up two life vests and made her way to Yana. "Here you go." She handed a vest to Yana, not meeting her eyes.

Her glossy dark-brown hair fell straight and sleek to her shoulders. How long had it taken her to straighten that morning? Four hours and twenty minutes. That was how long Yana had stood behind Naya in the fifth grade, running her friend's curls through the flat iron they had borrowed from the babysitter. That was how long Naya had stood, patient and unmoving, in spite of the burn that Yana had inadvertently left on her forehead.

The memory made Yana's throat tight, and that made her speak harshly. "Don't worry, Naya. I promise I won't throw up on you."

Naya gasped. "That's not what I was thinking!"

Didn't matter if it was the truth or a lie. There was no denying the past. The incident had hovered over their every interaction for the past five years, a row of faulty bricks built into the very foundation of their relationship.

The girls had been inseparable since kindergarten, when the teacher put them at the same table so that they could learn how to spell their names, which had the same letters. Inseparable, that is, until a cold winter day in the eighth grade. Yana had packed green curry for lunch, and Naya PB&J. They were carefully dividing up their lunches when Naya's crush, Mason Bryce, had approached them in the cafeteria.

Naya had gripped her best friend's hand under the table, her fingers trembling. And Yana, so anxious for her friend, so overcome by the poignant potential of young love and perhaps the clashing scents of curry and peanut butter, had vomited all over Naya's shirt.

The unfortunate regurgitation in itself might not have been fatal to their friendship. But Everly, ringleader of the popular crowd even then, had stood up on the long bench and dubbed her "Yana Yacks."

She had then extended an open hand to Naya and invited her to join them at *the* lunch table, the one in the center of the cafeteria, the one that might as well have had a spotlight shining upon it.

Naya, the laughter ringing in her ears, her pukey blouse exchanged for a gym shirt, had accepted. Who could blame her? Yana didn't. And yet she could never quite forgive her former best friend for deserting her, either.

With the memory of their past weighing heavily on their shoulders, the two girls fastened themselves into the life vests and checked each other's handiwork, making sure the straps were sufficiently tight. They didn't speak even when the yacht's horn blared, and the ship pushed off from the dock.

The others, however, whooped with excitement. Brett threaded the life vest between his legs like a diaper, and Taylor and Everly, argument paused, shrieked and each slapped one of his butt cheeks. Not to be outdone, Finn stripped down to his Speedo, leaving the life vest open over his six-pack. Meanwhile, a crew member fluttered around them helplessly, trying and failing to get them to practice the proper use of the life vest.

"Why are you friends with them?" Yana wasn't trying to be critical. She really wanted to know.

"They're not so bad," Naya said defensively, but her eyes were trained on the floor once more. "They understand me."

"But do they accept you?"

The question hung in the salt-scented air, and then Naya trudged back to her friends without a response.

Yana's stomach churned. Why did she bother? Their friendship had evaporated as quickly as cotton candy when it touched the tongue. That should have clued her in that their connection had been as insubstantial as those fragile threads.

And yet, when Naya joined Taylor and Everly, Yana didn't see any true joy lighting up her former friend's eyes. In fact, Naya looked lost and isolated. As forlorn as she had been when their eyes had met across the cafeteria, five long years ago.

March 1

Rumor Has It . . .

A tale as old as time . . . if time was measured by
the minutes between first and second periods!
She wears pearls and schoolgirl plaid and
has stars in her eyes. (Don't look here for any
discounts! I abhor a uniform.) *He* rocks sweater-
vests, day-old scruff, and (groan) khakis.

I know what you're thinking, but there's nothing
cliché about this love story.

One teaching assistant and one high school
senior here are in luuurve and have more reason
than most to count the days until graduation.

Time may not be able to heal their lovesickness,
but it can tell whether or not this TA will damage his
career before it's really even started. . . .

First lesson in Teacher School: You can't have S-E-X
with your students! What are they teaching over at OU?

I guess Mr. Sweater-Vest flunked that class.

Ever yours,
Everly

SIX

NAYA

3:42 P.M.

Naya trudged out of the library, leaving behind its cherry-wood bookshelf-lined walls, neat rows of leather-bound books, a rolling ladder fit for a Disney princess, and her Belle daydreams. She'd made one comment about going to find her sunglasses in the lounge, and suddenly she was on her way there with Everly's Celine bag in hand as she ran an errand for the author of *Rumor Has It.*

"Less Belle, more Cinderella with evil stepsister Everly...," she grumbled, rubbing the bag's buttery-soft leather.

But do they accept you?

Yana's question blazed through Naya's thoughts, and she nibbled on the tips of her self-manicured nails. Worry wriggled in her chest, and she stifled a cough.

No one can mess this up, she reminded herself as she approached the lounge. *I'm already here. I've made it. My life is perfect.*

"Be quiet." Amelia's hushed voice came from inside the lounge. "I don't want anyone to hear us."

Naya inched forward and peered around the thick drapes into the lavishly decorated room complete with floor-to-ceiling windows, a plush sectional that lined one wall, and a bar across another.

Amelia's back was against the bar, her Forbidden Love lilac lips pursed. Derek was in front of her, one hand at the nape of her neck, the other hiking her silky blue skirt up her thighs. She pushed his hand away and crossed her arms over her chest.

"But . . . you said . . . ," he breathed between kisses.

"I know what I said, Derek." Amelia turned away from him, and Naya scrambled for cover behind the heavy blackout curtains before she was caught spying. "But not now, okay?"

"Then when?" His shout was immediately followed by Amelia's hissed *"Shh!"*

"After what I did for you, Amelia, and everything you said . . . I practically got you into Harvard. Was any of it real? I risked my job, my scholarship—"

"Derek!" Amelia spat. "I'm not talking about this out in the open."

Naya chewed her bottom lip. She'd read about their taboo romance three months ago in Everly's column. . . . She hadn't believed it, hadn't thought that her studious, rule-following friend would be the least bit interested in their very average, very boring precalc teaching assistant. But that hadn't been the first time Naya didn't believe what she'd read on Everly's website. Luckily, her doubts about one particular rumor had yet to be proved correct.

And it won't be, she assured herself. *There are two other French exchange students, not just Étienne.*

Naya exhaled into the stifling space behind the curtains. The dense fabric didn't allow for much air, and the increasingly panicked part of her brain was sure she'd suffocate if she didn't escape soon.

Amelia cleared her throat, her voice turning to honey. "Let's just go to your cabin where we can get more comfortable."

Naya frowned. She was right to hide instead of interrupting, wasn't she? Before she could decide, there was a rustle of movement and then silence.

She sipped shallow breaths of stagnant air, waiting to emerge until she was sure the couple was gone. Footsteps sounded, and Naya tensed, clutching Everly's bag to her side. It was so hot behind the curtains, every cell in her body wanted to run, to breathe in lungfuls of crisp, clean air, but she remained cemented to her hiding spot. Amelia or Derek had probably forgotten something. In a minute they would be gone for good, and Naya would be able to breathe.

The footfalls receded, and Naya relaxed.

"You're freaking yourself out for no reason," she whispered, pushing the drapes to find the edge of the darkness.

She pawed at the side she'd entered from, but the curtains felt stuck, as though glued to the wall. As she slid her other hand up the curtain, trying to reach for the opposite side, the fabric tightened around her. The drapes pressed against her palms, against her chest, the lining clinging to her face. She opened her mouth to scream, but fabric filled her mouth.

Naya's heartbeat pounded in her ears as she struggled to free herself, struggled to take in oxygen. There was reason to panic. She was going to suffocate.

SEVEN

YANA

3:57 P.M.

Yana reached inside her duffel bag, which an efficient crew member had kindly moved to the cabin she shared with Amelia. Her nail clippers had to be in it. She was certain she'd dropped them into her leaf-print toiletry bag this morning. And since she'd emptied out that small bag, with no sign of the clippers, they must've fallen into the larger satchel.

Velvet curtains framed the portholes that offered a bisected view: half submerged under the ocean, half open to the brilliant sky. Every room on the lower level had this same perspective.

Both queen beds were outfitted with Egyptian sheets, a fluffy duvet with dusky-rose tassels, and a gold-paper-wrapped chocolate. Stained-glass lamps sat on the two night-stands, emitting a warm, cheerful glow, while tasteful seascapes in muted grays and sunrise pinks lined the walls. A robe and matching slippers adorned each bed, next to white bath towels folded up like swans. If that wasn't enough, a trail of rose petals led to a spacious, bigger-than-her-bedroom-at-home bathroom.

It was the most elegant room Yana had ever been in. Maybe the nicest she'd ever seen.

And she would take the time to appreciate it just as soon as she found those damn clippers. The tear in her fingernail wouldn't wait.

She moved her fingers along the sides of the bag. Aha! There was a slit in the lining, one she hadn't noticed before. She just managed to get her scrunched-up hand inside. After an intense minute of searching, her fingers brushed against . . . something. Not cold, clipper-shaped metal, but something flat, with sharp corners and a bumpy, plastic surface.

Yana frowned. *What on earth?*

Grasping the object, she wrenched it out of the liner, ripping the hole even further . . . and then she dropped it like she'd been burned.

A foil packet of pills, two rows across, five white tablets per row. Two pills were missing, the foil backing crumpled.

What . . . what *were* they? And what were they doing inside her bag?

Yana hesitantly flipped the packet over with one finger. Rohypnol. Wasn't that the date rape drug?

Her stomach seized, squeezing, squeezing, squeezing, until acid spurted up her throat. The room spun, and she had to grab the edge of the bed to remain on her feet.

These were *not* hers.

Her brain blared, but who would believe her panicked protestations, if they found the drugs in her possession? She'd get kicked out of the society before she had a chance to gather information for her exposé. Hell, the Yates might even airlift her right off the yacht.

She had to get rid of the pills . . . now.

She stumbled into the hallway and was blasted by air-conditioning. The cold brought her back to her senses—marginally.

Think, Yana ordered her jumbled mind. *You're a reporter. You're getting paid to connect the dots, not get rid of potentially incriminating evidence.*

But she was here to investigate cheating. Not sexual assault! No way it was coincidence, right? And yet she couldn't fathom how they were linked.

Two figures emerged at the end of the hallway, and Yana eased behind a corner, slipping the packet of pills into the pocket of her jean shorts.

A crew member—the stew who had whistled at Brett, if she wasn't mistaken. And Derek. Was the stew . . . drunk? The crew member lurched from side to side, singing "I Will Survive" off-key. His eyes were nearly closed. Only Derek's arm kept him upright.

Or was he *drugged*?

The pills burned a hole in her back pocket. Derek. The champagne toast. The one he had been so insistent on having with the crew. The one he prepared himself, shooing away both the head stew and Amelia. Could that champagne have been spiked?

You got it. The tattoo of the cheerful penguin crossed her mind. Motivating words, for sure. But what, exactly, did they motivate Derek to do?

Maybe the very bland, very boring math teacher was a key piece in this puzzle. Or maybe the crew member had simply gotten overzealous with his day drinking, and her imagination was working overtime.

Derek escorted the stew up the stairs, presumably to find him a place to rest. Yana waited a minute and then stepped back into the corridor, her thoughts whirling. She would go up to the main deck. Hide the pills, in a place where nobody would find them, one that wasn't in any way associated with her. Then, if the tablets became evidence, Yana would still be able to access them—

A person with a full-on Slender Man mask jumped out of the shadows at the next corner, practically landing on top of her. Screaming.

Yana screamed in unison with her attacker, sinking to her knees and shielding her face with a raised forearm. This was it. She hadn't figured out the mystery quickly enough. She would die, right here, right now, over a cheating scandal she had just begun to investigate.

She didn't want to die! She had so much life left to live. So much good left to do in this world.

The attacker loomed over her, ripped the stretchy white mask off his face . . . and laughed?

"Brett?" Yana wheezed.

"You should see your face!" Brett slapped his knees, head tilted back as laughter consumed him. "Priceless. I've always wanted to do that. Could never have predicted it would go that well."

"Scaring me half to death is your idea of a joke?" She straightened up, willing her heart to return to its rightful place in her chest.

"Well, yeah." He raised an eyebrow. "Didn't you think it was funny?"

"Not in the slightest."

Unperturbed, he shrugged. "Guess there's no accounting for sense of humor." He sauntered down the hallway, whistling cheerfully.

Yana stared after him, her heart thrumming in her ears. If this was Brett at his most fun, she'd hate to see him when he was angry.

EIGHT

NAYA

4:01 P.M.

Sweat clung to Naya's brow and dripped down her back as she twisted and fought against the suffocatingly thick drapes.

"Naya?" Étienne's hand broke through the slack edge of the curtains and found hers. Cool air brushed her damp skin and startlingly bright sunshine flooded her vision.

Everly's purse slid from Naya's arm as she fell right into Étienne's. "I thought . . . ," she choked out between gasps. "I couldn't—I couldn't breathe."

"You're okay," he murmured, hugging her to him. "The luggage rolled and pinned the curtains."

She frowned at the handmade beige Globe-Trotter suitcase three times the size of hers, complete with gold buckles and a matching gold *E* monogrammed in the center. She had most definitely freaked out for no reason. Although shouldn't one of the stewards have taken their things to their cabins by now? She winced at the assumption. Yes, she could get used to this lifestyle, but she also had to remember who she was, where she came from, and how others deserved to be treated.

"I think I had a panic attack." She released a pent-up breath, rippling Étienne's soft cotton shirt.

"I'm glad I found you," he said, bringing her hand to his mouth and brushing a kiss against her knuckles.

Safe in Étienne's arms, Naya gazed up at him. She glided her tongue along her bottom lip, unable to look at his mouth without thinking about how it felt on hers. They hadn't kissed since he'd surprised her. Not really. Not the way she wanted.

"I was told there is a killer view out front," he said, tucking her hand in the crook of his arm.

"Yes!" she almost shouted, following him out of the lounge, following him anywhere as long as it led away from the site of her meltdown, and to the bow. In front of the guardrail, the spiky points of the mermaid's steel-blue crown shone like azure rays of a setting sun.

"I'm so happy you're here," Naya said as Étienne stood behind her while they gazed out at the water and the thin line where the ocean touched the sky.

"*Tout pour toi,*" he whispered against her ear before kissing a trail of heat along her jaw, down her neck, and across her shoulder. *Anything for you.*

Naya closed her eyes and tipped her face to the sun, arching into him, her soft moan swept up in the hum of the boat and the crash of the waves.

But do they accept you?

Her heart began to race again, and her eyelids flew open as Yana's question scorched her fantasies, singeing the edges, turning them black.

She stiffened and shook her head, banishing every thought

of Yana and the final remnants of her panic attack. She wouldn't let her past decisions or her recent fit of terror ruin her present.

Étienne paused and whispered something that the steady breeze and raging waters muted with their white noise.

Naya cleared her throat and forced herself to focus on his warm, solid body against hers. Giving in to him felt good. It felt right. With Étienne, she'd never once questioned whether or not he accepted her. He'd made it clear from the beginning of their relationship that she was the only one for him.

He resumed his sweet kisses, and Naya's eyelids drooped, lulled into relaxation by Étienne's lips and the steady beat of his heart. If only he would never leave.

"Know what I want to do?" he asked.

Naya rested the back of her head against his shoulder. "Stay here forever?"

"That, *and . . .*" Étienne kicked off his flip-flops, and with his hands firmly gripping the sea-spray-dotted metal on either side of Naya's, he stepped onto the lowest rung of the guardrail. "I can't do it without you," he said, motioning for her to join him.

A giggle played on her lips as she climbed up. Silently—because she would most definitely never do it aloud—she thanked Everly for projecting *Titanic* onto the huge screen of her family's outdoor entertainment area during her twenties-themed eighteenth-birthday party and ignoring Amelia, who'd spent the entire three hours muttering that the *Titanic* did not, in fact, sink in the Roaring Twenties.

Naya held out her arms and envisioned a windswept Kate Winslet and a young Leonardo DiCaprio at the bow of the great ship.

Étienne's fingers tangled with hers. It was just the two of them. Her future—*their* future—stretched out ahead, glittering with possibility against the cerulean waves. She'd worked so hard to be awarded the Yates Society scholarship that made it possible for her to pursue her dream career at her dream university. She was accepted early decision to Johns Hopkins, and had crossed her fingers, toes, and every other crossable body part in hopes that she'd ace her Yates Society interviews the same way she had her classes. The scholarship was the only way she could afford to attend Hopkins and one day be the chief of the ER in a hospital far, *far* away from Yatesville, Oklahoma.

"Hello?" Everly's sharp tone bit through the warm fuzzies, and yes, cheesiness, of Naya and Étienne's reenactment. "I'm calling a meeting in ten minutes! Everyone has to be there."

Naya didn't have to turn around to envision Everly, hands pinned to her narrow hips, thin nose pointed to the sky as she tapped the toe of whatever designer shoe her daddy had recently gifted her.

"Think she will vanish if we ignore her?" Étienne asked, settling his chin on Naya's shoulder.

"I know you two can hear me!" Everly's nasally whine reminded Naya of a train whistle.

"I wish I couldn't," she grumbled, loud enough for her boyfriend to hear. He snorted.

"What was that?" Everly asked.

"Be down in a second." Naya shifted forward, leaning out over the railing and the biggest point of the iron starfish crown to stare at the frothy white waves tumbling against the sides of the boat as it cut through the water. She wasn't ready to climb down and submerge herself in the realities of traveling with this group.

But do they accept you?

There was Yana once more, like a gnat, her voice swirling through Naya's mind, sowing seeds of doubt and worry, battling with Everly for the title of Trip Ruiner. It shouldn't matter whether or not they accepted her, but it did. Naya wanted to belong.

She sighed and focused on what was before her instead of the dread that gnawed at her stomach. "Come on. Time to rejoin reality."

Étienne's warmth drained away as he hopped down from the guardrail and offered her his hand.

Naya pressed her thighs against the railing as she released the guardrail and turned to reach for him. One sandal slipped on the beads of moisture covering the metal, and she squealed as she fell forward, the gleaming point of the starfish inches from her face.

Étienne caught her shirt and wrenched her backward. She collided with him, the air knocked out of her lungs as she struck his solid form.

"Are you injured?" he asked, pulling her into a hug. "You were almost speared by that . . . that. . . ."

"Mermaid," Naya supplied as she sucked in a quaking breath.

Étienne was right. She had almost been killed—*again*—speared by the very thing that was supposed to ensure their safe travels. From now on, she would stay away from curtains and mermaids and keep her feet firmly on the floor.

"See, Naya," Everly clucked, her pale cheeks rounding with a smile, "you should really know by now that bad things happen when I'm annoyed."

NINE

YANA

4:08 P.M.

Gabe was walking across the library. No, that wasn't right. He wasn't just walking. He marched deliberately across the rich tapestry rug, stopping underneath the chandelier and the stunning feat of architecture that was composed of a dozen crescent-shaped panes of glass set into the ceiling. The main cabin sat directly on top of the library, or so Everly had gushed, and a matching set of glass panels in the cabin's ceiling meant that you could see straight up into the cloudless blue sky from the library.

With his back to Yana, Gabe squinted up, up, up at the dazzling shards of chandelier. He then jotted something on a piece of paper, tucked the paper and pen in the back pocket of his swim trunks, and squinted up some more.

What was he doing? Recording his musings on the architecture of the *Seraphina*?

Yana itched for her speckled composition notebook that

she jotted down notes in for her upcoming articles, but she'd left it in her cabin. Instead, she crept toward Gabe, grateful that the thick rug absorbed the patter of her tennis shoes. The illicit drugs were now safely tucked inside an old, dusty volume on a bookshelf, and no one else had appeared yet for Everly's so-called meeting. The silence soothed her following that afternoon's chaos.

Trays of hors d'oeuvres filled the mahogany side table beneath a large portrait of an old lady with long silver locks. Floor-to-ceiling bookshelves lined two walls, while the wall opposite the portrait was covered with a row of wooden filing cabinets.

These must be the very same cabinets referenced by Brett, the ones that contained files on each of them. Presumably they were locked, given the empty keyhole in the upper right corner of each cabinet. The stained wood and small metal nameplates stood out from the old-world charm of the library as though they were meant to be noticed. They wanted Yana to wonder: *What are you hiding? What secrets are sealed within you?* But what really caught Yana's eye was the paper sticking out of Gabe's pocket. She could make out a blueprint of sorts, along with penciled measurements. What was it? Why would Gabe need a blueprint?

"Wow," he said jokingly. "I'm actually blushing."

Yana dragged her eyes up. "Huh?"

He gestured at the back of his trunks. "My ass seems to have mesmerized you."

"What? No!" Fire lit her cheeks. She was not ogling his glutes. Obviously. But now he was cocking his butt playfully, as though to accommodate her scrutiny. Could the rug split apart and the floor swallow her up?

"Your pocket. I was looking at the paper in your pocket," Yana blurted. "Trying to figure out what you were doing."

"Sure you were," Gabe teased, turning around so that she could no longer see the diagram—nor his behind, which, admittedly, was very nice. Firm, probably. He had thrown a tropical-print shirt on over his tanned, muscular torso and left it unbuttoned. In all the weeks they had flirted, she had never seen—much less been this close—to his naked chest.

Yana had learned her lesson, though, so she kept her eyes trained on the bridge of his nose.

"You don't have to be embarrassed," Gabe said gently. "It's okay that you find me attractive. In fact, it makes me super happy."

"I don't find you attractive." Yana perched on the edge of an oversized leather armchair, trying to act nonchalant, which might have been easier if her cheeks weren't flaming.

He lifted an eyebrow. "What about those looks you used to give me across the classroom? They made me want to leap over the furniture in my way and sweep you up in a hug."

She flushed, even as she wondered how, exactly, she had gotten dragged into this conversation. Gabe was the enemy. Wasn't he?

"You've lost me," she said haughtily. "I don't remember any such looks."

He jumped nimbly over the sofa set at an angle from Yana's chair. At first Yana thought—with joy? with horror?—that he was going to follow through with his threat and hug her. Instead, he sank down beside her, his knee brushing hers. The armchair, unfortunately, had only one extrawide cushion, which was still entirely too small to share with someone a few inches north of six feet like Gabe.

"Compliments are great," he said. "Here, let me demonstrate." He picked up her hands and turned to face her. "Yana, I love how independent you are. How you don't care what other people think. How you always stand up for what's right. I've liked you since the fifth grade, when Finn tried to cut the lunch line in front of that scrawny second grader and you marched right up to him and sent him to the back. Oh, and you're hot, too. Can't forget that."

"Hmm," she said noncommittally, tugging back her hands. Contrary to the facade she had erected, Yana wasn't immune to flattery. And this . . . this was one of the nicest things anyone had ever said to her.

"What, no response?"

"That wasn't a compliment," she said. "You were only giving me an example."

Gabe grinned as though he looked forward to the challenge. "You don't give, do you?"

"You're one to talk," Yana retorted, since she was pushed. "Freshman year, you showed up at school with a quilt around your shoulders. When people asked why you had it, you simply raised your eyebrows and said, 'Why don't you have a blanket?' To which they were forced to respond, 'Fair point.'" She shook her head. "I always wondered how it felt to walk around in the world with that much self-confidence."

"It's not self-confidence so much as not caring what other people think."

"Same thing!"

"Maybe," he conceded. "But if it is high self-esteem, then it was hard-won. You must remember me in elementary school. Chubby cheeks? Thick glasses? Terribly uncoordinated?"

Yana nodded. Of course she remembered. She'd felt a kinship with him, even back then.

"My parents split up when I was in kindergarten, and they both shoved food at me rather than deal with my messy emotions," Gabe said slowly. "I may have grown up with Brett and Ev and the others 'cause our moms are friends, but that didn't exempt me from their jokes. It wasn't until middle school when I shot up a foot and took up swimming that I began to feel okay about myself." He peered at Yana. "But thank you. If that was a compliment."

Yana struggled to keep her face blank. She didn't like this guy! She wasn't about to give him a second chance to humiliate her. And yet a part of her softened at his confession. His magnetic brown eyes pulled her in. She leaned closer. And then closer. One more inch, and maybe she would forget that he ever snubbed her at prom. . . .

Blinking, Yana sat up straight. "Why should I say nice things about you when you're just going to turn around and ignore me?"

His face sobered. "Okay, I deserve that." He slouched down in the chair and put his flip-flopped feet on the edge of the glass table. "I'm bummed 'cause I was really enjoying seeing your walls come down, and when I thought we were getting somewhere . . . prom happened."

Yana snorted. "You say that like prom is to blame and you're an innocent bystander."

He glanced up at her, his curly hair falling into his eyes. Yana didn't want to think about the view he must have of her chin and nostrils.

"I'm very, genuinely sorry," Gabe said sincerely. "When I

apologized to you at the end of the night, you acted so cool and unbothered that I thought you didn't mind that I had gone AWOL."

Yana dropped her eyes as hot tears pricked the backs of her eyelids. That was fair, she supposed. Sometimes she was a little *too* good at covering up her feelings. But that didn't excuse his behavior.

"It wasn't until you didn't answer any of my texts and calls afterward that I realized how badly I had messed up. Will you give me another chance? Please?" Gabe continued.

A part of her wished she could. That was the problem, the reason her voice turned harsh. "You're sitting too close to me."

He scooted over a few inches, squishing himself against the other side of the armchair. "How about now? Will you forgive me now that I'm all the way over here?"

In spite of her resolve, Yana's lips twitched. Gabe was too cute for her own good. "I'll think about it."

He sprang up, hopped over the back of the chair, and then performed an exuberant cartwheel, his toned swimmer's muscles flexing.

Had the boy ever met a piece of furniture that he walked around? "That wasn't a yes," she protested.

He gave her a wide smile. "It also wasn't a no," he said cheerfully. "I'm a patient guy. And for you, Yana? I'll wait until I take my very last breath. Until my heart beats one final time."

Hyperbole, clearly.

And yet Yana was more confused than ever. Maybe she had misread the situation that balmy night in May. Perhaps he had never meant to snub her . . . and perhaps she was falling for his charms once more.

Everly sailed into the library, stopping short at the sight of Yana in the armchair—and Gabe executing a second cartwheel. "It's prom all over again." She smirked and pointed a finger directly at Yana. "Don't come crying to me when he ghosts you after this weekend."

With the mean girl around, no juicy tidbit went unremembered. No secret uncovered.

Fifteen minutes later, Yana's cheeks burned as she perused the customized schedule that Everly had bestowed upon her along with a map of the yacht. According to the piece of paper, she was supposed to be "reading in a dark, dusty corner of the library for the remainder of the trip." Classic Everly.

Judging from the outcries, protests, and grumbles of the rest of the inductees, no one was any happier about their day being dictated by Everly. And Amelia—Amelia was so angry that she crumpled her schedule into a ball and stormed out of the library and into the bathroom directly outside its doors.

"Who put you in charge?" Finn demanded. He stood hip to hip with Taylor. "I only showed up 'cause Captain what's-his-face was supposed to connect us to what's-her-name."

"The founder of the Yates Society, Seraphina Yates," Taylor chimed in. "Captain Andy was supposed to set up a video call so she could welcome us."

But Captain Andy wasn't here. Yana hadn't seen him since the safety presentation. In fact, outside of the guy stumbling down the hallway, she hadn't glimpsed *any* of the crew, neither a steward offering them drinks nor a deckhand maneuvering equipment. Weird. Surely, they couldn't *all* be drunk . . . or roofied. Right?

Out of the corner of her eye, Yana saw Amelia exiting the bathroom, sans paper. Instead of returning to the library, however, the former student council president disappeared around the corner. "Captain Andy told me and Gabe that the founder's on her deathbed." Brett nodded vigorously. "She's probably too sick to greet us."

"Seraphina's also supposed to be some sort of recluse," Gabe added from Yana's left. This was the first time he'd spoken to the group, but she had been acutely aware of his presence the entire meeting. "Apparently, she *never* talks to the new inductees. But this year's different. Something about her mystery progeny being on board."

"Her progeny?" Finn echoed as everyone turned toward the portrait of the old lady. "That's, like, family and shit, right?"

"Definitely *and shit*," Brett agreed. He looked at each of them in turn. "Okay, fess up. Who is it?"

"Well, we can probably rule out Naya or Yana," Finn said, leaning forward and twirling a lock of Naya's hair as though its texture were proof enough.

Frowning, Naya took two careful steps away, pulling her hair out of his grasp.

Taylor jumped in, as though to smooth over her boyfriend's gaffe. "It's you, isn't it, Everly? You've got her elegance."

Finn's eyes popped open. "Ev! You should've told us. Heir to the Yates Society!"

Everly shrugged prettily. "Heiress. And I didn't want anyone to feel weird around me. I love you all." She batted her eyes in Gabe's direction. "I don't care about the difference in our socioeconomic status."

How very kind. Everly had been queen bee-ing them ever since kindergarten, when she demanded that no one copy her "signature" hairstyle of two pigtails. Of course, she'd come from the oldest of old money.

Meeting apparently over, the group began to disperse. Yana casually but deliberately made her way to the bathroom that Amelia had exited. Once inside, she scanned its contents. Like the rest of the yacht, the bathroom was steeped in money, from the purple-veined countertops to the folded monogrammed napkins . . . that they were supposed to use to wipe their butts? She didn't see any toilet paper. Seriously?

To quote Adisorn, *rich people*. Yana shook her head, continuing her perusal. The expensive, engraved bar soap on the sink. A smart toilet, with more buttons than her remote control. Where was the trash?

She opened one of the cabinets. Aha! A gold wicker wastebasket that managed to feel delicate despite its function.

Yana peered inside the basket. A crumpled paper sat by itself at the very bottom. With her fingertips, she grasped the paper and pulled it out. She sat on the closed toilet seat, ignoring the beeps and whirling she set off, and smoothed out the paper in her lap.

It wasn't a personalized schedule for Amelia at all. Rather, it appeared to be one of her old exams—calculus, to be exact—with a big fat *F* scrawled in red marker at the top.

Yana sucked in a breath. The Harvard-bound student

council president had flunked a test? In a class that just happened to be partly taught by her secret lover/partner in crime? What about her tutors?

So, the tip about the cheating ring was legit and not just a ruse to get Yana on board the ship. This failed exam was exactly the kind of evidence that the anonymous texter had wanted her to find.

Yana closed her eyes, trying to make sense of the clues. Her mysterious late invitation and a society that was getting more suspicious by the minute. The text, the friction between Derek and Amelia, this failed test. The drugs stashed in her duffel bag. The incapacitated crew member whom Derek had escorted down the corridor. How did they all connect to one another? Unclear. Only one thing was for sure: it was going to be a long, long night.

TEN

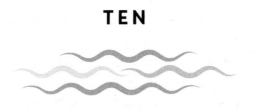

NAYA

4:47 P.M.

Naya stared at her schedule, one side of it crinkled in her fist. She was mad, *so* mad. At Finn. At Taylor. But most of all, at Everly. She was the ringleader. She always had been, and now Naya knew exactly why—Everly was a Yates, a family at the top of the food chain in Yatesville.

Naya smoothed her fingers through her hair—the hair Finn had used as evidence to prove there was no way she could be a Yates, as if he'd never seen *bi* or *multi* in front of the word *racial*. As if her mother could never have married into the elite family. "Diversity inductee . . ."

She tucked the map under her arm before balling up the schedule and throwing it over the side of the boat. It moved like a baseball in a slow, long arc, then sank into the choppy sea.

Naya blinked the tears from her eyes before they could fall. It didn't matter what Finn or Everly or anyone said or insinuated. She deserved to be here, and nothing could take that away from her.

She shook out the yacht map and studied it, trying to make sense of where she was. Below the main deck, where she was now, were the guest cabins, the game room, the theater, the beach club, and a section of the crew quarters only accessible from a separate entrance. The main level included two large decks and every *L* room: the lobby, the library, and the lounge. The wheelhouse, more guest cabins, and the dining room were upstairs, and the crow's nest a level above that. In addition, there were a number of unlabeled rooms on every level. Holy moly, this yacht was *huge*.

If she didn't hang on to this map, she was one hundred percent getting lost. Naya was to directions as cats were to water.

Just as a smile threatened to lift her cheeks, a gust of wind swirled around her, ripping the map from her hand and tossing it overboard.

Of course . . .

Behind her, the sound of bags being zipped and unzipped caught her attention. She turned, and her jaw tightened. She went back to the lounge, back to the panic and the struggle to breathe. But Étienne was there as he had been before.

"You're lucky you were able to skip that so-called *meeting*," she said to his broad shoulders as he stood with his back to her, hunched over the pile of bags. "It was such a waste of—"

The sentence died on her lips as Étienne spun around to face her, a long Tiffany-blue box clutched in his hands.

Naya's heart skipped a beat, and her grin finally broke through.

"Étienne," she breathed, and pressed one palm to her chest. "I don't know what to say." Emotion gripped her throat and each word came out a whisper.

His cheeks flushed pink, and his hazel eyes widened as he wordlessly moved his jaw.

"You always know exactly what to do to make me feel better." She beamed, joy lifting her onto her toes.

"*Non,* Naya—"

She rushed to him, throwing her arms around her boyfriend and nearly sending them both tumbling onto the bench. Although Naya could think of worse things than ending up on top of Étienne, the wind blowing and sun shining as they glided toward a subtropical island adventure.

"I love you." The words bubbled up her throat and escaped her lips before she had a chance to think. "Not because of this." She glanced down at the box he held between them. "But because you thought of me. You always think of me." She combed her fingers through his hair and pulled him down to her.

"Naya—"

She shook her head. She didn't need him to say it back. People didn't love in the same ways, much less at the same time. The only thing that mattered was that she'd expressed her true feelings. She knew too well how suddenly those she cared for could disappear completely.

"I love you," she whispered against his lips.

Sandals slapped the teakwood deck, and behind her, someone cleared their throat.

Naya deflated and dropped her arms from Étienne.

Taylor leaned against the doorway, dusting her cheek with the ends of her golden hair. "You two are almost as bad as Amelia and Derek."

If only she knew.

But that was a story for a different day, and most likely one Naya wouldn't tell. She'd leave the gossiping to someone far viler. "Taylor, you will not believe what I caught Étienne doing."

Taylor crossed her arms over her chest. "Try me."

"He was getting a surprise out of his bag." Naya motioned to the box Étienne clutched against his chest like a crucifix. "For me!"

Taylor cocked her round chin and lifted one brow. "Oh, was he?"

Naya nodded up at Étienne and fought the urge to run her hands through his hair and guide his mouth back to hers. "He is the absolute best."

Étienne's swallow was audible, and his cheeks pinkened again.

Naya bit her lower lip, realizing for the first time that she'd completely ruined his surprise and embarrassed him in the process.

"I'm sorry," she muttered. "We're on this gorgeous yacht, the most ideal setting for blue-box gift giving. There's no telling what you had planned or how long it took you to come up with it, and I killed the mood."

Étienne's hair brushed his brows as he shook his head. "No, Naya, please don't. You have no reason to be sorry. I do. I—"

"Keep dragging this out," Taylor groaned, dipping her chin to her chest and pretending to snore. "Don't leave the poor girl in suspense, Étienne. Give her the gift. I mean, it *is* hers, isn't it?"

"No, I—" He swallowed again and took a step back, his bare calves pressing against the bench.

"Look, I didn't mean to spoil everything, but Taylor is the first person I would show it to, so . . ." He didn't stop Naya as she pinched the slender rectangle between her thumb and forefinger and slid it out of his grasp.

Naya opened the Tiffany box. She gasped and clapped her hand over her mouth. The bracelet rested on a bed of white velvet. Each glittering rose gold link blinked up at her like Étienne had commissioned it from the stars themselves.

"It's beautiful." She nearly swooned, her hand shaking as she plucked the bracelet from the box and held it up. A delicate key charm hung from one of the oval links, its bow in the shape of a heart. *His* heart.

"The key to your heart." This time when the tears welled, Naya didn't keep them from falling.

"Wow." Sarcasm stretched the word from Taylor's lips like taffy. "Your boyfriend has *the best* taste in jewelry."

Or maybe Naya was just hearing Taylor's jealousy. The one main difference between Taylor and Finn—the one thing Naya had long suspected kept him bound to her no matter his true feelings—was money. Her family had it. His did not. The only gifts he ever gave her, she'd paid for.

"I love it." Naya set the box on the bench before fastening the bracelet around her wrist. She wrapped her arms around Étienne and bounced up and down, unable to contain her giddiness.

"On that note, I'll leave you two lovebirds. Says here I'm supposed to get my tan on because"—Taylor squinted at her folded schedule—"*glowing skin is always in.* But, Étienne, definitely find me later so we can talk jewelry."

Naya pushed aside the thorn of suspicion that threatened to pop her bubble of happiness. Instead, she let joy wash over her, warm and soft, while she wished she hadn't had to give up her phone, so she could send a photo to her mom, post a photo on social, reach out to every news outlet on the planet. Her life was only getting better.

Rumor Has It . . .

He flew in and stole the heart of one of our own.

But that wasn't the only thing he stole.

Fellow seniors at Yatesville High, as we close out our reign and are overtaken by graduation gifts, a word of advice: hold your loved ones close— and your loved things closer.

Class rings, Van Cleef necklaces, crisp green Benjamins—nothing is safe from our resident klepto.

His jaw may be square; his eyes, enigmatic; his accent, très, très sexy . . . but don't be fooled. Just when he's got you dreaming of stolen kisses, his hands are in your back pockets, stealing whatever he can find.

Don't say I didn't warn ya!

Ever yours,
Everly

ELEVEN

NAYA

7:04 P.M.

Naya had spent the past two hours adhering to Everly's strict schedule, which consisted of "sunbathing and tropical drinks on the lido deck." Translation: listening to Everly weigh the pros and cons of various island vacations while Taylor slept face down on a puffy white beach towel and Amelia had her nose in a romance novel. No sign of the boys, Yana, or any of the crew members, but Naya wouldn't be surprised if Everly had given the crew their own agenda to adhere to. After all, it was supposedly her family's boat.

At least Naya had had the chance to go back to the cabin she and Taylor shared for their scheduled hour of "makeup, etc." in preparation for what Everly had listed in bold on her Yacht Vibes Schedule as The Yacht Party to End All Yacht Parties! Followed by the Most Epic Fireworks Display Ever!

Now, she hesitated at the top of the stairs. Everly and

Gabe were chatting. Well, whispering was more accurate. Everly leaned back against the guardrail, her slender arms stretched out on either side, one foot propped on the railing behind her. It was like a perfume ad—the gorgeous, wind-swept blond being fawned over by the tall, handsome brooding boy. Gabe's mouth was so close to Everly's ear, if he stuck his tongue out, he could lick her.

He glanced over his shoulder, the tips of his ears turning cherry red as he locked eyes with Naya.

He gave her a stiff smile and hurried away.

"Wave bye to one of my many admirers." Everly grinned and pretended to study her manicure, but Naya didn't miss the way her brown eyes flicked up, trailing after Gabe.

"I see you're finally after someone not already taken," she mumbled.

Everly let out an annoyed huff. "You're seriously going to start that again?"

"*I* didn't start anything," Naya said, turning to face her. "You were the one half-dressed at your birthday party with your claws in Finn. I just wanted to find the bathroom. Believe me, if I could take it back and pee outside instead of finding you two practically midcoitus, I would."

"I hate to be *that girl*—"

Naya rolled her eyes and steeled herself for whatever insult Everly was about to fling. She reveled in being *that girl*.

"There's one secret you should know."

Everly placed her hand on Naya's arm. If Naya didn't know her, she'd actually think Everly was being sincere. "It's fine that you don't like me, much less trust me, but I never lie. Add a little flair, yes. But lie, never. And you need to know—"

As if an alarm had blared the moment Naya turned her back on the gossipmonger, Taylor, Étienne, Amelia, and Brett emerged from the stairwell.

"Where are the stewards?" Taylor asked, glancing around the nearly empty deck. "I was promised both a mani-pedi and massage, and no one ever showed up. Plus, I'm hurtling toward dehydration and would kill for some food."

Amelia patted the back of her coiffure and removed a speck of invisible lint from her pale-pink, scallop-edged Ted Baker cami. "Derek said they're in some sort of crew meeting and that he'd bring up drinks and snacks."

"Leave it to the help to be engaged when we most need them." Everly pouted and this time did in fact study her expertly foiled glass mani.

"Yeah, I'm sure they're MIA just to spite you," Taylor mumbled.

Naya bit the inside of her cheeks to keep from smiling.

"Who needs the stews when I have this?" Brett whipped out his phone from the pocket of his designer lounge shorts. A few taps later and dance music pulsed from the boat's speakers.

Taylor sashayed over to where Naya stood next to Everly and wiggled her butt against Naya's hip. "What are you two so buddy-buddy about? Don't need to worry about you stealing my bestie, do I, Ev?"

"Of course not." Everly's veneers glistened as she turned on her glamorous smile and stared out at the sunset. "Naya and I were just soaking up this gorgeous view."

"And Everly was about to let me in on one of her famous secrets. A secret that could *change everything.*" Naya held up her hands and wiggled her fingers as if summoning a ghost.

Again, Everly cocked her head, her long blond hair sliding from her thin shoulders as she eyed Naya.

"You are so weird. Étienne's lucky he'll go home to another continent after this trip," she said with a frown, before brushing past Naya and Taylor and disappearing into the shadows of the library.

Naya blinked, rendered speechless by Everly's one-eighty from concerned frenemy to complete jerk.

Taylor draped her arm over Naya's shoulders. "A life-changing secret, huh?"

"That's what she said." Naya narrowed her eyes in the direction of the library. She and Étienne weren't going to let separate continents ruin what they had.

We'll make long distance work.

As if summoned, Étienne slid up next to her and pressed his lips to her cheek.

~

8:15 P.M.

The music at Everly's yacht party changed without warning from a karaoke pop hit to a pulsing techno beat with everyone jumping and head-nodding.

Étienne held out his hand, palm up. "May I have this dance?"

Naya giggled at the formal request for such a fast song and placed her hand in his. She let her thoughts of the Taylor-Everly-Finn fiasco drop away as Étienne swept her around the expansive deck. They worked up a sweat as the sun dipped below the horizon. Completely worn out, she rested her head on his shoulder and closed her eyes when the yacht's lights clicked on and illuminated the deck with a soft glow.

Étienne guided them around the deck, snippets of conversations brushing against her like the breeze.

"And her thrift-store jumpsuit"—Taylor's words drifted to her as she and Étienne glided toward their friends—"it's three seasons old."

Naya's eyelids fluttered open, and her jaw tensed against Étienne's chest.

"Someone should really do us a favor and tell her that buying old designer is the same as buying brand-new, off-the-rack department store. Save her and her mom the money they obviously do not have."

Naya's gaze fell to her seasons-old pale-yellow Gucci jumpsuit. For someone like Everly, she knew she would never be enough, never *have* enough. But Taylor? She was harsh, sure—losing a parent would do that—but her cattiness had never been aimed at Naya. At least, she didn't think it ever had been.

"God, Taylor," Amelia said, disapproval sharpening her tone. "Naya's your best friend."

The song ended, and Naya stopped her pathetic attempts to keep up with the music in time to turn and catch Taylor glowering at Amelia as the petite brunette walked away.

"Naya!" Taylor cheered, and practically bounded over to her side.

She hooked her arm through Naya's and dragged her away from Étienne. "Amelia is *so* insecure. Did you hear what she said?"

Naya's mouth was dry, and her swallow felt stuck in the back of her throat. "I heard what *you* just said."

Taylor waved her hand as if her comments had been no more of a nuisance than a gnat.

"She was going on and on about being ugly and I was trying to make her feel better. You know you look absolutely amazing."

Taylor leaned into Naya, bumping her shoulder conspiratorially. "Money can't buy taste." She nodded toward Amelia, who was helping Derek bring out crystal glasses.

Naya's stomach squeezed. When had Taylor become so outright mean?

Feeling unsettled, Naya scanned the deck for Everly but didn't see a trace of the blond.

Perhaps she did need to know the rumor Everly had come to her with instead of posting on her site. Maybe she'd been too quick to dismiss her. After all, Everly did say this secret would change *everything*.

Rumor Has It . . .

Ah, so sweet, they said. So innocent.

The portrait of purity—wide eyes, pink lips . . . bare breasts?!

Yep, you read that right, friends and fiends. A certain junior girl has been fooling us all (except yours truly, obvs). She puts on an unassuming facade, but underneath that angelic face, a wild soul twirls and twerks. Topless!

And I've got the photos to prove it.

Go on. Take your best guess. I won't tell . . . much.

Ever yours,
Everly

TWELVE

YANA

8:32 P.M.

Sweat drenched her hair and trailed down the nape of her neck. It would've shown up on her minidress with the flouncy skirt and deep pockets if the material wasn't black. The dress was pretty enough, but who was she fooling? Yana's outfit was as inappropriate for the occasion as Yana herself.

Which meant that she had no business being at Everly's epic party. Feeling a little disgusted that she was falling in line with Everly's instructions but also craving silence and a good book, Yana wandered into the library. She wasn't alone. Someone was slumped in *her* armchair, the one that she and Gabe had shared. Her steps faltered as the person straightened and his chiseled features came into focus. Finn. The last person she expected to see here while a party raged outside. Did he even know how to read?

Okay, that was mean. Yana of all people should know not to judge others.

But she should proceed cautiously. Finn could very well have been sent by Everly to stop Yana's investigation.

Her foot clanged against the metal base of the coffee table, and Finn shot out of his seat. Her shoulders relaxed. He was as surprised to see her as she was to see him.

"Oh. It's you," he said. With a lazy smile, he settled back into the chair and proceeded to give her a slow perusal. "Looking good, Yana."

"You know my name?" she said pointedly as she sat on the love seat across from him.

"I make it a point to know the names of every pretty girl I'm around." He flashed straight white teeth.

Yana rolled her eyes. Finn was a notorious flirt. She was fairly sure he'd try to seduce the file cabinets if they could sigh and fawn in return. "Flirting, Finn?" she said lightly. "It would be more convincing if you hadn't stared at me blankly and refused to budge when I was trying to get through the door to history class last semester."

"Was that you?" he asked, unbothered.

"No, it was the *other* Asian girl at Yatesville High," she quipped, referring to the half-Korean freshman girl who looked nothing like Yana.

"Really?" His eyes heated. "You mean there's two of you? Now, *that's* a guy's dream come true. Or girl's. Not discriminating here."

If he wanted his ego inflated by stammers and blushes, he was wasting his breath. He was attractive; Yana wasn't so bitter that she couldn't see that. The requisite blond hair and blue eyes, accompanied by a bad-boy smirk. But she had witnessed his offhanded cruelty too often to fall for his shallow compliments. Cutting the line in front of powerless underclassmen was only one example.

"I like your dress," Finn continued, oblivious to her frostiness. "One of Taylor's hand-me-downs? Her mom loves to donate to secondhand stores. Makes her feel charitable." He made air quotes with his fingers around the last word, his voice sour.

Ah. There was the Finn Yana knew and *didn't* love.

Yet the insult still knocked the breath out of Yana. She wasn't ready. She hadn't prepared. She hadn't braced herself, the way she had before school every day, putting on her invisible shield and armor.

That was *her* fault. She never should've let down her guard for one moment. She shouldn't have allowed herself to be distracted by Derek or Amelia—even her interactions with Gabe.

This is what happened when she wasn't expecting the worst.

"I don't have to listen to this. You have no idea what it's like to be judged about what you have or don't have." Yana stood, prepared to leave, but Finn's hand shot out and grabbed her arm. Not in a hard, violent way. His touch was soft, maybe even beseeching.

"Wait. Where are you going?"

"Anywhere that's not here," she said coolly.

"I wasn't trying to insult you, I swear." He raked his free hand through his perfectly coiffed hair—he probably used more product than Yana. "That was my pitiful attempt at bonding. Sorry. Please sit. I could use the company."

His hand dropped from her arm. Yana was free to go, but she didn't.

Maybe it was the apology. Maybe it was the show of vulnerability, which always fascinated Yana since she could never imagine herself being that open. Or maybe she was just curious what Finn Kelley, someone who had barely looked at her in the past four years, could possibly have to say.

She sat back down, crossing her arms and legs.

"You want to talk about what I wear and where I shop? Honestly?"

He shrugged.

"Fine. This was my prom dress, which my parents bought for me." She lifted her chin, daring him to make fun of her. It was easy to tell him the truth, since she didn't care—had never cared—what he thought. "It's simple, a little black dress, but that's the whole point. My parents wanted me to be able to wear it again, not just for one silly night."

Finn sat up. (Not an easy task, given the lumpiness of the armchair.) His eyes widened, no longer bored. "Cool . . . I—I . . . uh . . ."

Stuttering, too? This encounter was getting stranger and stranger.

He shook his head, pulling himself together. "What you said earlier about me not getting judged. I do. Get it. This outfit?" He gestured to his shorts and polo shirt. "Taylor bought it. Just like she bought my gear for swim team. Last week, she came to my house, went through my closet, and decided that I didn't have anything nice enough for this trip. Nice enough for *her*. She's tried this crap before, but I never let her dictate my wardrobe, outside of the necessities. *We're not in high school anymore, Finn,* she said. So, if I want to be her grown-ass, adult boyfriend, I have to look the part."

Yana blinked. Golden Boy was just like her. Just like Naya. In one way at least. He didn't have as much money as the Taylors and Everlys of the world. She'd had no idea.

"Tay's so sure of herself," he continued. "That's one of the things that attracts me most—her absolute certainty about our future. Both of us, attending TU next year. Married three years after that. Her parents have already bought us a luxury condo downtown. We move in as soon as we get back from Bermuda. After college, we'll work if we feel like it. If not, her trust fund will take care of us."

He laughed, self-mockingly. "All I have to do is not piss her off, and my life is set."

Yana asked the obvious question, the one that should've been front and center in his dilemma. "Do you love her?"

He glanced up. The light painted shadows across that strong jaw, across his geometrically perfect nose, tilted 106 degrees at the tip. (Or so Taylor had announced on social media after she measured.) Yet his indecision was clear.

"Is it her, or how much she offers? I wish I knew," Finn said, and then shook his head, as though disgusted at the picture he'd painted of himself, disgusted at the light in which he appeared.

"It's not about the money, although I wouldn't blame you for thinking that. Hell, that's probably what Tay herself believes," he said. "The thing is, I crave predictability. Stability. You see, my sister is bipolar, and so my family life is always in upheaval. I adore Lily. Like my parents, I'd part the ocean for her. But I never know what will happen from one day to the next. And so, the kind of mapped-out future that Taylor promises is tempting. I just don't know if that's the life I see for myself."

His words hung in the air and turned solid.

An instant later, the moment was shattered by a scream that wrenched the night.

THIRTEEN

YANA

8:58 P.M.

Yana jumped to her feet, the cry icing her blood.

The feral howl was *that* bad. The stuff of nightmares. Worse, even. The mind has a way of protecting people from the things they can't handle or understand. And that sound had come straight from the abyss of the unimaginable.

Yana's eyes met Finn's. He was frozen in place, stymied by the fight-or-flight response. The *last* thing Yana wanted was to face whoever had released that anguished cry. Yet where, exactly, could they run when they were trapped on a yacht in the middle of the ocean?

"We should investigate," she offered. That was what she did, after all. "Someone might be in trouble."

Instead of responding, Finn just stared at her—eyes wide, knuckles clenched, a line of sweat forming along his hairline. She didn't wait for him to snap out of it. Whoever had cried out didn't have the luxury of time. Without another thought, Yana ran toward the noise. Fight, it was.

She wasn't much of an athlete; she'd only run track for one season, in the seventh grade, when her team had managed to squeak into a second-place finish in the relay race. But somehow she beat everyone else on the yacht to the bow.

Well. The ones who weren't *already* there.

The deck was dark. Shadows shrouded the white leather couch where she'd sat with Brett that afternoon, and the railing of the yacht blended with the turbulent black ocean. The wind whipped back her hair and pelted her skin with drops of water. Above the dull roar, she heard a low, animalistic moan.

Yana absently swiped at her face, her attention captured by the single spotlight shining on the hot tub—and the figure standing inside it.

Gabe. Fully clothed, the water rising to his waist. Wet cotton clung to his back. At first, Yana thought he was cradling some kind of wounded aquatic mammal. And then she realized that the keening was coming from *him*.

Shocked, she waded into the hot tub. Water sloshed against her dress and flooded her tennis shoes. "Gabe? What's wrong?"

Nothing. Either he didn't hear her or he wasn't capable of answering. She put a hand on his arm. It was surprisingly cold, given the heat of the water. He couldn't have been standing there long. "Gabe," she said, louder, trying to break through his trance. *"Gabe."*

His head snapped up, his eyes darting wildly around the deck. His breath was coming in quick, panicked gulps. And on his cheeks, were those . . . splatters of blood?

For the first time, Yana noticed that the water they were

standing in was murky. As though it had been mixed with another liquid.

"I told her to be careful," Gabe babbled. "I told her she couldn't go around blackmailing people. 'Cause one day, karma would collect." Gabe's face crumpled, and he lowered it to his hands.

"Slow down." Yana grabbed his hands and pulled them down to reveal his tortured expression. "Who are you talking about?"

"Everly," Gabe gasped, swaying on his feet. "We have to help her. She doesn't deserve this. Please."

His arm was wrapped around Yana's shoulders now, her shorter body functioning as a crutch, while she struggled to keep them both upright. "Where is she?" she asked. With a shaky finger, Gabe pointed toward the prow of the yacht, where the mermaid lifted her head high, guiding them toward safe and calm waters.

Except . . . something was obscuring the mermaid, some-thing more substantial than the dark.

Yana moved closer. Gabe's arm slipped off her shoulder; she would have to trust that he could float.

She could make out someone slumped in front of the mermaid.

"Everly?"

But what was she doing? Her body was pressed against the metal figurehead. Was she *hugging* the mermaid? Trying to set up some kind of selfie? Maybe her neck had gotten stuck on the statue, like a tongue licking a piece of ice. But how would that even happen on a balmy night in the middle of the ocean?

Yana pushed herself up and out of the hot tub, her soaked

dress weighing her down like an anchor. Every step was a struggle. Every inch forward, a win.

Or maybe her dress wasn't impeding her progress. Maybe it was the dread saturating the air.

When Yana was a foot away, she smelled it. Over the salt of the ocean, intermingled with the chlorine of the hot tub. Sharp, metallic. There was no mistaking it: blood.

It dripped down Everly's body and pooled around her feet. *That's going to stain,* Yana thought faintly. *Both her midriff-baring blue top and ruffled skirt as well as the teak flooring.*

She walked closer . . . and then wished she hadn't.

Everly *was* stuck to the mermaid. Specifically, the tallest spike of the mermaid crown impaled her neck. A bull's-eye of blood circled the spike, turning Everly into a gruesome corpse.

Yana was looking at the end of *Rumor Has It* . . . the end of countless blackmailing . . . the end of one girl's micro-aggressions . . . the end of Everly.

Her stomach heaved. She knew she shouldn't vomit, not here. The headlines would not be kind—*Crime Scene Destroyed by Avalanche of Puke*—but she couldn't help herself. She threw up all over the corpse.

FOURTEEN

NAYA

9:01 P.M.

"Everly's dead!"

The words exploded in Naya's ears as she charged toward the bow. The voice was disembodied, far away, a shriek against the wind that sent a trail of ice down her spine.

And then she saw it. She saw *them*.

Naya stared at the red water lapping against the sides of the hot tub, shimmering in the yacht's low light like red Kool-Aid.

She froze, feet cemented to the glossy deck, vision blurring as she stared unblinking at Yana. Crimson droplets rained around her feet, splattering her white shoes, now dyed pink with blood.

Everly's blood.

It cascaded down the metal railing, encircled her sandals, swirled with vomit, and dripped into the hot tub.

Gabe pulled himself out of the water. He moved as though

his legs were bags of wet cement as he crept closer to the body.

Naya pressed her eyelids shut. If she kept her eyes closed, she could rewrite the scene—imagine that Everly was draped over the mermaid in a perfect pose.

But there was so much blood . . .

Naya's heart climbed into her throat, and she struggled to breathe. While volunteering with the Red Cross last summer, she'd seen firsthand how tragedies affected people, but those had been *other* people. She hadn't known them, had had no personal connection to their suffering. She'd approached each person with a measure of impersonality learned from visiting area hospitals. But this . . . Everly . . . wasn't a nameless patient.

Tennis shoes squeaked against the deck and heavy footfalls forced her eyelids open.

Finn wound around Yana and Gabe until he was inches from Everly. He flattened his hand against her rounded back, his fingers climbing toward the metal spike that pierced her neck. Like a TV doctor, he shook his head back and forth. He swiped his hand across his forehead, leaving a streak of red behind, and turned to face Gabe and Yana. His mouth moved, but Naya only heard the roar of her pulse and the splash of the North Atlantic's waves.

She had to do something to help. She was the only one of them who could.

Naya surged forward, ready to put her training to use. A shadow fell over her, and goose bumps crested along her arms when Taylor grabbed her hand. The numbness dripping into Naya's fingertips receded as Taylor yanked. Naya shuffled backward, pulled by the currents of fear and panic that swept across the bow.

"Naya!" Taylor's shout ricocheted between her ears. "We have to find the captain!"

Naya fell into step with Taylor and Étienne, squished between them as they rushed up the stairs to the wheelhouse.

Footfalls sounded behind them, harsh clanks against the polished steps that pushed Naya forward, faster, away from Everly and the blood and the three who were streaked with it.

The door to the wheelhouse was open, and the group exploded into the navigation center, cries for Captain Andy perched on their lips.

Naya took in the crescent-shaped panel covered in levers and buttons that spanned the front of the room, the six laptop-sized monitors glowing above it, and the cushioned leather chair where Captain Andy sat in front of the control panel.

"Captain!" Naya nearly sobbed with relief. She had told her mother she was an adult, but now she needed someone older and more experienced who would be better prepared for something like this.

She rounded the chair and froze. Captain Andy's eyes were closed, his chin rested on his chest, and a line of drool stained the front of his uniform.

"Captain?" Naya shook his shoulder. "Captain Andy, wake up!"

Finn charged in, his blood-streaked forehead beaded with sweat, Yana and Gabe on his heels.

Taylor nodded at the champagne glass dangling from the captain's fingertips. "I think he's drunk."

Finn spun the chair around. Captain Andy's legs dragged like anchors, his shoes squeaking against the floor.

"*Arrêt!*" Étienne reached out, but he was too late to stop Finn.

Captain Andy slid out of the chair, landing on the floor with a *thwack* that set Naya's teeth on edge.

Finn mumbled something indecipherable and bent over the captain.

"Hey!" He swatted his cheeks. "Wake up!"

"That won't work," Naya said.

Sure enough, Captain Andy didn't flinch, the only sign of life the gentle rise and fall of his chest.

"How long do you think he's been like this?" Yana asked, her voice shaky.

Taylor sucked in a ragged breath. "Who's been steering?"

Yana approached the control panel, her shoes squelching with each step. "Didn't he say something about it being on autopilot?"

Étienne pressed his hand against Naya's back. "We will figure this out," he whispered, smoothing slow circles between her shoulder blades. "Everything will be okay."

"What about this?" Taylor held up a white plastic box with a red cross stamped on its center.

"Seriously, Taylor?" Gabe peeled off his soaked T-shirt and draped it over one shoulder. Red droplets fell onto his chest. "What's a first-aid kit going to fix? Last time I checked they came with Band-Aids, not Narcan. Oh, and Everly is *fucking dead*!"

Taylor's bottom lip quivered. "I'm just trying to help."

"Well, you're not. No one is! Least of all *him*." He jabbed the captain with the toe of his wet sneaker. "The only thing that would help is going back in time and never getting on this boat."

Yana placed her hand on Gabe's arm, and he recoiled.

"Bro, calm down." Finn wiped his hands on his jeans, painting them with streaks of scarlet. "Yelling at Taylor isn't going to solve anything."

"Calm down? You want me to calm down?" Gabe wrapped one hand around his shirt, his knuckles blanching with each passing second. "I found a dead body. One of our friends has been skewered by a metal mermaid, and you want me to relax?"

Taylor crossed her arms over her chest, narrowing her eyes at Yana. "And to make things worse, Yana went and did the most disrespectful thing ever and puked all over Everly."

Finn tilted his chin. "How do you know it was Yana?"

"Who else would it be?" Taylor snapped.

Yana hugged her arms around her stomach and scooted backward.

Naya's stomach roiled in sympathy, and she shrugged away from her boyfriend, stepping into the center of the small, cramped room. "Stop. That's not important right now." Her hands trembled as she tucked her hair behind her ears, the ends now frizzing as much as her edges. With all eyes on her, she felt like she stood in the volatile, molten core of the earth. "Obviously Captain Andy is . . . indisposed, so *we* have to figure this out on our own. We should call—"

"The Coast Guard," Finn interjected, taking the focus off Naya.

Étienne threw up his hands. "With what? Mrs. Stewart took our phones. The only one with a phone is Brett, and who knows where he is."

"Wait." Taylor stepped forward. "Where *is* Brett? Or Derek and Amelia, for that matter?"

The wheelhouse erupted with angry shouts. First Gabe, then Taylor, followed by Finn, and ending with Étienne, who was trying his best to smooth everything over. It went on like this for a few minutes, a savage symphony building to an even more explosive crescendo. Besides Naya, the only other person silent was Yana.

Their eyes met, and Yana's jaw ticked once, twice, before she glanced away. Naya swallowed, her gaze sweeping around the room.

There has to be something here that can send out a signal. That can let people know we need help.

Her eyes traveled over a wall that had twelve monitors linked to the various cameras she'd seen around the ship, before landing on the expansive window that overlooked the blood-filled hot tub, Everly's limp body, and—*Brett?*

"Guys?" Naya pawed at the air behind her, unable to take her focus off Brett. But the cacophony of arguing continued. "Guys!" She released a bark that quieted the room. "I found Brett"—she shook her head, continuing to watch him as he crouched down next to Everly—"examining Everly's body?"

Taylor approached, her hands clenched into fists. "Get away from her, you creep!"

The hairs on Naya's neck rose as Brett continued his perusal of the corpse. "He can't hear you through the glass."

Yana snatched the boxy two-way radio receiver and held it up to her lips. "Mayday! Mayday! Mayday!"

The room fell silent as they waited for a response.

"Mayday! Mayday! Mayday!" she repeated.

Again there was no reply.

Anxiety swelled, forcing them all to the control panel. Buttons clicked and indicator lights flashed as they desperately tried to make contact with someone who could rouse the captain and assist them with Everly's body.

Gabe grabbed the corded phone receiver attached to the control panel and pressed it against his ear, repeating the question, "Can anyone hear me?" over and over again until it blended with the beeps and clicks of the group's feverish attempts.

A sharp *beep*, and the deck lights switched off. Naya's breath caught as the bow went dark and the glow from the bulbs illuminating the inside of the hot tub burned like an open sore against the deck.

"Shit," Finn hissed. "I can't get the main lights back on."

"You broke them?" Taylor shouted. Gabe grumbled a series of four-letter words under his breath as he sagged against the wall.

"We need to find the rest of the crew," Finn said, flicking a switch that changed the screen in front of him from gleaming white to night-vision green and then back again. "One of them will know how to work all this."

Étienne's hand found Naya's, and he gripped it tightly. "Finally, a good plan."

Finn pulled the only flashlight from its charging station by the door and turned it on as he stepped out of the room and into the darkness.

"Hopefully someone can find the right switch or change out the spark plugs or whatever's needed to fix the electricity," Taylor said, looping her arm through Naya's free one.

They left in a group, clustered together like grapes, the

only sounds coming from the hum of the engine, the crash of the waves, and their shoes on the stairs.

Naya pressed herself against Étienne as Finn led the pack.

"Brett!" Finn's shout made Naya flinch. "What the hell are you doing?" he asked, shining the flashlight in Brett's direction.

Brett jumped and held up one hand, shielding his eyes from the beam of light. "Christ! You scared me half to—" He clamped his mouth shut and cast his gaze toward Everly, her body aglow in the red light of the hot tub. "Well, *death*. But that seems inappropriate."

"That's rich, coming from you," Finn muttered.

Taylor released Naya's arm and ran down the rest of the stairs to her boyfriend's side. "Yeah. Not as inappropriate as you doing . . . What exactly *are* you doing?"

Brett shrugged. "Looking for clues."

"Clues for what? This was an accident," Gabe said, wringing out his shirt.

Brett sighed and shook his head like they were the most ridiculous people on earth. "We're on a megayacht, at night, in the middle of the ocean. This is Agatha Christie *Death on the Nile*–level gold. How does the untimely passing of our dear gossipmonger Everly not seem suspect to anyone else?"

Taylor crossed her arms over her chest. "What seems suspect is you. Give us your phone so I can see what you've been doing and call for a medic."

"Can't." Brett shrugged, unconcerned. "Battery's dead. I doubt I'd get a signal out here anyway."

A chorus of voices rose again, accusing Brett of being careless—and worse.

"Everyone, chill out. What happened to Everly was an

accident," Naya said. "Earlier, I slipped and almost . . ." Her throat tightened, and with her free hand she rubbed her neck where she, too, could have been impaled.

Étienne's hold on her hand intensified.

"I was there and caught her, but if I hadn't been—" He broke off, battling the same emotions Naya felt. "I'm sure Everly went up on the railing and fell over. It could have happened to any of us."

Gabe put his shirt back on, and Naya's lungs squeezed at the band of pink that stained the bottom half. He, Yana, and Finn were covered in Everly.

"The captain's passed out, so we're going belowdecks to find the rest of the crew," Gabe said to his old teammate, motioning in the direction of the crew access door. "You coming with or staying up here to play Inspector Gadget?"

"Inspector *Lestrade*," Brett corrected, clearly whodunit stan. "Although Detective Poirot would be more accurate. Lead the way."

Brett fell into line, and they all followed Finn as he guided the flashlight along the deck until they reached a white door that blended almost seamlessly into the prow. It opened noiselessly and a narrow beam of light glowed from the main deck pantry.

Naya released a pent-up breath. The entire ship *wasn't* dark.

"The emergency lights are switching on," Finn said, clicking off the flashlight.

As they crammed into the space, Taylor found Naya and tugged her to the front of the line. "Please tell me I'm not the only one massively creeped out right now."

"You're definitely not," Naya muttered as they descended the winding staircase that led to the crew quarters.

She shivered as her arm brushed against steel refrigerator and freezer doors as they crept along the narrow hallway and through the open galley. Aside from the low hum of the engine, the crew's area was eerily quiet. Too quiet. The kind of quiet that made Naya feel like she was being watched.

"Hello?" Her voice cracked from her dry throat. "Anyone down here?"

She hoped to hear the voice of a steward, but the steady growl of the yacht's engine was the only reply.

Naya and Taylor nearly smacked into Finn when he came to a stop in the cramped doorway that opened on the crew mess.

Naya lifted onto her tiptoes and peered over Finn's shoulder. The dark, windowless room contained a section of cabinets, a sink, a dishwasher, a minifridge, and a panel of switches and buttons they should probably stay away from.

"Oh my God." Taylor's sharp inhale drew Naya's attention to the large wooden table and banquette on the other side of the room.

The open fridge's sharp rectangle of icy white light sliced across the table, illuminating the crew members in an eerie glow. Eight of them sat slumped over as if boneless, their faces pressed against the tabletop. Half-empty champagne glasses littered the table, some still clutched in the crew members' hands.

Naya slipped between Finn and Taylor and rushed to a crew member crumpled on the tile floor, one hand outstretched toward the door. She checked his pulse. Feeling a steady, slow rhythm, she shook his shoulders.

No response.

"Can you hear me?" she shouted close to his ear.

No response.

"We need that stuff Gabe mentioned." Finn snapped his fingers, searching for the word. "Narcan!"

"With this many people unconscious, they've likely been drugged with benzos, ketamine, GHB. . . ." Naya stood, shaking her head. "Naloxone won't be effective. It only works on opioid overdose."

Shouts and curses rose from the others as they rushed past her into the dining hall and tried and failed to rouse even one crew member. Naya waded backward through her friends, putting more space between her and the unconscious people draped over the table and on the floor like cast-off dolls lit only by the haunting glow of the refrigerator.

She couldn't save them, couldn't help them, any of them. Her thoughts spun and her stomach dropped as if she were falling, hurtling toward the earth until—

Oof!

Naya slammed into a solid form. She whirled around to face them.

"Brett!" she hissed, pressing her palms against her chest.

"They're passed out," he said, his eyes never leaving the doorway to the crew mess and their friends' frenzied actions as they shook and yelled at each crew member.

It wasn't a question, but Naya answered anyway. "Yeah, like Captain Andy."

She bit her lower lip and stared up at him. He was unmoving, unphased by what they'd discovered.

"They were drugged. Who would do something like this?" Naya swallowed as Brett's unflinching gaze met hers. "And if they could do this, would they kill Everly?"

"Now, that is the million-dollar question."

FIFTEEN

NAYA

9:17 P.M.

The group operated with one mind, running back down the hall, up the staircase, and exploding onto the deck now dimly lit with fluorescent white emergency lights. They stampeded back down the main stairs to the guest quarters in a mad dash to find the only other "adult" on board.

Naya was glad they were together, not only because there was safety in numbers but also because she would have gotten lost a hundred times over without them. Plus, there was someone on this boat who wanted the crew out of the way. Why?

They turned another corner toward Derek's room. The muffled, tinny drone of music through the expensive oak door filled the shadowy hallway.

Yana reached the room first and slammed her fist against the door. "Derek!" she shouted between strikes. "There's been an incident. Something's wrong. We need your help!"

Taylor stormed up to the door. "Something isn't just wrong," she spat, her narrowed gaze never leaving Yana. "Everly was murdered. This was personal."

Shaking her head, Naya took a step back. "As in intentional?"

"What are you saying, Taylor?" Gabe asked, pushing through the others to stand next to Yana.

"The captain and the crew are unconscious," she said, ticking the points off on her fingers. "Everly's dead. That was no accident. She was a direct threat to Yana. Everyone knows Yana was jealous that her little articles didn't get as much attention as *Rumor Has It*."

Yana crossed her arms over her chest as the group's attention darted from one girl to the other. "I wasn't threatened by Everly."

"The internship!" Taylor shouted, her eyes wide and wild. "The *Yatesville Sun!*"

"I got the internship!" Yana countered. "There was nothing Everly could do about it."

"She knew exactly how you got that position: your parents' secret connection with the editor-in-chief." Taylor turned to the group as if she'd just finished a closing argument.

"What?" Yana sputtered. "She used to come into the restaurant sometimes. She liked our crab rangoon. That was literally our only so-called connection."

"Yana wouldn't kill anyone, especially over a job," Naya said without thinking. She was no longer best friends with Yana, but she didn't have to be to know that Yana wasn't a murderer.

"And, if you're looking for motive, all of us had one," Gabe added.

Finn opened his mouth as if to protest but closed it just as quickly.

Taylor brushed her hair from her face and leveled her gaze back on Yana. "There's only one of us who wasn't friends with her."

Gabe let out a rush of air and scrubbed his palm against his brow. "Who here has been blackmailed by Everly?"

One by one, everyone raised their hand. Everyone except Yana.

"So, Ev was a bit manipulative." Taylor shrugged. "That doesn't prove anything."

"Nobody would've offed Everly because she blackmailed them," Finn said slowly. "More likely, someone had a secret that she knew. A secret they would kill to protect."

"Oh, really? And what was your secret, Finn?" His girlfriend rounded on him. "That you secretly had the hots for her?"

As the rest of their friends continued arguing, Étienne leaned into Naya. "What did Everly threaten you with?"

Goose bumps raised on Naya's arms, and she smoothed them down with a quick swipe of her hands. "Nothing yet." She thought of Everly approaching her that evening with her "life-changing secret." "But I think she was about to. What about you?"

Before he could answer, another series of punishing knocks echoed on Derek's door. "No one cares that you're in there *discussing next year's student council transition* with Amelia!" Taylor called. "We graduated. She's legal. Whatever."

Naya's gaze went to Yana. She hadn't heard the rest of their conversation or whatever other accusations Taylor may have flung at her. The mass drugging and Everly's murder had everyone tense, on edge. There was someone on this boat with ulterior motives, and Naya had no idea who it was.

Yana blinked up at Taylor, an unreadable expression ghosting her features.

"What?" Taylor glanced back at her and shrugged. "She *has* graduated, and she *is* eighteen. Amelia's not as young as our sweet Naya." She leaned back and pushed Naya's shoulder. "Right, babe?"

Naya gave a weak smile. It seemed that, for the moment, things were back to normal. Well, as normal as they could be given the circumstances. Still, this didn't feel like the time to comment about how she hated always being the last one to reach the coveted milestones of a driver's permit, a driver's license, and now, getting in unaccompanied to R-rated movies. Not that she had any interest in seeing a scary movie ever again. Witnessing Everly's speared neck was enough horror for the rest of her life.

Brett cracked his knuckles and gave a loud clap as if about to start a swim meet. "We should break down the door."

Gabe, Étienne, and Finn turned to him before warily eyeing the solid slab of wood.

"What? We're big, strapping young men, aren't we?" Brett crossed his arms over his chest. "Plus, brute force usually works."

Couldn't argue with that logic.

Yana stepped back, making room for Gabe as he motioned to the door. "If you think you can knock it down, go for it."

Naya winced, her shoulders aching with the thought of ramming them into the thick, expensive oak.

Brett inhaled, his muscled chest swelling as he tested

the door's strength with a quick practice shove. "On second thought," he said, "we should get the ax."

Étienne let out an exasperated exhale. "Where are you going to find an ax?"

"Dude, watch a movie. There's always an ax on a boat." Brett stroked his smooth chin and turned to Yana. "It's usually by an exit, right?"

"How would she know?" Naya clamped her mouth shut. She hadn't meant to be so rude and say the question aloud. But really, how *would* Yana know? She'd never been on a boat. Although, until this trip, she and Naya had barely made eye contact for five years. A lot could happen in that time.

Yana put her hands on her hips. "I have watched movies, you know."

"I know. I just meant that . . ." Naya cleared her throat. This wasn't how she wanted their second conversation in years to go.

"What?" Yana cocked her head, her dark eyes narrowing. "That I'm too poor to have ever streamed a movie set on a yacht much less take a trip on one?"

"No, that's not—"

"It's fine." Yana held up her hands. "Whatever. I'm just being sensitive because there's a freaking dead body on board. And, you know, a murderer roaming around. But you do you." She opened her mouth to say more, but instead turned and strode back down the hall.

"I don't think you killed anyone!" Naya called after her. "I don't think any of us did it. We might not all be friends, but none of us is a murderer. That's just . . . ridiculous. Right?"

No one met her eyes as her gaze swept her friends' face, but that didn't change her opinion. She knew these people.

She had faith in these people. It was someone else. Someone who had snuck aboard. Someone who had to be stopped.

"So . . ." Brett clicked his tongue in the tense silence. "I'm off to find an ax."

"I'll come, too." Finn gave Taylor a quick peck on the cheek before joining Brett.

"Yeah." Gabe ran his hands through his hair, his eyes searching the corridor. "Me too."

Naya blinked. Had she single-handedly torn apart the group with her comment?

Taylor slung her arm over Naya's shoulders and leaned against her. "Yana was completely out of line. Major attention-seeking behavior in a time of crisis, and I know attention-seeking behavior."

"I didn't know she and Brett talked about movies together. I never—" Naya's lungs tightened and she let out a weak cough. "I would never say that she's poor."

Taylor scoffed. "She *is*."

Naya shrugged out of Taylor's reach. "So am I."

"Yeah, but that's different." Taylor pulled out her lipstick and applied another coat. "You're closer to being one of us than she ever will be."

She'd said it so easily.

But do they accept you?

Naya's fingers tingled, and she tightened her hands into fists. She'd planned on keeping in touch with Taylor after high school. But *this* Taylor, the one on the megayacht, the one she'd quite possibly been for years, was not someone Naya wanted to stay friends with.

I don't need to be one of you. The words sat on her tongue, but she couldn't bring herself to say them. She didn't even know if she believed them. Could she reach her goals without people like Taylor?

"Hey." Étienne grabbed Naya's hand, his golden gaze dropping to the floor. "Listen, there's something I must tell you."

Naya's stomach squeezed. "That's almost as bad as being told 'We need to talk.'" She forced a chuckle, but he didn't return it.

"It's about this." He smoothed his thumb over the links of the bracelet. "It's not yours. It's not mine."

Naya took her hand from his and clutched it against her chest. "I don't understand."

Even as she said the words, she knew they weren't true.

"I took it," he said, his gaze not lifting from the floor. "I stole it. I've stolen . . . a lot of things."

Naya swore she heard a gasp, but with how far away and out of her body she felt, it could have been her own. She sucked in another breath and pressed her fingers to her lips.

Finally, Étienne glanced up at her. "It's amazing the things you discover about people when they don't know you are watching."

Naya took a step back as if increasing the distance between them could keep her from his admission. Everly had let her in on this secret months ago. She'd let everyone in.

"I didn't want to believe what she wrote." Naya's eyes burned and her throat squeezed, but she wouldn't cry. She would no longer be *that girl*—the one surrounded by sharks and too naive to know it. Now Naya would be honest with herself even though her boyfriend hadn't been. "Whose is it, Étienne? Who did you steal this bracelet from?"

"It's Everly's." Taylor pushed away from the wall like a shadow. "At least, it *was*."

"Are you serious?" Naya found the clasp and tore the bracelet from her wrist, shock and disgust clawing up her throat.

"Here. Take it," she said, thrusting it at Étienne. "Take it!"

The delicate jewelry danced in the air, vibrating in Naya's shaking grasp.

"Naya, there's more." He shuffled forward, and she took another step back.

"Don't, Étienne." Her vision blurred as tears threatened to spill. "I can't—" She shook her head. "I don't want to hear anything else."

Naya thought back. Taylor had known. When Taylor had found her and Étienne together, when he'd given Naya the gift, she had known. It wasn't Taylor's jealousy Naya had felt. It was her judgment.

Why didn't she say anything? Knowing that Étienne was lying to her face? But Naya was guilty of the same transgression. She'd lied to Taylor, too.

She bit the inside of her cheeks as a sob cracked in her throat.

"You should've gone back to Paris," she whispered before dropping the bracelet and running away like Yana, too upset to be concerned with her safety.

SIXTEEN

YANA

9:28 P.M.

Yana slumped against the wall by the partially open door. Not one of them knew she was there because not one of them bothered to notice where she had gone: to her own cabin, opposite Derek's. She'd hoped against hope that she would find Amelia sleeping in her own bed. But alas, she wasn't in the room. Her roommate must be where the others suspected, ensconced with Derek.

Stay calm, Yana ordered herself, wringing her hands. Amelia was probably fine. Derek wasn't necessarily the murderer nor a sexual predator. She had no actual proof that the champagne had been spiked. Anyone could've drugged the crew and put the Rohypnol in her bag. A disgruntled crew member. A stowaway. Everyone in their group had a motive to kill Everly. One thing was for sure: her death had been premeditated.

Yana pulled out her notebook, the one she used to record

her observations for upcoming stories, and began to write down the list of suspects.

Amelia. If the gossip queen had threatened to pin the cheating on her.

Derek. For the same reason, he had motive to cover up his role in the scandal.

Finn, who stood, frozen, at the sound of Gabe's anguished cry. His flirtation with Everly might have pissed off Taylor and threatened his perfect future with her. Offing Taylor's competition would set his life back on track.

Taylor. Likewise, she could be the killer, if Finn and Everly's flirtation had crossed an emotional or physical line. If she was ragey-jealous enough to retaliate.

They could've Bonnie-and-Clyde'd the situation.

Brett??? Ah, good ole Brett. Wacky—and violent—sense of humor. Brought a Slender Mask on the yacht . . . for what reason? As a practical joke? Tons of tension between him and Everly over his supposed steroid use. And he was snooping around her body, for pra Buddha cho's sake!

Étienne. We can't rule him out. He had admitted that he was blackmailed by Everly like the others. She had called him a thief—a huge accusation. Foreign thieves didn't get to stay in the US.

Gabe and Naya . . . Well, they were harder to explain. Yana's gut told her that neither of them were murderers, but what did she know? They had raised their hands in the confession circle. Plus, with her interest in medicine, Naya could've figured out just how much Rohypnol to give the crew to render them unconscious.

And now that Yana thought about it, why had Gabe measured the very library where she was sitting when she heard his anguished cry? Could he have been calculating how long it would take for someone to run to the scene of the crime?

Finally, herself. Yana. Taylor had been right. She *was* a suspect. An outsider. A long-standing competitor of the dead girl. Just because she didn't raise her hand didn't mean she'd had no bad blood with Everly. Naya, Brett, and the others could easily believe that Everly had stumbled upon a secret of Yana's, something shadier than her boss being a patron of Siam Garden.

Yana rolled her neck, closing her notebook. Her brain hurt. There were too many suspects. Too many questions. Not enough answers.

Grief clawed at her throat. Yana hadn't been close to Everly. She wasn't sure she could dredge up one positive interaction between them. Yet a girl she knew, with whom she had competed, year after year, was dead. Everly had pushed Yana to do her best, without even knowing it. Everly might not have been kind, but she'd had a bright future. She had an impressive talent for rooting out the truth. A fun, clever way with words. Her death was such a waste.

Tears burned the backs of Yana's eyes. Before they could spill out, she rose to her knees and peered out the crack of the cabin door.

In the hallway, Étienne clawed at the air, grasping at nothing, while Naya's hair whipped around the corner.

"Naya, wait," he pleaded. "It's not safe—"

He slumped to the floor, right where the tapestry rug ended and six inches of hardwood began. Taylor patted him on the shoulder.

"I can't believe Naya won't even talk to me," Étienne mumbled to his knees.

"Um, I can. She just found out her boyfriend's a klepto," Taylor said. "She needs a little time."

"We don't have time! I go back to France right after this trip." He slammed one hand against the wall, hard enough that a loud crack sounded and an indentation formed in the wall.

Taylor jumped. *Yana* jumped. She had never seen Étienne violent before, and she doubted Taylor had, either.

"Dude. Calm down!" Taylor huffed.

Étienne stretched out his bruised hand and studied the wall. "*Mon dieu.* I don't know what's wrong with me."

"My mom will send you a bill for property damage on behalf of the Yates Foundation," Taylor said crisply. "In the meantime, try keeping your sticky fingers to yourself."

He pushed to his feet. "I have to find Naya." He yanked up his pants and pulled something from his calf. "And I can't hold on to this thing any longer."

Yana squinted. A gleaming curved handle with a long serrated blade. Holy crap, was that a hunting knife?

"Whoa, whoa, whoa!" Taylor scooted backward across the rug, strands of her hair sticking to the wall with static electricity. "Where did you get that?"

"From a blue duffel bag in the lounge," Étienne said. "Not sure whose. It came with a calf strap and everything."

Taylor stared at him. "Exactly how many of us have you stolen from?"

Yana stiffened. If Étienne had lifted objects from multiple bags, could he also have put items *into* their luggage? Had he been the one who stashed the Rohypnol in her duffel? He had as much to lose as anyone else if Everly had gone to the authorities with proof of his thieving ways.

Goose bumps popped out along her arms. It was one thing to speculate about the others' motives. Quite another to see Naya's boyfriend holding a very dangerous knife that had no business being on board.

"You can't go after Naya holding a knife!" Taylor exclaimed. "Do you have any idea how scary and suspicious you seem right now?"

Étienne glanced down at the hunting knife, which looked entirely too comfortable in his hand. He was either a natural . . . or he'd had experience wielding deadly weapons.

"I thought knowing I had something to defend us with might bring Naya some comfort," he said. "Since there's a killer on the loose." Apparently, he too had reached the same conclusion as Yana, as Taylor, as anyone with any sense on this yacht.

Everly was murdered, and the murderer might very well be *him*. How many killers lied to their friends' faces in the movies before slashing them?

"Think, Étienne! How's she going to react if you attempt to apologize holding *that*?"

"You're right." He grimaced. "I'm . . . not thinking clearly. But I have to go to her, whether or not she wants me around. She can't be alone. And neither should you."

Carefully, he hid the knife behind a potted plant, on the elegantly carved sideboard. He and Taylor walked down the hall, presumably to the cabin that she and Naya shared. Yana waited a beat, and then she slipped out of her room, picked up the knife from its hiding place—and slid it into one of the deep side pockets of her dress.

Yana crept upstairs. The hunting knife weighed down one side of her dress, banging against her hip every two steps, while her mini composition notebook pulled down the other side.

She could hardly believe it. She, Yana Bunpraserit, was wandering around a yacht with a deadly weapon concealed in her flouncy dress. A razor-sharp steel blade with a grip that wouldn't get slippery even when covered in blood. A knife that could puncture flesh with a single twitch of the wrist. She'd run away and scream if she thought about it too deeply. Except for one problem: there was nowhere to run. She was trapped in the freaking Atlantic Ocean.

A squeak sounded above her, and Yana whimpered, clinging onto the railing for dear life. This was it. The murderer was descending upon her. The Slender Man prank earlier was just a warm-up. This was the real deal. She was going to die in a cheap dress in a fancy stairwell, far away from the only people who truly loved her.

She squeezed her eyes shut . . . but nothing happened. The only noise she heard was the thudding of her own heart. No killer, then.

Get a grip, she ordered herself. Her stomach churned, twisting and contorting and folding in on itself. Nothing new there. Years of therapy had taught her exactly how to calm her physical symptoms before they resulted in regurgitation.

Deep breath in—*one, two, three, four*—and out—*one, two, three, four.*

Alphabetical cognitive game with animals. *A* is for aardvark; *B,* bear; *C,* camel.

Homing in with her senses, she eyed the runner on the stairs, plush underneath the thin soles of her tennis shoes.

Heard the ocean crashing against the yacht. Felt a burning sensation at the back of her throat.

When she regained some semblance of steadiness, she continued up the stairs. Were those . . . footsteps behind her? She stopped again to listen. No. Just her imagination, again. She'd need a whole lot more courage if she was going to survive her chosen career in investigative journalism, let alone this night.

She'd been too hasty to storm off by herself. In every horror movie ever, bad things happened when a person peeled off from the group. Which was what they'd all done, for reasons that only seemed rational at the time. She had to find someone else, quick. For her protection. For her sanity.

At long last, she stepped onto the deck and took a deep breath of night air, trying to get rid of the smell of dead corpse. Well, not *the* deck, the one where they had found Everly, but the crow's nest, which was on the tippy top of the four-floor yacht.

The coast was clear, except for a couple of cans of soda canoodling on the ledge of a hot tub—because, you know, one wasn't enough on a yacht this size. Yana walked to the railing and gazed out over the ocean. That was when she saw the silhouette sitting in front of the railing, twenty feet away, legs dangling over the edge, almost invisible in the shadows of the hot tub.

Gabe. It was becoming easier and easier to identify him at a glance. That long, lean figure. That messy mop of hair.

Should she trust him? Of course not. But there was safety in numbers. And he and Naya were the two people she knew best in this group, even though that wasn't saying much.

Indecision gripped her, but she finally took the knife out

of her pocket and laid it on one of the bar tables, along with her notebook. She wanted the weapon close by in case she needed it for protection. Besides, Gabe had no reason to trust her. For once, she agreed with Taylor. Deadly weapons weren't exactly conducive to gaining someone's confidence.

She crossed the deck and hesitantly sat down next to Gabe. They were concealed by the bulk of the hot tub and the partial roof rising above their heads. A dozen yards below, the water prowled up the sides of the yacht. The black of the sea almost matched the sky's deep navy. Similar colors, different textures. The sky was highlighted by the brilliant pinpricks of stars.

"I'm okay," Gabe said finally, his eyes on the ceaseless surge-and-retreat of the ocean. "You don't have to babysit me. It's just . . . I can't believe she's dead."

"Maybe I'm not thinking about you." Yana's tone was light, given the sorrow-soaked air. "Maybe I'm freaked out and don't want to be alone. I wasn't as close as you were to Everly. I don't have any special claim to sadness—" She broke off, a sob clogging her throat.

She hadn't even liked the girl, but respect and a deep, ferocious regret saturated her veins.

Gabe raised his hooded gaze. He was wrecked. Eyes bloodshot. His composure only held together by his sheer resolve to continue.

This was not the fake grief of a cold-blooded killer. She'd hang up her journalist's cap if her instincts were wrong. The knots in her stomach loosened. She was safe here, in these shadows, next to Gabe. No one would be able to spot them from the door with a cursory glance.

"I'm sad, yeah," he said in a low voice. "But I also feel

guilty. Countless times, I hoped she would just go away." He moved his shoulders. "I can't help but wonder if the universe granted my wish 'cause I prayed for it so hard."

Yana blinked. Now, *that* was unexpected. She'd thought there was a flirtatious vibe between Everly and Gabe. Maybe not now, but definitely in the past. Definitely on prom night. She could still hear Everly's delighted squeals as Gabe whirled her around the dance floor. Could still see the way Ev looped her arms around his neck as the tempo slowed to a sultry ballad.

"To the outside observer, the two of you seemed to get along well enough."

"We were neighbors. I've known Everly since we were both in diapers." He rested his forehead against the middle rail. "She wasn't necessarily warm and fuzzy, but she did have her moments. In elementary school she would bring an extra sandwich for me every Monday and Tuesday because she knew that those were the days my dad had me, and he always forgot to buy groceries. He and I practically lived on takeout.

"And once, she found a dead baby bird, and we had a full-blown funeral for it next to the brook that ran behind our houses. We picked wildflowers, I played 'Twinkle, Twinkle, Little Star' on my violin, and Ev gave a little speech." He shook his head. "The tombstone we made out of her mom's crystal paperweight is still there. I saw it just the other day during my run." He squeezed his eyes shut, as though the memory was too painful. "I hate that I've been so mad at her these last couple months."

"You weren't the only person who wished she would disappear," Yana said gently. In spite of their long-standing friendship, Gabe had raised his hand. Everly had blackmailed him, too. "Everly had more enemies than she did tubes of lipstick."

"She was the one who invited you here, you know," he burst out. "Bragged to me about it before the party tonight. She pulled some strings—aka asked Daddy, who was the society's chairman of the board, for a favor—because she wanted you to report on some major reveal that was supposed to take place tonight. She said the news would be taken more seriously coming from you."

"Are you sure that's what she said?" Yana creased her brow. "She hated me. If she was behind my invitation, I'm sure it was for some very petty reason."

"Nah. Ev was like that to everybody. It was just her personality. But she respected you. Said she didn't trust anyone else to break this story."

Yana blinked. And then blinked again. So, the respect had been mutual. Her chest tightened and her eyes burned all over again. For a minute or ten, the hardwood bit into her thighs, the salt clung to the air, and they looked at the night rippling out into oblivion.

"Why are you being so nice to me?" Gabe asked, his voice riding the wind that buffeted them.

"This is nice?" Yana gave a short laugh. "Am I so cold that I get brownie points for being a decent person?"

"Not cold . . . complex. You feel things really deeply, I can tell. You just don't share them with the rest of the world." He shook his head. "After I ignored you at prom, you had every right not to speak to me again."

Fair point. Prom conjured up a whole mix of feelings—anger, humiliation, insecurity, regret. She had sworn she'd never make herself vulnerable to him again.

And yet . . . she'd seen his face crumple in despair less than an hour ago. She'd supported his staggering weight as hot jets of water swirled around their legs. A classmate was dead, speared on the spike of a mermaid, only months before she was supposed to start the next chapter of her life. At the moment, his betrayal seemed insignificant, even frivolous.

"That's in the past," she said.

"I want to explain." Gabe cleared his throat. "Everly was the reason I ditched you on prom night."

Yana dug her fingernails into her palms, not sure she wanted to hear this.

Gabe slung his hands over the railing. "My sister Ava was dating Everly's brother." His mouth twisted. "They got into a huge fight the night before prom and broke up. I guess he ran crying to Everly, 'cause next thing I know, Ev's got me backed against a wall at the dance, shoving a phone with revealing photos of Ava in my face. My little *sister*."

He shuddered. "I was so pissed. The only thing worse would've been the rest of the world seeing them, too. Everly said I had to do *exactly* what she demanded, or she would go beyond a *Rumor Has It* teaser and post the photos on her site." He ducked his head. "My first task was to drop you immediately and spend the rest of the dance catering to her every need. Never mind that her poor date was also doing the same thing." He laughed, unamused. "Some friend, huh?"

Yana shook her head, trying to wrap her mind around Gabe's confession. "I don't understand. Was she upset for her brother? Or did she have a crush on you?"

"She's always been flirty, but I think she was madder at you. Respect or not, she was raging that you'd gotten that summer internship. She probably wanted to hurt you any way she could." Gabe slowly rubbed his temples. "I should've told you. I wish I hadn't let her use me as a tool in her petty revenge. But Ev held the photos over me. I couldn't tell anyone." He shook his head again, disgusted. "I was her puppet."

"You were a caring brother." Somewhat to herself, somewhat to him, she whispered, "I thought you ghosted me because I wouldn't have sex with you."

"What?" He turned to her, wide-eyed. "No. That was never my expectation."

"It was just, you know. That *Rumor Has It* post said that the varsity athlete was dating this girl for only one reason—"

"You thought that was about *us*?"

He was so incredulous, it was cute.

"Um, yeah. Why would Everly put up such a scathing post if it didn't concern one of her inner circle dating someone *beneath him*?" Yana put the last two words in air quotes.

Gabe shook his head. "I'm hardly inner circle."

"Given the way she ogled you, you were the very core of her group."

For the first time in the conversation, his mouth quirked. "Must have something to do with my hot bod."

A paltry attempt at humor, but she laughed anyway.

But then his eyes dropped to her bare legs, and the laugh died in her throat. Her dress had ridden up, so a good length of her thighs shone in the moonlight. He raised his eyes an instant later, but the glance had been undeniable.

The air went still. If the wind blew against her cheeks, she didn't feel it. If the waves continued to pummel the yacht, she didn't hear them. The only thing she was aware of was her knee, nestled against his. Her hand, lying on the teakwood next to his larger one. His lips, inches from her own.

"Can you forgive me?" he asked, his voice scratchy.

"I'd be a jerk not to."

"And we've established that you're a nice, decent person." A shadow of a smile crossed his lips.

"True. But," she warned, "no more compliments."

Gabe lifted his eyebrows. "I guess you *don't* want to hear how pretty you looked on prom night? I . . . always wanted to tell you that."

"Okay. You can keep *those* compliments coming." Yana motioned to the lacy black minidress with a sweeping neckline. "I'm wearing the same dress that I wore at prom," she confessed.

"I know. I think about it more than I should probably admit." His pupils darkened. His head bent. And then she lifted her face, pulled by an invisible magnet. Yet, when he was an inch away, he stopped.

"I'm sorry," he said hoarsely. "Everly just died. Her body is lifeless on this yacht. This . . . this doesn't feel right."

Disappointment landed in her belly with a thud, but Yana nodded, refusing to let it show. "Yeah. I get it. Bad timing."

She got to her feet, and he stood up next to her. They both gazed awkwardly out at the water. In the distance, directly at eye level, a white light flashed—and then flashed again.

"Another yacht?" Yana blurted. "Maybe they can help us."

Gabe shook his head. "Too far. And we have no way to flag them down. But you just gave me an idea," he mused. "I could swim out to the rescue tender. You know, the speedboat that the yacht is towing, in case of emergencies? I swim much greater distances every day."

Not among the swells of the ocean, though, in the middle

of the night, with who-knows-what marine life just waiting to take a bite.

But Yana didn't voice her protests out loud. Because she knew—with a dead body, no communication, and zero adults—they had to consider every option.

"You'll need a life vest."

SEVENTEEN

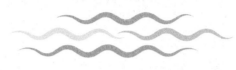

YANA

10:14 P.M.

Gabe insisted that they split up.

He wanted to check on the crew to see if any of them had woken up. In the meantime, Yana would retrieve life vests from the main deck. Efficiency of time and movement.

Separating was the practical thing to do, Yana assured herself. Yet she couldn't help but feel rejected. Just a bit. She understood the reason—even agreed with it—but the facts were indisputable.

Gabe hadn't wanted to kiss her minutes ago.

And now, he preferred *not* to be in her company.

Not to mention the pesky detail that a killer was on the loose.

Feet heavy, Yana turned to go.

"Wait." Gabe caught her arm, his voice low and urgent. "I, uh, wanted to say you look pretty now, too. Not just on prom night. 'Cause I said you were pretty then, and I didn't want you to think that I didn't think so now. Even if it's the same dress. *Especially* if it's the same dress. You don't need clothes to look pretty." He flushed. "I mean—"

Yana grinned. She had never seen Gabe so flustered, and it did a lot to boost her bruised ego.

Taking a risk, she stepped forward and touched his cheek, enjoying the roughness of his stubble against her palm. "Thank you."

"Be careful. I'll find you as soon as I can." He covered her hand, flashing his signature smile—suave Gabe was back, if only for a moment—and then he loped down the stairs.

She stared at the opaque black space where he'd disappeared. Unlike him, she needed a few minutes to recover. It wasn't every day she went from the possibility of romance to the reality of a dead body and a killer in a split second.

A figure stepped out of the shadows.

Yana screamed, nearly jumping overboard.

"Whoa. It's just me. Again." Brett moved forward, twirling an ax as though it were a baton. Even in the night, the blade caught a glimmer of moonlight. "Your friendly neighborhood ax murderer."

"Hilarious." Yana frowned. "Maybe I just didn't recognize you without your Slender Man mask. Although I suppose a dangerous weapon is a fair substitute."

"Relax," he said soothingly. "I'm just trying to ease the tension."

"Swinging a blade through the air is not the comfort you think it is."

He shook his head with mock disappointment. "Come on, Yans. I wouldn't hurt a fly."

She snorted. She enjoyed Brett's sense of humor, but it meant as little as his protestations of innocence. Because if he had actually killed Everly, he wouldn't come right out and say it. She wouldn't.

"So, you found an ax," she said carefully. "Where's Finn?"

Brett shrugged. "With Gabe, I guess."

"Gabe went belowdecks to check on the crew." She tore her eyes from the mesmerizing spin of the ax to look at Brett's freckled face, realizing for the first time that he had emerged not from the door, but from the back corner of the crow's nest. Which meant he should've *already* known what Gabe was doing. "How long have you been here?"

Brett smirked. "Long enough to hear my best bud hit on his dream girl."

She flushed in spite of her suspicions. "We were just talking."

"Oh, really?" He waggled his brows. "Is that what the cool kids are calling it these days?"

"You oughta know." Her cheeks got even hotter. "Can you put the ax down? You're making me nervous."

"That's not the only thing raising your heart rate," he teased, but then he complied, and the moment the ax hit the bar table, his demeanor changed. "So, there's a reason I waited for Gabe to leave. I'm going to get to the bottom of this murder." He pointed both thumbs to his chest. "That's the least I can do for our dear Everly, after she's done so much for us." His voice was soaked with sarcasm. "And you're going to help me."

Yana's eyes widened. "Um, no? Why me?"

"You're an outsider to our group. You might see things the rest of us miss. It's like in *Knives Out*, when Benoit Blanc enlists the help of Marta because she isn't family. Hell, you even throw up like her."

"First, Marta and I are not remotely similar, other than our unfortunate but medically based tendency to regurgitate," Yana said primly. "And second, are you seriously comparing yourself to a famous fictional detective?"

"If I don't, then who will?"

Couldn't fault his confidence. "Okay, Supersleuth. Did you forget that *Marta* has her own secrets? Maybe I'm the one who shoved Everly onto the spike."

"That's cute, Yana." Brett shook his head. "But you didn't kill her."

Her heart stuttered. "And you know this because . . . ?" *You killed her yourself?* she thought but didn't say.

"Easy. You throw up when you're stressed. And according to Gabe, there wasn't a speck of vomit on Everly's body when he found her. You couldn't have cleaned up your own vomit without also smearing the blood."

"If I'm a sociopath, I wouldn't get stressed by my murderous ways," she countered.

"Maybe. But your first time? That'd make anyone anxious."

She nodded slowly, following his logic. "Okay, I'm in." She wasn't sure she could trust him. That said, if he found any clues, she wanted to be the first to know about them. "Motive for the killer? What do you think?" She had her theories, but like Brett said, he was an insider. That was where the best tips came.

"Blackmail." Brett moved to the hot tub and into the light, yanking off his T-shirt. "The problem will be narrowing down the suspects."

Yana stared. Not because of his muscular physique (she'd

already admired that), but because *his* shirt was splattered with blood, something she hadn't noticed when he was standing in the shadows.

She took a shaky breath. "Why is your shirt bloody?"

"Oh, this thing?" He dunked it into the hot tub and began to wring out the fabric. Strands of red swirled in the jets of water. "I got bloody when I was checking out Ev's body for clues."

"Way to not disturb the crime scene, Benoit Blanc."

He snorted. "Who cares about the crime scene when we're stuck on a yacht with a killer?"

Yana exhaled. "You were one of Everly's victims."

He gave a short bark of a laugh. "What gave it away? My raised hand, or the oh-so-cozy tension between me and the deceased?"

Brett held up his shirt, which was stretched out from the weight of the water. The blood had faded to smears of pink. "Long story short, my dad's the kind of guy who would do anything to win, for him *or* his son. Ev overheard us arguing about steroids. He wanted me to take them, I refused, yada yada yada. He got pretty abusive, but that's a bedtime story for another time," he said grimly. "Ev threatened to throw my state championships into question. I told her to go screw herself." He allowed himself a tight smile.

"She got pissed and published the rumor," he continued, "but it's not true. I've never taken performance-enhancing drugs. *Ever.* So long as it doesn't interfere with my scholarship, I don't give a shit what Ev's readers think of me."

He put on the wet shirt and then, thinking better of it, ripped off the tee and hurled it into a dark corner. His rage, just from recounting the story, was palpable. But that didn't have to mean anything. Their emotions were all heightened after the events of the evening.

Testing him, Yana said, "Pretty clever of Everly to dictate our schedules earlier. She basically gave us a map of everyone's location at the time of her death."

"*If* they stayed in their assigned spots," Brett muttered.

"Do you think Everly knew she was in danger?" Yana ventured. "Or was the schedule just part of her typical controlling behavior?"

"I don't know." Brett's brow furrowed. "The schedule kept Everly attached at the hip with Finn and Taylor. Away from Naya. And *you* isolated in the library." He gazed into Yana's eyes. "Did she have anything to fear from either of you?"

"Not that I know of. But here's something interesting: Amelia didn't have an assigned spot," Yana said, remembering the crumpled-up exam. "Instead of a schedule, Everly handed her one of her old math tests, one that she had failed. Don't ask how I know." She held up one hand when Brett's lips parted. "But that means Everly didn't even attempt to control Amelia's whereabouts. And she's been missing since Everly's murder."

Brett nodded briskly. "Derek, too. I rewatched the video of him preparing the toast. He definitely dropped *something* into each drink." He nodded, two, three, four times.

"You have video evidence?" Yana nearly shrieked. "Why didn't you lead with that?"

"We're still getting to know each other, partner," he drawled.

Facts. And while she didn't have to reveal everything she knew, she had to give a little in order to gain his confidence.

"Rohypnol," she said slowly. "I found a packet of pills in my duffel bag. It's not mine. Which means someone stashed it there."

Brett sucked in air. "So, we think Derek's our guy?"

"Maybe. Maybe not." She tilted her head, thinking. "Show me the video."

"My phone's dead, remember? It didn't magically revive itself in the last hour."

"But your battery was full when we sat on the sofa!"

"You really are next-level observant," he said admiringly. "The guys probably drained my battery when they borrowed my cell to watch the finals."

"So you say." She held out her hand. "Hand over the phone."

"Can't." Brett shook his head. "It went missing sometime between me examining Ev's body and us trying to shake the crew awake."

Yana blinked. "And you just expect me to believe that?"

"It's the truth." He raised one shoulder. "You're going to have to put your faith in me if we're going to team up."

Not a chance. But he didn't have to know that. "Change of plans. You go retrieve the life vests," she said, mind whirling. Maybe she was safer by herself if she couldn't figure out whom to trust. "Gabe wanted to swim to the tender—"

"I'm not letting him swim that alone!"

"We figured. Gabe asked me to bring *three* life vests: for him, you, and Finn. Better you than me, since you clearly have no problem being on the main deck near Everly's body." Yana shuddered. "I'll go back to the wheelhouse. There were surveillance monitors up there. Maybe I can find footage of the time leading up to the discovery of Everly's body."

"Done." Brett snatched the ax off the bar table. "Better keep this baby safe."

"And I'd better keep . . ." Yana turned to the other bar table, where she had carefully laid the knife and her notebook and sucked in a breath. "Did you take them?"

"Take what?" He spread out his arms as if inviting her to search him. The only item of clothing he wore was a pair of lounge shorts, in spite of the buffeting wind. The thin shorts weren't hiding a credit card, much less a deadly weapon. Which meant . . .

Her notebook was gone . . . and so was the knife.

EIGHTEEN

NAYA

10:32 P.M.

Boom! "Naya!" *Boom!* "Ma chère." *Boom!* "Please."

Étienne knocked on the door to Naya and Taylor's shared bathroom. And, yes, maybe his knocks were purposeful yet respectful and not the loud bangs against the door that Naya heard them as, but she definitely deserved the right to be a little dramatic. After all, her worst fear had just been confirmed: Étienne, her delicious, smooth-accented, muscle-chested, curly haired beau had been stealing from . . . well, quite possibly everyone she knew.

And he'd given her a dead girl's bracelet. How messed up was that?

She turned on the faucet and thrust her wrist under the deluge, washing away the ghost of Everly's bracelet.

"Naya." Étienne punctuated his call with another series of knocks. "You said you needed time. I gave you forty-five minutes."

How kind.

"Don't give in," she scolded her reflection. "He's a thief."

"Quoi?" *What?* He tried the doorknob again, jiggling it when it refused him entry. "I cannot hear you."

Naya released a calming breath and tucked her hair behind her ears, silently wishing she had a scrunchie, before turning and unlocking the door.

It flew open and Étienne nearly tumbled to the floor.

"Serves you right." Naya crossed her arms over her chest. She wasn't vindictive or resentful—not normally, at least—but the fact that he'd lied to her, the fact that people knew, or at the very least suspected, while she went around talking about how perfect he was and snot-crying at the mere memory of their post–high school goodbyes . . . She swallowed against the lump that formed in her throat.

She loved him. Did he even love her back, or did he only want something from her?

"Mon coeur—"

"Don't 'my heart' me," she snapped. "Why did you do it—steal the bracelet—steal any of it?"

Étienne's head hung low, the albatross of his actions no doubt weighing him down.

"You know what? It doesn't matter. In a few days, you really will be on a plane headed back to Paris. I won't ever have to see you again. I won't ever have to feel this naive or embarrassed or deluded again."

"Naya, I am sorry." He held out his hands and moved closer. "Let me prove it to you."

"I'm good." She shrugged. She didn't want to be this person, rude and bitter and hurt. "It doesn't matter anymore."

Taylor poked her head into the room. Her blond hair, lit by

the emergency lighting, seemed to glow against the navy wall-paper and mahogany wainscoting. "Everything okay in here?"

Naya pasted on the fake smile she'd perfected over the years of attending parties she would have rather avoided and brushed past her boyfriend. Or maybe he was now her ex.

Her smile nearly faltered.

"Everything's fine," she chimed, her plastic smile in place. She hooked her arm through Taylor's and steered them toward one of the stairways that would take her farther away from Étienne and whatever else he'd kept hidden from her.

"So, how'd that go?" Taylor asked as they ascended the steps to the aft deck.

Naya's jaw tensed. She wanted to dissolve into tears and admit she was utterly wrecked and that she now understood every tear shed by every sad heroine in every romance movie ever, but the words wouldn't come.

"That bad, huh?" Sympathy creased Taylor's forehead. "Guys are trash."

Naya stared out at the unending night sky that had swallowed the once-beautiful horizon. There were ship lights in the distance. Too bad it hadn't been close enough to hear their screams.

Naya tried to blink away the thoughts about Everly's death, their panicked shrieks that had echoed in the dark, and the truth about her first love, and stared up at the clouds rolling in to cover the stars as she and Taylor headed toward the glow of emergency lights emanating from the library.

"Minus Finn, of course."

"Of course," Naya muttered, while Taylor continued to drone on about her own love life.

As if to remind Naya that she'd been a terrible friend to

not one but two people, images of Finn and Everly sparked to life in Naya's mind. Taylor was going on and on about her boyfriend, just like Naya had about Étienne, completely oblivious that his lies were out there waiting to strike.

Naya chewed her bottom lip as she watched Taylor.

She can't already know the truth. Can she?

They turned the corner, and Taylor stopped short.

Her round chin quivered, and her face distorted. Her knees buckled, and Naya clung to Taylor's arm to keep her from sinking.

The glass doors to the library were open. On the floor in the center of the room, Finn's blond hair drowned in a puddle of scarlet that stretched from his body, broken, smashed, and impaled beneath the massive chandelier.

A wail tore from Taylor, a keening as shrill as a coyote at nightfall.

Shit. It was happening again. Panic shot through Naya, piercing her bones as she inhaled the metallic scent that stained the air, and a fresh wave of terror pressed against her like a shadow, cold and dark.

Taylor lurched from Naya's side and ran to Finn.

"No, no, no!" Her hands plucked the air above the chandelier as if she were too worried about harming him further to act. But she couldn't do any more damage.

"Finn! Get up!" she shrieked. "Oh God, Naya." Taylor whirled around, frenzy flashing in her green eyes. "Help me get it off him. Help me!" She turned back to the chandelier, clamped her hands onto the metal, and pulled. "It's too heavy!"

Naya's legs felt detached from her body as they carried her to Taylor's side. Blood squelched under her shoes, warm and thick. Naya couldn't make out Finn's face, couldn't find where his flesh ended and the filigreed metal began. They were one, crystal and bone, steel and tendon.

"Taylor, he—" She wet her dry lips. "Finn's gone."

Taylor's scream shattered against Naya's ears.

"Finn!" His name was an oath, a curse she howled over and over. It rippled through the lake of crimson and stained Naya's skin. She would never be able to wash herself clean.

"He's gone," she repeated, wrapping her arms around her friend. Taylor struggled, her shoes slipping in the blood, painting the wooden floor with streaks of ruby as Naya dragged her away. But neither of them could keep from staring at the mass of crystal and bronze and the boy who once was.

"He's gone. Finn's gone." Naya didn't know what else to say, so she repeated the words as she took in the horrifying scene. "He's gone."

The chain above the hanger loop snagged Naya's attention, and she froze.

Naya's breath stuck in her chest as she studied the silky gold fabric covering the chandelier's chain-link mount. The material had been cut, and the clean slices revealed the chain beneath.

She retraced her steps back to the chandelier. She skirted the pool of Finn's blood and his mangled hand, reaching out to her like a ghoul from the grave. She leaned forward to inspect the chain.

There were gashes in one exposed link, each deeper than the next, until a final cut had set the monstrous fixture free.

The hedge trimmers . . .

Naya had seen Finn throw them overboard.

The edges of Naya's vision pulsed with each rapid beat of her heart. She could no longer cling to the notion—the hope—that Everly's death had been an accident. More than one body equaled homicide. But why had Finn had the weapon that ultimately led to his death?

"Holy shit!"

Naya spun around as Gabe and Yana skidded to a stop inside the library.

"Finn?" Yana went pale, and she flattened her hands against her stomach.

"He's dead," Taylor croaked, lowering herself to the floor and drawing her knees to her chest.

Gabe dragged his hands through his hair and steadied himself against a nearby armchair.

"Yeah . . . dead," Naya repeated, unable to sort through the onslaught of questions and worries that swirled between her ears.

"I heard shouting!" Brett bounded through the open doors, ax and life vests in hand, his heavy footsteps booming like thunderclaps against her raw nerves.

"This ship might be massive and expensive, but it's falling apart," Gabe whispered. "The whole thing's a giant death trap."

"It's not—" Naya swallowed. "It's not falling apart." She motioned to the silk-covered chain, its cut end dangling above the slick pool of red. "But it *is* a death trap."

Brett set his loot down on the floor, his steps now slow and silent as he crept toward the chandelier and Finn's crushed corpse. "Someone cut it."

Yana jogged over to join Brett and Naya, clapping her hands over her mouth to stifle a dry heave.

"You were with him last." Taylor was on her feet, her words sizzling with rage. "Both of you." Her gaze sliced through the room, beheading both Brett and Gabe.

Gabe held up his hands in a show of innocence. "I was

with Yana and then I went to check on the crew. Everyone's still passed out. Brett's the one who stayed with Finn."

Taylor narrowed her vicious gaze at Brett.

"Wait." Brett took a step back. "I *was* with Finn. We got the ax, then split up. He was *alive* the last time I saw him. And do I look like I can fly?" He pointed to the ornate ceiling medallion where the chandelier once hung.

Naya tilted her head back and stared up. It was at least fifteen feet high, but it wasn't impossible to reach. Not with the lofty bookshelves and their accompanying ladder. "You'd have to be tall, but—"

"With the right tool and a little flexibility, anyone could have done it," Yana finished, miming hanging onto the ladder and reaching toward the chandelier.

The four of them stood there for a moment, the reality of her statement settling in.

Anyone could have done it.

Maybe the chandelier hadn't been cut with the hedge trimmers. Maybe it'd been cut with the ax.

Naya rushed to Taylor when new sobs shook her shoulders. She clutched at Naya as if she could save her from this devastation. But Naya wasn't even sure she could save herself.

"Anyone could have, but who would?" she asked. "What reason would anyone have to do"—she swallowed and glanced down at Finn—"this?"

Gabe dragged his hands down his cheeks. "Someone from the crew?"

Brett shook his head. "The whole crew was drugged."

"How do we know they were *all* drugged? One of them could've been faking it," Gabe countered. "We're friends. None of us would do this."

Yana shifted uncomfortably under the weight of the word *friends*, and Naya's suspicion softened.

"Well . . . one of us might kill," Brett said, his brows lifting. "That is, if she found out what Finn had been hiding."

Taylor lifted her head from Naya's shoulder and sniffled. "I knew about Finn and Everly."

Naya took a step back. "You did?"

"She may have been really good at keeping other people's secrets, but she was terrible at keeping her own." Taylor wiped her tear-streaked cheeks and turned to face Brett. "And for you to even think that I'd—" She clapped her hands over her mouth, muffling her sobs.

"Her boyfriend's just been murdered, Brett," Naya scolded, wrapping her arms around Taylor. "Try not to be so heartless."

"If anyone here is suspicious, it's Yana," Taylor raged. "*She* was sitting right here, whispering to him in the dark, while the rest of us were at the party. She probably lured him down here, once again."

Yana's mouth opened and then closed at the accusation. Why was Taylor so fixated on Naya's former best friend?

"What? You thought I didn't know?" Taylor bit out. "I saw the two of you together." Naya guided Taylor to the opposite end of the library, but not too far. The other set of glass doors would lead them to Everly's body, another sea of red stretching out like a living thing along the deck.

Two dead former classmates. So much blood. So much death.

"It might not have been anyone in this room," Naya said. "But someone did this. Someone *murdered* Finn and Everly. And there's no telling who's next."

NINETEEN

YANA

10:52 P.M.

Yana retched over the toilet. Nothing came out. Surprise. She was pretty sure she'd already emptied the entire contents of her stomach near Everly.

Standing, Yana gargled with the complimentary mouthwash. She examined the bottle. Rich-people mouthwash even *tasted* delicious. Tingly, but not stinging; minty, but not medicinal.

With renewed energy, she walked back into the adjoining library—and the sounds of Taylor's wild sobs. Étienne had joined the group while Yana had been indisposed.

"Yo, Yans!" Brett called out over the wailing. "Are there any earplugs in the bathroom?"

Naya kicked him in the shin from where she was sitting on the floor next to Taylor.

"*Ow!*" Brett yelped, hopping on one foot. He met Yana's eyes from across the room. "It was just a joke. Jeez."

Yana allowed her lips to curve. His humor and timing were clearly inappropriate, but you had to give the guy points for trying.

"Can you be serious right now?" Naya hissed.

"Fine. What did you find on the surveillance footage? Any incriminating evidence?" he asked Yana. As an aside to Naya, he muttered, "How's that for serious?"

Yana stared. What was Brett doing, asking her in front of the entire group? The last thing she wanted to do was tip off the killer.

So, she wasn't about to reveal that she'd spied Étienne on the surveillance video, plucking a set of keys from the head stew's pocket moments before Derek had lifted his champagne flute in a toast. Not just any keys, either.

The primary set. The ones that would unlock the doors of every guest cabin.

"Nothing," she lied. "This evening's footage had already been erased."

"Maybe because *you* erased it!" Taylor raged.

"Hey, can we keep the accusations to a minimum?" Gabe asked in a calm voice. "We're all in this together."

"Like hell!" Taylor screamed. "My boyfriend's dead. I can accuse every single one of you. Like your best buddy, who's holding the ax that probably cut down the chandelier." She glared at Brett over Gabe's shoulder.

Brett let the ax slide through his fingers. It hit the floor with a thud. "If we're really pointing the finger, we should think about Derek and Amelia. No one's seen them since before Everly's death. How did we get sidetracked from breaking down their door?"

They fell silent as Taylor's sobs filled the air. Naya stroked her friend's hair, her mouth issuing a *shh*. Étienne placed his hand on Naya's shoulder, creating a chain of comfort. As though startled, Naya looked around the library, bewildered and helpless—until her gaze met her boyfriend's. She visibly relaxed, shoulders drooping, forehead smoothing. A few seconds later, Naya shook herself and broke their eye contact. The confession that Yana had overheard from her cabin had clearly disrupted the flow of their relationship. But before tonight, Étienne had been Naya's safe haven.

Yana shifted her feet, her outsider status clearer than ever. In spite of the arguing and the accusations, the five of them were so natural with each other, so *comfortable*. They were clearly a tight-knit group of friends. One that didn't include Yana.

As if reading her thoughts, Gabe turned and beckoned her over.

Yana didn't need anyone's pity. And yet the expression on Gabe's face was anything but. Quickly, before her brain came up with an excuse not to, she crossed the room. He draped an arm over her shoulder, pulling her into his chest.

Her body was pressed against his in a long line from her cheek to her hip, his T-shirt warm and soothing. The smell of sandalwood wrapped around her, and she could hear the rhythmic beating of his heart.

It was . . . nice. She felt, dare she say, protected. But she and Gabe didn't have that kind of connection. Not yet, and maybe never. She had only begun thawing toward him that afternoon, in this very library, when he was staring up at the chandelier.

The chandelier.

At the moment, it pinned Finn's dead body to the ground,

glass shards sprinkled across the room like confetti. Seven hours ago, Gabe had been gazing up at it as though it were an enigma he had to decipher. *Had* he found a solution to his puzzle? And did it involve cutting through a silk-covered chain?

Suddenly, the heavy thuds of Gabe's heart felt a lot more menacing. He was genuinely grieving over Everly's death. That much was clear. But that didn't mean he hadn't played a part in it. He was the one who had found Everly's body, after all, and he had insisted, in spite of Yana's reluctance, that they split up. Who was to say that he didn't sneak into the library to kill Finn? Did they have some animosity toward each other she didn't know about? And could these secret entanglements have something to do with Everly's big secret, be it the cheating ring or otherwise?

Besides, her notebook was missing. That meant some-body knew exactly what her suspicions were. For all she knew, Gabe was the one who had taken the composition pad—and he was merely pretending to be supportive. Keep your en-emies closer and all that.

Yana pulled away, just a few inches—and met Brett's eyes. *Do you trust him?* she mouthed.

With my life, he returned.

Yana forced her shoulders to relax, even though Brett wasn't any more trustworthy than Gabe. Still, he was osten-sibly her partner, and she could kinda sorta rely on him. At least for the moment.

Taylor leaped to her feet, her sobbing turned to babbling. "I can't. I just can't. Get me off this boat. Now!"

"A thousand bucks and it's done," Brett said, straight-faced.

"What he means is, the two of us can swim to the boat

we're towing," Gabe said, his voice even. Yana could hear it vibrating in his chest. "Yana and I saw the lights of another boat in the distance. With any luck, once we secure the speedboat, we can reach the other vessel and get help."

Brett gestured at the orange life vests. "And it'll only cost you fifty bucks each to rent these."

The vests were the same ones they had tried on during the safety training. They appeared fairly standard—zip closure, snap belts, even a dangling flashlight and whistle. They didn't evoke a hint of suspicion . . . except that there were two of them and not three.

Finn had been on the swim team, too. In fact, his skills had rivaled Gabe's. Yana had specifically asked Brett to bring three life vests. Did he only bring two because he *knew* that Finn wouldn't be around to use one? Or did he just decide—on his own—that only two swimmers were needed on the mission?

"Didn't I ask you to bring three life vests?" Yana asked.

"Did you?" Brett blinked. "I don't remember that."

Truth . . . or lie? That was the question that plagued her every interaction.

"The swim sounds . . . dangerous," Naya said haltingly.

"It's a risk I'm willing to take," Gabe said. "What other choice do we have?"

Not to be outdone, Étienne dropped a kiss on Naya's cheek. "I'd risk everything to save you, too. But alas, I don't know how to swim." Naya frowned and pulled away, apparently not ready to forgive.

Brett extended his hand. "Let's head to the beach club!"

"For what?" Naya said, exasperated.

"Weren't you listening during the safety meeting? Naya,

Naya, Naya." Brett tsked. "That's what they call the garage thingy that holds the inflatable slides and other water toys. It's also the platform where the speedboat is moored."

Continuing to bicker, they migrated toward the exit, with Taylor sprinting ahead and Gabe and Yana bringing up the rear.

"Stick together, please," Yana pleaded. "We don't need anyone else to wander off on their own again and . . ."

No one listened. Too much anxiety and adrenaline pumped through their veins, and they raced ahead at various speeds.

No one listened, that is, except Gabe.

"Don't worry," he said, slipping his hand into hers. "I'll stick by you."

They'd held hands before, during their weeks of flirtation leading up to prom. The physical contact had been thrilling, but she hadn't marked it as any kind of milestone. *This* handholding . . . well . . . it meant something.

Fear? Excitement? Yana couldn't tell. Her pulse raced, her mouth ran dry—the symptoms were eerily similar.

"I made a mistake earlier," Gabe said as they descended the darkened stairwell. Despite the clatter of the footsteps ahead and Taylor's periodic shrieks of grief, Yana could almost believe they were alone.

"What's that?" she asked.

He didn't respond right away. They walked down the twisty stairs hand in hand. The silence pulsed with the suspicions and nerves jostling for space inside Yana's brain.

When they reached the bottom, he faced her. "Ev and Finn." He closed his eyes, as though pained. "I don't understand what happened to them. It's awful and gutting and unfair. But their deaths remind me that nothing's certain in life—least of all, time. We have to seize every moment because we don't know how many we'll have left." His eyes opened, and they reflected the stars, even though the two of them were inside. "I should've kissed you earlier, up in the crow's nest."

Yana wondered if the others would judge her for wanting to give in to Gabe on such a horrendous night. Then his gaze flickered to her lips, and the air around them turned hot and sauna-like. Yana swayed forward, her lips parting. Gabe was right. They had to seize the present. Besides, she had never cared what this group thought of her, and she wasn't about to start now. . . .

"There you are!" Naya burst into the vestibule. "We thought you two had gotten lost—"

She broke off, taking in the position of their bodies. Her eyes widened, ever so slightly, and then she broke into a shimmy, alternating her shoulders back and forth, as she swayed from side to side.

Yana burst out laughing. So much for Naya judging her. That was their signature move back in middle school, before their friendship fell apart. Every time one of them aced a test, or got their braces off, or worked up the courage to talk to a boy, the other would do a little shimmy. It was their equivalent of a thumbs-up, a way to connect from across the room.

This was what Yana had always loved about Naya. She was happy for Yana, and she wouldn't allow anything, even their awkward history, even this nightmare of a trip, to prevent her from expressing her joy.

"Naya! Come here, please." The voice was Étienne's, but Yana had never heard him sound so terrified.

The grins fell from both girls' faces, and the three of them ran through the doorway onto the swim deck that jutted out from the beach club.

Taylor hugged herself to stay warm, while Étienne crouched by the cleat, the metal base designed to keep the towline in place. Brett stood next to him, holding a double-braided nylon line that *should've* disappeared into the current, attached to the tender and tugging it behind the yacht.

Except it didn't. The bitter end dangled from Brett's hand. Like the chandelier chain, the line had been cut all the way through.

No. No way. No freaking way.

Yana spun around and met Gabe's grim expression. The light in his eyes had faded; their nightmare reality had charged back in. First, the chandelier. Now the towline. The blade that had been briefly in Yana's possession—if it was indeed the same knife—had been busy.

That was when Yana let the truth of the situation sink into her bones.

The speedboat was no longer an option. Their exit strategy had evaporated like the salty mist rising from the ocean.

TWENTY

NAYA

11:16 P.M.
Rain began to fall. A sudden deluge of fat, cold drops that slapped Naya right in the face. Overhead, the sky cracked, and a flash of lightning splintered the black blanket of night. As if energized by the discharge of electricity, the waves swelled. They clawed at the oversized yacht—Poseidon come to life to drag them down to the ocean's depths.

Or maybe Naya was being dramatic. Not that being on a boat with a murderer didn't entitle her to some overwrought emotions.

"One of you did this!" Taylor's shout was highlighted by another clap of thunder. "And I'm not waiting around for you to kill me, too. I'm going to my room and locking myself in." Lightning flashed, illuminating her pale skin and wide, frenzied eyes.

"Taylor—" Naya stepped forward, but Taylor held up her hands.

"Naya, if you were smart, you'd come with me or find someplace else to hide." She backed away. "I don't trust any of them, and you shouldn't, either."

Thunder rolled overhead like a train as Taylor turned and sprinted from the beach club.

Naya rushed after her. Taylor wasn't thinking clearly. She'd just lost one of her friends and her boyfriend in the most horrific ways, but she couldn't keep running off by herself. There was strength in numbers, and Naya genuinely believed that her friends were innocent. It had to be a third party. Besides, if one of her friends *was* responsible, they had to remain in a group to subdue the killer when they struck again.

The thought made Naya cold even as she ran, lungs burning and heart beating against her ribs.

Naya galloped down the hallway, as the door to their room slammed shut and the lock clicked into place.

Music continued to play, wafting into the corridor from Derek's cabin, where he and Amelia remained tucked away, blatantly ignoring the chaos tearing the boat apart. To be honest, she couldn't blame them.

"Taylor!" Naya shouted, knocking on the cabin door. "What are you doing? It's not safe, and I don't have my key. Open up."

"Leave me alone!" came Taylor's muted reply.

"Taylor—"

"Leave me alone!"

"Fine." Naya sighed. She supposed that if she'd just seen Étienne's dead body, she wouldn't want to be around anyone, either. "But stay locked in our room and don't open the door for anyone."

"Leave me alone!"

Naya backed away from the door, hands up in surrender. "I am! I'll just find my way back, then."

She walked past Derek's door, throwing it a cutting glance before going back down the corridor. She and Étienne should have locked themselves in her room as soon as she'd found out he was on the boat and *before* he'd confessed to being a complete klepto. Ignorance was sometimes bliss.

Naya let out a long exhale and stopped in the center of the hall where it branched off to the right and the left. Turn or keep going straight? She'd never approached the beach club from this part of the boat. To be honest, she'd been too lost in thought to even be sure of how many turns she'd already taken. There were too many options and too many doors that looked exactly the same.

"Shit."

A muffled roar of thunder echoed as her attention moved down the hall on her right, the emergency lights like beacons on an airport runway. She turned and peered left. The lights flickered, occasionally plunging the passage into darkness.

Naya wrapped her arms around her middle, digging her fingers into her rain-soaked jumpsuit. She was alone. Worse, she had no idea how to get back to Taylor or anyone else.

Three rights and a left.

No, that didn't make any sense.

Two lefts and a right?

Naya chewed her lower lip. She needed the map Everly had passed out. Or her phone—that was usually the way she kept from getting lost.

"But I'm not lost," she reassured herself.

No, she knew exactly where she was—on a megayacht

in the middle of the ocean with an unknown murderer. She swallowed as another distant boom of thunder echoed.

Footsteps padded along the lush runner, and Naya whirled to her left, a scream coiled in her throat.

No one was there.

Her wet flip-flops let out burbling sighs as she crept away from the footsteps, imagined or otherwise. The emergency lights buzzed and went silent, throwing a cloak of darkness over the corridor.

This had been a very bad idea. If Naya's life were a movie, anyone watching would tell her to run.

She placed her fingertips on the wallpaper, tracing it as she walked farther down the hall.

There was a pattern to the darkness, to the lights.

Buzz buzz. Buzz. Buzz. Silence.

The darkness lasted longer than a blink, longer than a breath, longer than two tentative footsteps.

Naya's fingers hit wood. She froze, tracing the intricate carvings, waiting for the light.

Buzz buzz. Buzz. Buzz.

Her eyes widened as the hall fell into blackness again. She stepped closer to the wall, her fingers hurrying across the painting as if it were alive, as if in the darkness she could confirm what she'd seen in the light.

Finally, the light returned.

Naya yanked her hand back as if stung. A portrait of a young Seraphina Yates stared back at her, round nose lifted high and catlike eyes cast down. Naya traced her fingers over her own round nose and thought of the shape of her own eyes.

Do we—look alike?

She sank into darkness. Alone with her thoughts and Seraphina.

"No." Naya shook her head.

This was a trick of the light and of fear and adrenaline.

As if they'd heard her thoughts, the emergency lights buzzed back to life. Naya studied the image of young Seraphina. She let out a pent-up breath and couldn't help but roll her eyes at her ridiculousness. She'd seen a thousand photos of Everly with the same expression. She'd even snapped pictures of Taylor and Amelia with a similar stink-faced, sucked-a-lemon expression.

"Maybe we're *all* your progenies," Naya said to Seraphina before the buzzing ceased. "Is that why we're inductees together? Because we're related? Did you want us to fight to the death for our inheritance?"

Naya smirked at herself, but her amusement vanished when darkness fell once more. She blinked and squinted back the way she'd come. She couldn't see anything, but she knew she'd wandered too far.

A warm breath tickled the nape of Naya's neck. Goose bumps sprang out along her skin as her heart, a living bird in her chest, hurled itself against the bars of its cage.

Strong hands clamped around Naya's waist, and she screamed as they pulled her farther into the dark.

TWENTY-ONE

YANA

11:17 P.M.

Taylor sprinted from the swim deck, her hair streaming behind her like a wet flag. Before any of them could react, Naya took off after her.

"Naya, wait!" Yana called, but her words were swallowed by the rain's steady patter. "Why won't anyone listen to me? We seriously need to stick together," she mumbled as Naya disappeared into the stairwell.

The boys had wisely retreated inside the beach club and out of the rain. Yana joined them. Brett had found one of the deckhands' uniforms and was putting on a polo shirt, and Gabe was saying that he didn't think the Jet Skis tucked in a corner of the garage would have enough fuel to reach land.

Étienne suddenly spun around, as though to go search for his girlfriend, but Gabe hooked an arm through his, keeping the French boy in place. "We can't be chasing each other all over the yacht. That's easy pickings."

Étienne's nostrils flared. "You cannot expect me to not care that my girlfriend is off alone."

"Relax, bro. The girls will hole up in their cabin and be fine." Brett hooked his arm through Étienne's other arm, mirroring Gabe. "We, on the other hand, get to hunt for a killer!" he said gleefully.

Gabe and Étienne stared at him balefully, and he faltered. "Too much?"

"By about a million decibels," Gabe grumbled.

"Focus," Yana said, trying to keep them on track. "Derek. Amelia. We need to find them. Enough is enough."

Étienne blinked. "Amelia does not even kill spiders. She wraps them up in a tissue and carries them outside."

"Not saying they're the killers," Yana clarified. "But Brett saw Derek spiking the champagne, and I saw our so-called chaperone escorting a drugged crew member down the hall. We have to question him."

Brett nodded vigorously. "I'll get the ax. I left it in the library."

"Slow down." Gabe clapped both hands on Brett's shoulders. Gabe was the taller of the two, but Brett was more muscular. It wasn't clear who would win if it came to blows. "Would you use the ax to break down the door or as a weapon?"

Brett shrugged. "Both?"

"Listen to yourself." Gabe massaged his temples. "He's our nerdy-ass *math TA*."

"Shouldn't have given me that C in calc, then."

Étienne groaned, and Gabe shook his head.

"Fine," he sighed. "We'll get the ax. But keep your hands—and your weapon—to yourself."

They trooped to the stairs, single file. Gabe led the way, but not before catching Yana's eyes and mouthing, *Are you okay?*

She would have joined him at the front. In fact, maybe that's what he'd hoped. But she had something else in mind.

They began to climb, and in the dim light, Yana scrutinized Naya's boyfriend's backside, encased in a pair of tight white jeans.

A giggle crept up Yana's throat as she imagined Naya's reaction. *Can't fault you, hon,* her former best friend would've said, winking.

But that's not why Yana was staring. She'd thought she'd glimpsed a lump in Étienne's back pocket—and she was right. Did it appear key-shaped? Hard to tell, but Yana would bet her big little brother's basketball career that there, less than twelve inches from her face, were the primary keys that Étienne had lifted.

Yana didn't think. She just acted.

She deliberately tripped, falling forward into Étienne and knocking him to his knees. "Sorry! I'm so sorry!" she babbled, her hands *everywhere.* She'd blush about it later, but right now she was on a mission. Dip into his pocket, crook a finger . . . got it! Plastic wrist coil, jagged metal grooves. She'd found the keys. In a flash, she dropped them into the deep side pocket of her dress.

Étienne pushed himself to his feet, dusting off his hands. He glanced over his shoulder, his eyes narrowed.

"Jé suis désolée," Yana said solemnly, deliberately butchering the pronunciation of the apology because she knew it would annoy him. At least her sorry excuse for a French teacher had been good for something: how *not* to speak the language.

He winced, tormented by her accent. "Pas de problème." *No problem.* He turned back around.

Okay. She'd succeeded in both distracting and grossly

manhandling him. Yana followed the group to the top of the stairs. When she reached the main level, she bent down to retie her shoe, forming exaggerated bunny ears. Her fingers were clumsy; her pace slow. When she looked up, one of Étienne's tasseled suede loafers and an inch of his bare ankle were just disappearing into the library.

Yana allowed herself a small smile. Just like that, she'd managed to detach herself from the group.

Yana raced up the stairs and down the hallway that led to the main guest cabin, as lightly and quickly as possible. The boys would be exiting the library at any moment. How many male athletes did it take to get one ax?

The primary keys gave her an idea. If Brett was right, Taylor and Naya had ensconced themselves in their cabin. Which meant that Yana could safely search Everly's bedroom for any clues.

She halted in front of the main cabin and fumbled with the keys. *Please, please, please.* She couldn't afford—literally—to rely on a disinterested universe. But for once, could luck be on her side?

The door opened. Yana slipped inside, shut the door, and slid to the floor. Sweat dripped down her face, and her heart could win a drum solo competition.

When she could breathe again, she took in her surroundings. No wonder Everly had claimed the main bedroom for herself. Yana hadn't seen so much splendor since she'd visited Bangkok's Wat Phra Kaew—the Temple of the Emerald Buddha—five years earlier.

An intricately carved golden headboard with crystal insets anchored the king-sized mattress, which boasted cream silk sheets and a dozen gold-tasseled pillows. Gold trim lined the walls, while the oak nightstand, drawers, and vanity featured a raised floral design, also studded with crystals.

The true grandeur of the room, however, lay in its architectural design—the same one that Gabe had so admired. Large crescent-shaped glass panels were set into the hardwood floor, which looked into the library underneath. In the ceiling, these same panels—perfectly aligned with those below—functioned as skylights.

Everly would've felt like true royalty had she reclined in this bed and bathed in the moonlight. Too bad the thunderclouds and pelting rain obscured the stars. Even worse that she hadn't made it to this hour.

Yana pushed herself off the floor. Enough gawking. She had a mission to accomplish.

She crossed the room to the vanity, where Everly's personal laptop lay. The password was her next hurdle. Yana sat on the decorated stool and lifted her eyes to the ceiling. What could the gossip queen's password be?

Yana typed:

RumorH@slt

Error message.

3v3rYours

Damn it! Another error.

She tried various iterations of the above two. Error, error, error.

Only one guess left before she would be locked out.

Yana gazed up at the crescent-shaped skylights for inspiration. She tried to put herself into Everly's mind. What word or phrase would be meaningful to the mean girl? Yana lowered her eyes until they were reflected in the vanity mirror. What affirmation would Everly say to herself as she looked into this mirror every morning?

In a flash it came to her. It was definitely a stretch, but Yana felt in her gut that she was right.

I@mBe@utiful

Bingo! She was in.

Couldn't knock the girl's confidence.

Opening the Documents folder, she clicked to sort the files by date. She wasn't sure exactly what she was searching for, but she knew it would be something incriminating. She scanned the files for a few precious minutes.

Now, *this* seemed promising.

"Draft: *Rumor Has It . . .*" blazed across the top, along with a publication date in June . . . two days from now. Yana checked the time that the file was last saved—1:47 p.m., that very afternoon. Only an hour before she'd arrived on the yacht. The school year was over, and many of her sources and subjects were about to leave for college, but Yana guessed that Everly hadn't been ready to close down her website. Maybe she had planned a sophisticated rebranding and launch at Cornell that fall. They, unfortunately, would never know.

With her stomach flipping over itself, Yana began to read:

I've got a secret.

Yes, yes, I know. That's what this entire column is about. Covert whispers in the dark. Furtive glances when you think no one is watching. Rumors, mostly corroborated and completely life-changing.

Secrets.

But this one's different. This one's special.

All year, I've exposed the dark underbelly of Yatesville High. Students' shameful behavior has ranged from petty crime to jailable offenses, a little light cheating to actual fraud. (No need to hold your applause; I gladly take credit where credit is due.)

But alas, all brilliant and beautiful things must come to an end. And what better way to wrap up this column than to unveil the biggest secret of all? One that's been passed down through the years. One with the ability to either make or destroy a life. One that will have you hyperventilating in shock.

Should I tell . . . or should I not?

That, my dear readers, is—and always has been—the million-dollar question.

Ever yours,
Everly

Yana's breath came faster and faster, until she was afraid that she might hyperventilate. So *this* was the motive, Yana thought. Finn was right. Everly hadn't been murdered because someone was fed up with her blackmail. Rather, she died because someone had a secret they would kill to protect.

Yana scrubbed a hand down her face. At least, that was the best theory she had at the moment. Could the secret be about the cheating ring? Possibly, depending on how deep it went. As far as she knew, Everly had never posted about it, so there hadn't been any speculation around it. That would explain why two people were dead. Everly, for the secret she was about to expose. And the anonymous texter—Finn?— who had shown by their text message that they were willing to reveal the scheme.

The back of her neck suddenly prickled. A third person knew about the cheating. In fact, she was running around the yacht tracking down clues. Yana herself.

Did that mean she would be next? Did the killer know about her secret mission?

Her body was racked by trembling. No. She was only guessing. According to the text message, Everly was part of the scandal. Yana had yet to come up with a logical reason why she would have wanted to incriminate herself. No, the reason Everly was dead could have stemmed from *anyone's* secret. Even her own.

Yana's fingers slipped on the keyboard, and a jumble of letters in blue appeared on the document. Oh. Someone had toggled on Track Changes.

On a whim, Yana clicked on Show Comments. An instant later, she sucked in her breath. A long string of editing notes appeared in the margins.

[Guest]: A little pathetic, Ev. I didn't know you were such a tease.

[Ever Yours]: I'm not going to *publish* the post yet. I just want to be ready—you know, if and when.

[Guest]: Look, you need to calm down. Derek's not telling. Neither is Amelia. She was just upset that you demanded she keep stringing along the math assistant until we got to college. Nobody will care then that he snuck us a few exam answers. But you know Amelia. She was all, *I draw the line at sex.* Whatever. I'm not losing everything because she can't play along.

[Ever Yours]: I'm not talking about Mel.

[Guest]: What else is there? I didn't know you had any more secrets.

[Ever Yours]: You never were a very good liar.

Yana's mouth dropped open . . . and stayed open. Amelia had seduced—er, *not* seduced Derek to get answers to exams? And not just one, but a whole batch of them? There it was, black and white. Not rumors, not insinuation. *Proof.* She now had a foundation for her exposé. She could write her article. Impress her editor. Build her résumé. Something good could come of this nightmare.

Yet that was the least of her concerns. Was it possible that she was reading a conversation between Everly and her killer written mere hours before Everly's absolutely grue-some death?

That was quite possibly the creepiest thought ever.

Yana pressed a hand to her stomach. She was going to be sick. *Breathe!* she coached herself. *Come on now. In and out for four counts each.*

When she was no longer afraid of regurgitating, she tilted her gaze back up to the crescent-shaped panels. The night sky, more than any cognitive alphabet game, would serve to distract her.

Did the comments rule out Derek and Amelia as sus-pects? And the cheating scandal as the "biggest secret of all"? At first glance, yes. But after a few seconds of thought . . . no. No way. Both Everly and the guest user could be lying. There might be an undercurrent to the conversation that Yana didn't understand. So, she had to stay wary. She couldn't fully trust anyone.

Yana glanced at her watch. Twenty minutes had passed. The guys were probably already searching for her. She couldn't let them catch her here, rifling through Everly's things. She had to find her way back to them; she had to come up with a believable excuse. . . .

Screeeech.

Yana leaped to her feet, glancing around wildly.

There it was again. The noise came from one of the glass panels set into the floor. She cocked her head, listening. It was the one by the far pedestal of the bed.

As Yana watched, her throat pulsing, the sheet of glass *lifted up and moved to one side.*

And then Gabe hoisted himself through.

TWENTY-TWO

YANA

11:36 P.M.

Yana's blood turned to ice. The cold spread to her fingers, to her toes. Ears, nose. Every last bit of her body.

"What are you doing here?" Her gaze bounced around the room, searching for a weapon. "You're supposed to be with the group."

How had she calculated so wrongly? She'd trusted Gabe . . . as much as she could trust anyone on a yacht with two dead bodies and a comatose crew.

And here he was, squeezing through a crescent-shaped panel. Into a dead girl's cabin.

This was bad. Very, very bad.

"So are you, Miss We-Have-to-Stick-Together," Gabe said slowly. His hair was mussed, his T-shirt bloodstained. No weapons—at least not in his hands. Thank pra Buddha cho for *that*. "You snuck off without a word to anyone. Doesn't that make you a hypocrite?" He shook his head. "Or do you have something to hide?"

Clever, throwing suspicion back on her. But she wasn't going to fall for it.

He took a step forward, and she backed away. The lamp. She grabbed it, but the damn thing wouldn't budge. Rich people and their rich, heavy decor! Compromising, she swept up a hairbrush. Not the best weapon ever. Who was she kidding? It wouldn't bat away a mouse, let alone a six-foot-three, two-hundred-pound athlete built of solid muscle. But it was better than nothing.

"Stay where you are!" Yana shrieked. "Don't come any closer."

Gabe halted. "You think I would hurt you?"

"I don't know what to think."

Turning, he reached for the laptop on the vanity. Okay. So it would be the slender but heftier computer versus a puny old hairbrush. Not exactly fair.

Gabe raised the laptop over his head, moments away from flinging it at Yana.

She tightened her grip on the brush. She could see the headline now: *Teen Killed by Blow to Head While Defending Herself with Beauty Product.*

But she wasn't going down without a fight. Maybe, just maybe, with the element of surprise and a supernatural shot of adrenaline, she could get out of here alive.

She exhaled until the breath left her body. And then she charged, sprinting at him with all her might . . .

. . . just as he slammed the laptop onto the floor with all *his* might.

A split second later, she crashed into him, and they both fell to the floor.

"Oof," Gabe moaned, rubbing his head. "Can't say I haven't been dreaming about this moment, but I thought it would go a bit differently."

"Not funny." Yana twisted her head. Pieces of the laptop—circuit board, wires, metal parts—were scattered across the floor. She groped in the wreckage and came up with a jagged piece of metal, which she jammed against Gabe's neck. "You have ten seconds to tell me why you broke into Everly's room."

He held up both hands. "Not for any nefarious reason! I promise. I wanted to destroy the photos of my sister," he explained. "I figured now was as good a time as any. Why are *you* in here?" His gaze zeroed in on the key ring on the vanity. "Ah. Very smooth," he mused. "Why didn't I think of that?"

"I didn't steal it," Yana bit out. "Étienne lifted the key ring from the head stew, and I, um, borrowed it from him."

"So, secondhand stealing," Gabe quipped, placing a hand on her head.

Yana froze. Not sure why, since she was still lying on top of him, but *this* was the action that made her return to her physical body.

She already knew his chest was rock solid. But his abs, his thighs—she felt like she was lying on a slab of marble.

She slid off him, and they both sat up. "You know, you might have just destroyed a major piece of evidence," she said, struggling to sound sensible and not flustered. "With luck, any valuable information will be on the cloud. And so might the photos of your sister."

Gabe nodded gravely. "One count of destruction of property at a time." He hooked Yana's arm with his hand as she began to move away.

"Stay with me for a minute," he murmured. "I need a break from dead and drugged bodies." He tucked her against his side so that they both leaned back against the bed.

"How do I know you're not the killer again?"

Gabe's lips quirked. "You could always search me."

Yana shook her head exasperatedly, and his expression sobered.

"Yana, I'm not the murderer. I would prove it to you if I knew how. For all I know, *you're* the one plotting my demise. But I'll take my chances."

They stared at one another, faces inches apart. She wanted to believe him. She wished, more than anything, that they were just a girl and a boy who had reconnected on a relaxing, boring cruise, devoid of mayhem and murder. As an aspiring investigative reporter, she relied on her logical mind, a painstaking attention to detail, and her gut instincts. Her gut was saying now that Gabe was telling the truth.

She cleared her throat. "We're alone again. No one to interrupt us. Secure, for the moment. Were you, um, thinking about kissing me?"

His eyes darkened. "Do you want me to?"

"Yes," she said, and she hoped he understood that she was offering more than her lips. She did trust him. She always had. The betrayal at prom had given her pause. It was so out of character that it had made her doubt everything—her feelings, his sincerity, her instincts. But the reason she had been attracted to Gabe in the first place, out of every boy at their school, was because he was a genuinely stand-up guy. He had a way of drawing her out. He made her feel safe.

With his index finger, he lifted her chin and then slowly, carefully, softly, he fit his lips against hers. The kiss that followed was as tender as the brush of butterfly wings, as electric as a jolt of fire. Yana felt the tingle in every cell of her body.

She had known he was good at this, that they were good together. But their kisses before, no matter how crave-worthy, were fleeting, ephemeral. They ceased to exist the moment their lips lost contact. But this kiss felt weightier, built from pain and loss, in hope and in faith. It pinned its memory into Yana's brain, and she knew it would be a long, long time before its edges faded away.

Presently, they eased apart, and Yana pressed her cheek against his chest, resuming what was quickly becoming her favorite position. Gabe pressed a kiss on the top of her head. "Yana? Could I ask you something?"

"Hmm?" she murmured, the closest to relaxed she had been since she'd stepped foot on this yacht.

"You still haven't told me why you broke into Everly's room."

Oh. That pesky little detail.

Spell broken, she pulled out of his embrace and scooted back so that a full foot separated them. "I was looking for clues," she muttered.

He lifted his eyebrows. "Um, okay, *Brett*. Do I have to give you a detective name, too? Because you didn't have to break away from the group to do that. In fact, you could've told us and we could've done it together."

She shrugged, as casually as possible. "I saw the keys in Étienne's back pocket. And I didn't think about it too hard. I just went with it."

"Uh-uh. You're being evasive again. Do you know how I know? This right here." He traced a finger down her forehead. "This is your tell. You get a crease, right there, when you're trying to push me away."

"So, pretty much all the time, then?" she joked weakly.

"Yeah, pretty much." His hand moved to cup her chin. "I'm not the enemy here. I'm on *your* side."

Yana looked into his handsome face—the dependable eyes, the playful smile. It made sense to confide in Gabe. She needed one ally whom she could fully trust. Besides, she *wanted* to tell him.

"Do you promise that you didn't steal my notebook?" she asked.

He furrowed his brow, genuinely confused. "What notebook?"

"Never mind." Taking a deep breath, she summarized the draft of Everly's column and the comments. She probably talked too fast and shared too much, but Gabe didn't seem to mind.

"So, you think the guest commenter could be involved in the murders?" he asked when she was finished.

Yana shrugged. "Seems that way." She paused, gathering her thoughts. "This secret. The life-changing one that Everly was hinting about. That's the key. We figure out the secret, we find our killer."

"Sex, greed, and money," Gabe mused. "The holy trinity of homicide."

"Is that true?" Yana asked.

"Hell if I know." He shrugged. "I've been spending too much time with Brett watching suspense movies."

Yana glanced at her smartwatch. Thirty minutes had passed since she had broken off from the group. Way too long. "Speaking of the burgeoning detective, should we re-join the group?"

Gabe groaned. "If we must."

Slowly, they got to their feet, hesitant to leave the bubble of peace they'd created in the midst of the chaos. But as care-free and effervescent as bubbles were, they always popped.

They were almost at the door when Gabe turned to her with a mischievous grin. "I don't think that kiss was my best work. Dead bodies and killers, you know. They throw me off my game."

Yana shrugged, red blossoming in her cheeks. "Felt pretty good to me."

"We'll have to do it again. And again. And again." He smirked. "Believe me, you ain't seen nothing yet."

She punched his shoulder. "Watch the ego! You have to fit through the door."

Yana reached for the doorknob, but he turned her to face him, placing both hands on her shoulders. "When this is over and the only danger we face is flunking biology at Northwestern, I'm going to give you a kiss that you'll re-member when you're eighty-five and gray. A kiss that will curl your toes. A kiss that will have you forgetting your name but shouting mine at the top of your lungs."

"We'll see," Yana said noncommittally, but inside she was smiling. She wanted that kiss.

But what she wanted even more was for her and Gabe to make it to Northwestern, alive.

TWENTY-THREE

NAYA

11:42 P.M.

Naya bucked and squirmed, but the hold around her waist only grew tighter. She let out another scream and drove her elbow back. It connected, and with a sharp, wheezing exhale, her attacker released her.

She lurched forward, steadying herself against the wall of the dark corridor.

Buzz. Buzz. Buzz buzz.

The lights clicked on, and she forced herself to make eye contact with her attacker.

"Naya." Étienne coughed, rubbing at a spot just below his ribs. "I know you are mad, but—"

"You scared the shit out of me!" she hissed.

"It was a hug," he coughed. "Not meant to be scary."

"You snuck up behind me, in the dark, on a . . . a . . . *murder yacht*!"

"I did not sneak. I said your name, but you were too busy

staring at that picture," he said, motioning to the painting of Seraphina.

"And we were *not* hugging," Naya continued as if he hadn't spoken. Whether or not he'd snuck up on her or had been calling her name for the past five minutes didn't matter. Not when he'd finally revealed his secret. "You lied to me. You've *been* lying to me for our entire relationship." A thought dawned, and a sick feeling bubbled up in her gut. "Was that a lie, too?"

The buzzing ceased and they were drenched in darkness again. Silence burned around them, and Naya was relieved she didn't have to hide her fear of his answer. What if none of it had been true? What if it had been one big farce, the ultimate joke that he could take with him back to Paris? Would he tell his friends about the typical American who fell for his sexy accent and European allure?

"You are the truest thing in my life." Étienne's voice was thick with emotion as he neared her. "I will never forgive myself for making you believe what we have is not real."

Naya's skin tingled. She wanted him to tell her everything would be okay. She wanted his lips on hers, to feel nothing except him. More than that, she wanted to believe what he said.

Buzz. Buzz. Buzz buzz.

Étienne stared down at her, his brilliant gold gaze making her fuzzy and giddy—drunk on him as she had been for the past six months, oblivious to the red flags waving in her periphery.

He took her hands in his and drew slow, mesmerizing circles against her skin.

Could this be his only secret? If so, was it too big for them to be together?

Naya glanced down at their joined hands and back up at him. "Étienne, why do you steal?"

"It started as a thrill—fun with my friends." He inhaled, shaking his head. "They quit when it no longer gave them a rush, but I could not. The *need* to steal took over. No matter what I do, I can't stop."

A loud *bang* rang out. Footsteps rushed toward them, and Étienne pulled Naya against him, wrapping her in a protective embrace.

Naya buried her face in his chest, inhaling his scent of sandalwood and pine and feeling the safest she had since they began their journey.

They stood there for what felt like hours waiting for what the night would bring next.

Buzz. Buzz. Buzz buzz.

Brett skidded to a stop a few feet from them. "Oh shit!" He pressed one hand to his chest and took a step back. "What are you two doing standing in the dark in the middle of the hall? This is not your grandma's soap opera. Why is everyone sneaking off to bone?"

Naya wrinkled her nose at Brett's crassness before reluctantly releasing Étienne.

"*Merde*, Brett." Étienne dragged one hand through his hair while keeping the other firmly wrapped around Naya's fingers. "You cannot sneak up on people."

Naya, not quite ready to forgive her *maybe* boyfriend, pulled her hand from Étienne's grasp. "You literally just did the same thing to me."

"I was searching for you. Brett is running around like a chicken with no head. Alone. Looking guilty."

Brett stiffened and crossed his arms over his chest. "If I didn't like being the center of attention, I'd be really pissed at how many of you have accused me of murder when I'm the only one actually trying to solve these crimes. Unfortunately, for the rest of you, I'm not the one with a gun."

"A gun . . . ," Étienne whispered.

"That's what that bang was—a gunshot?" Without thinking, Naya groped the space between them, searching for Étienne's hand. She squeezed it. "What about an explosive? There was a fireworks show listed on the schedule. Couldn't it have been one of those?"

Brett's sigh told Naya how ridiculous he thought it was that she didn't know a gunshot when she heard one. "Either way, are we going to investigate, or are we going to stand in this very creepy, very murdery hallway?"

More racing footsteps thudded on the carpet, and Naya stiffened. At least this time she wasn't alone. Hopefully, the three of them would be able to take down the killer.

Taylor sprinted down the hall in a blaze of wild blond hair, flushed cheeks, and wide, frenzied eyes.

"Taylor!" Naya reached out to grab her friend, slow her down, keep her safe with them. Her fingertips grazed the straps of Taylor's life vest as she ran by in a whoosh of air.

"I'm getting off this boat!" Taylor shrieked, her footsteps getting farther away.

"We have to go after her." Naya started after Taylor the way she had when the blond darted from the beach club, but this time Étienne pulled her back.

"You did that before. I can't let you do it again. It's too dangerous."

"She's my best friend."

"And she'll be safer if we can stop this person. We all will," Brett said.

Naya chewed her bottom lip. She couldn't argue with that.

Something caught Brett's eye, and he bent down and plucked a black and silver device off the floor. "My phone. Must've dropped it in all the excitement." He shoved it into his pocket before Naya could tell what it was. "Don't bother asking. I still can't find my charger."

Étienne ran his hand through his tousled hair. "We have bigger things to worry about than your dead cell phone. Are we going to catch this asshole or not?"

His chest swelled and his eyes narrowed as he turned to Brett, nodded, and took off down the hall. Brett clapped his hands, apparently ending a group meeting and went after him.

As if drawing a curtain on the scene, the lights went out.

<hr>

Naya ran behind them, each ground-eating stride bringing her closer to the fluorescent white and the shooter.

"Two things," she called after Brett and Étienne. "One, I really don't like how you both just assumed I would follow. And two, we don't actually have a plan. What do we do when we find this person?"

They rounded another corner, and she scrunched her nose. The hall smelled like fireworks, the invisible cloud of charcoal and sulfur seemed to be overtaken by a hauntingly slow ballad. Piano notes stabbed the air in time with a mournful bass and a singer's voice, muffled by Derek's closed door. It hadn't been long since they were here trying and failing to get their former teacher's attention. It had been even less time since Naya had stood a few rooms down, pleading with Taylor to come with her or stay locked in their quarters for the rest of the trip. Her friend hadn't listened to either instruction.

"I have this side," Étienne said, motioning toward the three closed cabin doors on the left side of the hall. "Brett, you take the two on the other side. We will open each room. The killer must be here. We're in the middle of the ocean. They have nowhere else to go."

Brett rushed to the closest door on the right and flung it open before raising his fists to attack.

"Naya, that room is empty." Étienne nodded at the cabin Brett had just cleared. "You should hide in there. We'll call out if we need you."

She took a step toward the vacant cabin, her body more than eager to follow his directive. At the last second, she stopped. Her whole life she'd been going with the flow, doing what she was told—who to be friends with, who *not* to be friends with, which clothes to wear and classes to take, how to style her hair. She would do anything, be anyone, to make sure this group tolerated her presence. Not respected, not cherished, not even accepted . . . *tolerated.*

Brett busted down another door, which might have been more impressive if it had been locked, and Étienne stiffened, glancing over Naya's shoulder at the empty room.

She'd been chasing her future without realizing she was sacrificing her present. Only looking ahead had gotten her here, and by the end of this trip, she might have no future to realize.

It hadn't been worth it.

"Hide?" Naya shook out her curls and tilted her chin. "Not a chance." Before Étienne had the chance, she strode to the next door, twisted the handle, and pushed it open. Empty except for the two queen beds, luxurious linens, and tufted velvet armchairs that faced the expansive window. The tension coiled in her stomach didn't ease, however. The killer was here, and she, Étienne, and Brett would find them.

"C'est ma petite louve." *My little wolf.* Étienne joined Naya, and together they stalked to the next cabin. They were back in front of Derek's room and the locked door that had shielded him and Amelia from the horrors on the deck.

"What if it's still locked?" she asked.

Brett crossed the hall and threw open another door, and Naya and Étienne paused, waiting for him to call out. When he did, Étienne drew his knee up to his core.

"What if it isn't?" This time, when his foot struck, the door flew open, slamming with a loud *thwack* against the stopper.

Étienne charged in, then froze before staggering back as if the floor beneath him had lurched and it was all he could do to stay upright.

Brett rushed to his side and clamped a steadying hand on his shoulder before leaning forward to peer into the cabin. He pressed his palm to his mouth and retreated. "Oh God. Oh no." He shook his head. "No, no, no."

"What? What is it?" Naya asked, inching forward, the scent of copper stinging her nose.

"Naya!" Étienne threw himself between her and the open door. He gripped both sides of the doorframe, shielding her from what was inside. "Don't go in there."

The song ended, and silence hummed against her ears

as she glanced from Étienne to Brett and back again. She placed her hand on Étienne's bicep and pursed her lips. It was her life, and she was going to do with it what she wanted.

"I can handle it. Actually, I can handle a lot," she said before ducking under his arm and slipping through the space between his body and the doorframe.

Naya hadn't lied. She was stronger than she seemed, both physically and mentally. Just today, she'd seen a body impaled by a metal spike and another crushed and oozing beneath a chandelier, and still she'd run headlong toward a mysterious shooter instead of breaking down. And now, she'd seen this.

Naya took in Derek's and Amelia's lifeless bodies—his on top of hers, suspended in time like Romeo and Juliet. Yet another tragedy.

Her gaze crept over Derek's naked back, landing on the slick blood and thin wound that punctured his shoulder blade.

Her stomach clenched, and she suppressed a sob.

Naya was cold, her skin clammy, her heart thundering up her throat. She wasn't numb. She was delayed, her mind thick as molasses, trying to slow down time, hoping it would change. But it hadn't. Derek was dead. Naya's gaze slid down his spine, following the river of blood to the waist of his khakis now stained scarlet.

And beneath him, Amelia, unnaturally pale and unmoving.

Naya pawed at her throat. She couldn't breathe, couldn't swallow. Another of her friends was gone—murdered.

The edges of Naya's vision went dark even as Étienne's hand found hers. Tunnel vision. That's what it was called when the world closed in and all that could be seen was dead center.

Dead center.

Naya bit the inside of her cheeks to stifle a bubble of hysterical laughter. This was the worst time for a pun. An even worse time to lose her grip on reality. She needed to stay calm and focused. She could handle the hard stuff. Her life and the lives of her remaining friends depended on it.

She inhaled and smoothed her free hand down her stained jumpsuit. She was a pro at this, after all. Derek and Amelia weren't her first or even second dead bodies. Naya would break down later. Right now, she needed to survive.

TWENTY-FOUR

NAYA

11:59 P.M.

"We have to find her," she said out loud.

Taylor's alone.

That was her foremost thought, the one that rose to the surface, even as she stared at the entwined dead lovers.

She shouldn't have believed herself to be a hero. She should have stayed focused, should have gone after Taylor and made sure her best friend wasn't by herself. They weren't going to find the murderer before they were rescued.

"Find who?" Rushing footfalls merged with Naya's thundering heart as Gabe tore around the corner. A few moments later, Yana appeared. Naya couldn't tell whether they'd arrived together or separately. She supposed it didn't matter. There was no chance either of them—any of them—were capable of this.

Yana and Gabe's chorus of shocked and anguished exclamations pummeled Naya's ears and drove a stake through her heart. She pressed her fist against her chest as if she could soothe the wound, stop the fissures from cracking it in two.

Naya's eyes met Yana's and another splinter dug into her chest. How long would they be safe?

Naya pushed down her fear. Yana and Étienne were right here, right now. There was only one person she cared about who was missing. "Taylor. She's alone."

She let the words hang in the air knowing full well that she was asking her former best friend to help save the one who'd replaced her.

"I know her," Naya continued. "I know she didn't do this."

Yana's eyes met Naya's again, and she shrugged. *What are we waiting for?*

The two of them had always been able to speak without words. It was one of the many things only they shared.

"Taylor should still be in your room," Gabe supplied. "I checked in on her right before I, uh, investigated something with Yana." His gaze drifted to the girl at his side. "She's fine. I told her to lock her door so the killer doesn't get her."

Naya shook her head. "We saw her run down the hall after we heard the shot. She tore past us with a life vest."

Brett turned his back to the bodies and scrubbed one hand down his cheek. "She said she was getting off the yacht."

"How? We've already tried everything," Naya said, her hand finding Étienne's without instruction from her brain. He was always there, proving that she wasn't alone.

Brett's brows lifted. "Not *everything* . . . Maybe she swam for help."

Gabe paced the hallway just outside the open door, shaking his head. "No, you and I couldn't swim to that ship we saw in the distance in the best of conditions, much less Taylor in the middle of the night with this kind of storm. She wouldn't think about doing something so reckless."

"She might," Naya said quietly, "if she spotted another boat."

Étienne squeezed Naya's hand once, twice, three times before letting go. "You and Yana stay here," he murmured, pressing a kiss to Naya's temple. "Lock yourselves in. Brett, Gabe, and I will go find Taylor before she does something she will regret."

"Wait." Yana spoke up before Naya had a chance to protest. "You're not leaving us in a room with two dead people while you're gone for who knows how long." Her gaze darted around the room.

Heat drained from Naya's cheeks as the prospect became more real now that it'd been said aloud. "I agree with Yana. We're not staying in here like sitting ducks with—"

"The murderer has already been here," Brett interrupted, his attention returning to Derek and Amelia. "Serial killers are like tornadoes. They don't double back."

"What about when they return to the scene of the crime because they're raging narcissists?" Yana asked, crossing her arms over her chest. "Like most of the people on this yacht are. And like you did when you were sneaking around Everly's body."

Gabe snorted. "Brett didn't kill anyone."

"Et dis moi, how would you know?" Étienne asked.

"Because we've been teammates since we were in swim diapers." Brett leaned forward, inspecting Derek's wound. "Trust me, you get to know someone who shits next to you in a pool."

"Trust you? Look around." Étienne motioned to the

blood-spattered carpet and bedding. "Il n'y a qu'une seule personne en qui je peux avoir confiance sur ce bateau, et ce n'est pas toi."

"We don't speak French!" Gabe and Brett shouted in unison.

Naya tucked her hair behind her ears and groaned inwardly. "This isn't helping!"

Liquid splattered against porcelain and the toilet flushed, silencing everyone.

Yana winced as she hobbled out of the adjoining bathroom. "Sorry, I'm a little stressed." She heaved again, and the boys took a collective step back.

Naya grimaced and pressed a hand to her stomach. "I'll stay with Yana. She obviously needs to take a breather. You three go find Taylor."

Yana cleared her throat and wiped her mouth with the back of her hand. "No, wait. I just have to sit down for a second." With Gabe's help, she shuffled over to the two armchairs in the corner of the room and plopped down in the one facing the picture window that looked out on the charcoal-black sea.

"We *will* find Taylor," Étienne said, cupping Naya's face in his hands. "Then we will come back here and stay together as a group until we reach Bermuda. No more chasing the killer. They won't come for us when we're together." He feathered a kiss against her lips, so light and gentle she couldn't help but sigh.

And then he was gone, following Gabe out the door, taking with him his warmth and protection.

Brett rolled his eyes. "I cannot wait until we're off this floating anus," he mumbled as he closed the door behind him.

Immediately, Naya pressed the lock, her anxiety barely easing as it clicked into place. "Be careful, Étienne," she whispered, leaning her forehead against the cool wood. Even after everything that had happened, maybe *because of* everything that had happened, she couldn't imagine a life without him in it.

"Sorry." Yana's voice, small and quiet, came from behind her.

"For what?" Naya asked, walking to the bathroom.

"For being the reason you're stuck here . . . with them." In the mirror, Yana's face twisted, her throat tightening with a swallow.

"You're not the reason." Naya picked up an empty glass next to the sink and filled it before turning off the faucet and heading back to Yana. She handed Yana the glass and sat in the armchair opposite her. The one that faced the room instead of the window. The one that faced the massacre.

They lay sideways across one of the queen-sized beds. Derek's lifeless arms framed Amelia, his head buried in her chest.

Amelia's pale-pink cami was stained with the blood that had run down Derek's back, onto his khakis, and dripped from his side onto the former student council president.

It wouldn't be long until livor mortis set in—the first stage after death, when the blood settles in the lowest parts of the body—and Amelia's skin was as snow white as her skirt.

Naya rubbed the spot on her chest where her heart ached beneath her ribs and brought her attention back to Yana. "I make my own decisions. They haven't always been good, but they've never been because of anything you did."

An apology would be better. A clear *I'm sorry for abandoning you in eighth grade. I wanted to be popular, to be like everyone else. I saw my chance, and I took it.* But Naya wasn't ready for that admission yet. In truth, her heart couldn't handle another emotional injury. And even though they'd taken steps to get back to where they once were, Yana had every right to inflict one.

"Oh." Yana blinked, her dark eyes shining with unshed tears. "I thought . . ." She shrugged, the tip of her nose turning pink.

Say it! Naya scolded herself. *This could be your last opportunity. Rip off the Band-Aid and tell her that you were the worst friend on the entire planet and that you're sorry and that you've missed her and beg her not to hate you.*

You used to bring out the best version of me. The fun side of me. I can truly be myself with you.

Say it!

"Yana, I—"

A flutter of movement caught Naya's attention, and she sprang to her feet, the armchair nearly toppling over from her swift movement.

"What is it?" Yana rose just as quickly and joined Naya.

Side by side like they always should have been.

"Amelia," Naya whispered, wrapping her arm around Yana as they huddled together and inched closer to the bodies. "I think she's—"

Amelia's fingers twitched, her ballet-slipper-pink nails stabbing the duvet.

"Alive."

TWENTY-FIVE

YANA

12:11 A.M.

They both stared at Amelia's slender hand. Her veins gleamed ghostly blue. It was as though her spirit were already haunting them.

"Amelia! Amelia!" Naya dropped to the floor. "Can you hear me? Wake up?"

No response. Thirty seconds passed, and still no response.

"What do we do?" Acid surged up Yana's throat, but she shoved it back down. Yeah, she'd just thrown up. Yeah, she'd revealed her weakness in front of this group—not once, or twice, but three different times.

But that didn't mean she was weak. Exactly the opposite. She'd spent her whole life trying to convince herself. Now it was time to prove it.

"If Amelia's alive, we need to get Derek off her," Naya said shakily. "If the bullet didn't get her, then suffocation will."

"We?" Yana asked, buckling at the knees.

Naya tightened her grip on Yana's arm, pulling her back up. "Of course *we*! You and me, we're the strongest of the bunch. The boys couldn't even handle a little bodily fluid."

Yana turned to her former friend, meeting those familiar brown eyes. "You *were* the only one who stayed behind. They *all* took off, even Gabe."

"What are old friends for? I couldn't leave you to stand guard over a couple of dead bodies all by your lonesome," Naya said, and that's how Yana knew *her* Naya was back. The loyal, protective one she had known in childhood.

Yana smiled. "Right. Well, let's save Amelia from possible suffocation."

Actually moving roughly 180 pounds of dead weight was no joke. Naya grabbed Derek's arms and Yana took the legs. They pushed, pulled, yanked. Put their legs into it. Their backs, their core. They worked every major muscle group, and still, Derek didn't budge.

"Try his middle." Yana swiped at her forehead. The sweat dripped past her barely there eyebrows and straight into her eyes. Yet another reason to envy Naya's thick brows. "Maybe we can roll him."

Naya perked up, as though receiving a burst of energy. "One big shove, and gravity should take care of the rest."

Naya mimed pushing up her sleeves, even though she was wearing a sleeveless jumpsuit. Yana pretended to hitch up her pants (er, dress) and fastened invisible suspenders.

Exchanging small smiles, they positioned themselves on the same side of Derek's body.

"On three," Naya said. "One, two . . . three!"

They shoved. And thank the mother hen and her six chicks reincarnated as stars! It worked. Derek's body rolled.

Naya crawled over to Amelia, positioning her friend on her side and tilting back her head. "This will keep her airways open," she muttered, lifting one of Amelia's wrists. "She's warm. That's a good sign."

"Fingers crossed that's Derek's blood, not hers." Yana gestured to Amelia's white skirt and pink top, now stained red.

"She has a pulse! It's slow, but steady. That's to be expected in a resting state." Naya slid her hands over Amelia's body, checking for injuries. Her movements were efficient, competent. Professional.

Yana blinked. "How do you know how to do this? Don't tell me you've already started med school. Is it still your dream to be a doctor?"

"Always." Naya blushed. "I'm, um, president of the pre-med club. Plus, I read medical textbooks for fun and volunteer for the Red Cross. Taylor doesn't understand why I'd wake up in the middle of the night to hand out blankets to people whose homes have caught on fire. She'd much rather just write a huge check than do any real work. So I had to tell her that it's for the hot guys who also volunteer."

"Taylor's a spoiled princess," Yana said shortly. "I mean— I think what you're doing is amazing."

"Thanks," Naya said, continuing her examination. "Amelia has no sign of any physical injuries. No bullet wounds. Nothing."

"Why is she unconscious, then?"

Naya shook her head. "No clue." She turned her attention to Derek, who was now lying face up on the carpet. Yana peered over Naya's shoulder, zeroing in on Derek's face with its frozen lips, Botox-like skin, and rigid cheeks.

"Does Derek look weird?" Yana asked abruptly.

"He looks dead," Naya said, shuddering. "I honestly can't believe it. He was just making that toast to the crew a few hours ago! Tedious, yes. Yet also charming, in his quirky math TA way, you know? And now . . . he's gone."

Emotion swelled up Yana's throat, nearly closing it. Derek might have gotten caught up in a cheating ring over a girl. His intentions toward Amelia were definitely inappropriate. He deserved to be fired, not killed. He was a real human being. Someone's son, maybe a brother. Definitely a proud teacher. He had helped Yana decipher multivariable calculus more than once, during his office hours, and for that alone, she wanted to rage at the unfairness of it all. This murderer who was so intent on taking them out one by one had to be made of pure evil.

Did Naya know about the cheating? Two of her friends, Amelia and Everly, were involved, but Yana doubted that Naya had helped herself to any test answers. She was too conscientious for that. But with his cold body in front of them, she couldn't bring herself to disparage the dead.

Instead, Yana said, "No, look. His face. It's so stiff."

"Rigor mortis," Naya said, continuing to examine Derek's body. "It starts in the face, about two hours after death." Her jaw dropped, as though the implication was just sinking in. "But if Derek died two hours ago, that must mean—"

"He didn't die from the gunshot we heard," Yana finished grimly.

"He didn't die from a gunshot at all." Naya's eyes widened as she stared down at Derek's exposed ribs. "There are multiple wounds here." Shaking her head, she met Yana's gaze. "Derek was stabbed."

Naya jumped to her feet and began pacing from the gilded

armchairs to the matching bed, neatly sidestepping Derek's body. "I knew what we heard wasn't a gunshot. It was more than likely a firecracker. But I don't get it. Why light a fire-cracker?"

"What if it was just the killer's way of luring us here?" Yana asked. "They're manipulating us. For their own reasons, they must want us here. In this room, locked away. Either to keep us away from the action—or maybe because we'll be easier to find."

"The lounge is directly above us," Naya said thoughtfully. "If the shot didn't come from here, it must've originated from up there."

She extended her hand to Yana. A peace offering? An agreement, to be sealed with a handshake? Or simply a desire to reconnect?

Perhaps, maybe, probably all of the above.

"I have keys to this room—don't ask," Yana said. As a display of trust, she took the plastic coil of keys out of her pocket and tossed it to Naya. "We can lock Amelia in to keep her safe."

Naya nodded. "Good thinking."

"So, we're getting the phuk tong out of this room?" Yana asked. Once upon a time, two little girls used to curse with the Thai word for pumpkin.

"Yes." Naya emitted a giggle-sob. They both walked out of the cabin. Naya shut the door and locked it. "Or, as Étienne would say, phoque yeah!"

"What does that mean?" Yana asked curiously.

"Seal." One side of Naya's mouth curved. "As in the animal."

Six years later, those same two girls, marginally grown up, exited a cabin on a megayacht arm in arm, in search of a killer.

TWENTY-SIX

YANA

12:27 A.M.

"This is creepy," Naya grumbled as they groped their way through the dark and up the staircase.

Yana gritted her teeth but said nothing. No point in adding her panic to the chorus. It wouldn't make the shadows any less long. Wouldn't dampen the metallic scent of blood that tinged the air.

She let the anger build inside her, until it blotted out every last trace of fear. This freaking enemy. *Yana* was supposed to be the only one sneaking around this yacht. *She* had her own mystery to solve. This exposé on Yatesville's cheating elite would've been the ideal start to her internship. Whoever this subversive was, they were wrecking her plans.

"Lights." Naya sighed as the overbright lounge, with its glaring emergency lights that actually worked, came into view. "Finally."

They stepped inside, aware of every creak and groan that the hardwood floor made beneath their shoes.

"Someone forgot to clean up," Naya remarked.

The wind howled through the propped-open glass door. A cluster of unwashed champagne glasses waited in the sink of the wet bar, and cushions from the L-shaped couch were scattered haphazardly over every surface.

However, the glass walls, framed by heavy brocade curtains held back by gold cords, were intact and bullet-free.

"Maybe the crew passed out before they got the chance to clean." Yana ran to the door, kicking out the wedge of wood so that it slammed shut.

"I use that excuse with my mom, too," Naya said. "Luckily, she can't tell the difference between sleepy passed-out and drunk passed-out."

"Or at least Auntie Rose pretends not to know."

Yana used the familiar name without thinking—and then winced. In Thai culture, it was customary to refer to elders with an honorific, and the parents of close friends fell into the category of *aunties* and *uncles*. "I didn't mean—"

"She asks about you, you know," Naya said softly. "She even cuts out articles about you from the local paper and scrapbooks them. State champion in journalism, two years in a row? She's so proud of you." Naya stared down at her gladiator sandals. "We both are."

Yana swallowed, but the gunk in her throat remained. "My own mother doesn't even do that."

"Auntie Ae's too busy keeping you and the rest of the town fed."

The girls met each other's gazes—and then turned away.

Naya used to be a fixture next to Yana, as they sat in her family's restaurant, gossiping and wrapping egg rolls. In fact, her technique was even better than Yana's. Her rolls were always tighter; the creases, neater.

As far as Yana knew, since their falling out, Naya hadn't come to the restaurant once.

Not that Yana expected differently. She had to stop being so soft. She had no proof that Naya was innocent. Reuniting with her former best friend felt amazing. Yet how well did Yana truly know the girl that she was today? People changed, especially when they surrounded themselves with toxic friends.

Lighting zigzagged across the sky, followed a few seconds later by the sharp crack of thunder. Naya jumped, but then she straightened her shoulders and walked to the wet bar, as if determined to stay on track.

She snatched up a champagne flute and held it up to the light. "Yana, look!" She rotated the glass, displaying the lipstick stain on the rim. "Amelia's lipstick, Forbidden Love. I thought Amelia had copied the shade from Everly, since Ev was a rep for the brand. Turns out, Amelia discovered the lipstick *first*, and then Everly approached the company about repping them. Ev then had the audacity to tell us that Amelia had never had an original thought in her life."

Naya shook her head, a shadow of a smile on her face. "Isn't it funny how things that annoy you in life are kinda endearing in death? Everly was a giant pain, but I already miss her messy ass."

That was what Yana had always admired most about Naya—her ability to love, to *feel*, without restraint, without hesitation. Oh, Yana had feelings, too. She just didn't know how to put them out there like Naya.

Much easier to put up a wall, a fortress that didn't allow anyone in—even as it prevented the real Yana from getting out.

She *wanted* to put her hand on Naya's shoulder and squeeze. She wished she could share her own weird sorrow about her archenemy. But she was—and always had been—crap at knowing how.

"If Amelia drank some of the spiked champagne, it would explain why she's passed out, like the rest of the crew," Naya offered.

"Yeah. But why would Derek drug her?" Yana chewed the inside of her cheek, thinking hard. "He seemed like the prime suspect. On account of the champagne toast, the drugs, Brett's video footage of him spiking the drinks. But he's dead now. Does that make him more or less likely to be involved? Instead of answers, we have even more questions."

"So you don't think it was one of the crew?" Naya asked in a small voice.

Yana met her former—kinda sorta current—friend's eyes from across the room. "No," she said quietly. "I don't. Not anymore. There are too many secrets in this group. Too much resentment for it to be a stranger. And I didn't recognize any of the crew's faces. Did you?"

Naya shook her head. "A mysterious stowaway, then?"

"It would be one hell of a coincidence if it wasn't one of us." Frustrated, Yana kicked at the burgundy-and-gold curtain fringe in front of her. The brocade curtain swung back—and she caught a glint of metal next to a fire-scorched tube.

She dropped to her knees. "The hunting knife!" she exclaimed. The sharp steel blade with a rough grip. If it wasn't the same weapon she'd carried before, then it had to be its twin. And what looked like the burned remains of a firecracker. Shreds of red and white paper with singed edges were scattered on the floor next to the knife. "You were right. That must've been the bang we heard."

"Yay, me," Naya said with no enthusiasm. "Don't touch the knife. We don't want your fingerprints on that thing."

"My fingerprints are already on it," Yana said distractedly.

"What do you mean?" Naya came and kneeled beside Yana.

To Naya's credit, she didn't even flinch. It had never entered her mind that Yana could be the serial murderer taking out their classmates. Maybe Naya was naive, but the foundation of their friendship couldn't be forgotten. She trusted Yana with her life. Yana would have to remember that.

"There's something I have to tell you," she started, "about Étienne."

"If it concerns him being a klepto, I already know." Naya rocked back onto her heels in exasperation. "Did the entire world know about my boyfriend's penchant for petty theft before me?"

"It's not about that. Well, only partly." Yana took a deep breath. She'd delayed for as long as possible, but there was only so much she could do to shield her friend. "I saw him with a knife. This knife, maybe." She lifted the weapon gingerly.

"He said he found it in someone's bag, but he doesn't know whose." Yana licked her lips. "I, uh, took it from him when he wasn't paying attention, but then it went missing shortly afterward." She waited a beat. "Unless there's more than one hunting knife on board, this is the weapon the killer used to stab Derek."

Naya searched the coffered ceiling as though it might have answers. "So, he's lying to me again."

"There's one more thing," Yana said, the secrets rushing out of her. "The keys. The ones we used to lock Amelia inside. I took them from Étienne, who stole them from the head stew."

Naya shook her head. "Of course you did."

"Do you think . . ." Yana licked her lips again. "Is it possible that Étienne is involved in the —"

"Murders?" Naya's forehead creased. "I don't know why he took the keys or the knife. Maybe it was just—I don't know—part of his stealing addiction. Or something? But I know he's not a killer. I'd bet my life on it."

She was so certain, so resolute. Yana would think her love was sweet . . . if she wasn't afraid that her friend was wrong. Dead wrong. Étienne's behavior screamed suspicious.

The knob of the inner door rattled. Quickly, Yana shoved the hunting knife in the pocket of her dress before turning around.

Gabe stood in the doorway, holding a cue stick from a billiards table. How long had he been there? "There you are!" He crossed the lounge, heading toward them. "The search is taking longer than we thought, so I volunteered to rescue you two from the, um . . . cabin at the end of the residential floor."

It was kinda cute how he avoided saying *the room with the bodies*. "But the door was locked, and you two weren't in any of the other cabins, so I came up to the main deck," he finished.

"Amelia's alive, just unconscious," Yana said. "We locked her in to keep her safe."

"Thank goodness for that!" Gabe exclaimed. "But what about keeping yourselves safe?"

"We couldn't just stay in the room," Naya said slowly. "Derek had stab wounds, not a gunshot wound." She gestured to the remains of the firecracker on the floor. "We found what made the noise like a gunshot."

Gabe bent down to examine the burned paper, and Naya didn't say any more, particularly about the knife they had just found. Yana was glad. She trusted Gabe . . . far enough to kiss him. But people were dropping dead left and right. That meant all of them should only be sharing information on a need-to-know basis.

He stood up. "Good work," he said. And then, in a lower voice to Yana, "I missed you."

Yana blushed, even as guilt coursed through her from the thought she'd just had.

After making a pit stop to use the restroom, they snuck downstairs and peeked in the crew mess. The nine crew members remained either slumped on the table or against each other. Yana lifted the head stew's arm. The moment she let go, it flopped limply onto the table. Naya and Gabe proceeded down either side of the table, nudging, tapping, and tugging on the various bodies. Still unconscious. Still utterly unhelpful.

"We've gotta stop checking on them, Gabe," Naya said exasperatedly. "They're never going to wake up."

"That is patently untrue," he said blandly.

Yana cleared her throat. "What she means is, whoever the killer is, they must've been smart enough to give the crew a large enough dose to keep them out of the way until at least the morning. I don't think we can expect any assistance from them."

"Well, then, I guess we'll just have to save ourselves."

Squaring his shoulders, Gabe led them back down the darkened hall, smashing cameras with the cue stick as he went. The very same cameras whose footage could be viewed from the wheelhouse. It was smart. Once the cameras were destroyed, the killer would have no way of knowing their location. Gabe's reach was long, and made even lengthier by the stick, and he destroyed each camera with a precise and controlled strike. "I've already smashed the cameras in the game room, the library, and the main deck," he relayed.

It was, if Yana were pressed, mildly attractive.

The girls trailed behind him, and Naya threaded her arm through Yana's.

"He's adorable," she whispered into Yana's ear.

"Persistent, at least."

"He has to be to break down your walls."

It was amazing—and a little disconcerting—how well Naya could read the situation, even after all these years.

Up ahead, Gabe turned a corner, and Naya tugged Yana to the side, halting her stride.

"Listen, Yana," Naya said, her tone serious. "My boyfriend lied to me, and my best friend abandoned me. I can see now that you're the only one here I can trust."

Yana startled. There was a lot of talk about trust going around. First Gabe, and now Naya. She'd never been the object of so much confidence in her life. She didn't know what to make of it. "Gabe thinks he knows you, but I grew up with you," Naya continued. "You and I, we became actual *people* together. And there's no evil in your core. You couldn't do this, kill anyone. You're good people."

All of a sudden, Yana's eyes were . . . wet? How was that possible? She never cried. Not when Naya ditched their friendship. Not even when A-ma (her beloved grandmother) passed away.

Crying revealed to others that you were vulnerable, and as a journalist, she had to be tough. Empathetic, but not overly sensitive.

"Let's keep that I have a weapon between us," Yana said in a rush. "The boys don't need to know."

"Of course. I can feel the lump at my side. *Super* cute dress, by the way. Love the pockets." Naya's voice filled with the smile that Yana could almost see.

The girls continued down the corridor, Gabe's outline just visible in the shadows.

Somehow, some way, the girls had regained each other's trust, the one that was formed back before Yana had learned how to protect herself. Back before she even knew that she needed protecting.

Tonight, that trust would be tested—and Yana hoped to the pra Buddha cho that it would be confirmed.

TWENTY-SEVEN

NAYA

12:42 A.M.

Naya's thoughts swirled. Étienne kept lying.

It's not like I asked him if he had a weapon. The excuse—or maybe it was just a thought, an innocent observation—sprang to the front of her mind.

But still, he hadn't told her. And wasn't he, her boyfriend of six months, supposed to tell her everything? That was a huge secret to withhold given the circumstances.

Naya released Yana's arm as they filed behind Gabe into one of the many rooms Naya had yet to explore.

"What happened in here?" she asked, stepping over a couch cushion that had been haphazardly thrown near the door as she took in the sleek leather chairs and matching couch that flanked an ornately carved wooden pool table. The far wall was glass. During the day, the partially submerged view offered a breathtaking glimpse into the ocean.

Right now, however, the inky-black waves surging against the glass, lit from above by the bright fluorescent white of the emergency lights, turned the water into an abyss, a gaping maw, a grave.

Yana nudged a striped billiard ball with the toe of her tennis shoe. "It's like a bomb went off." The ball rolled into an autographed Kansas City Chiefs helmet that had also been thrown from its original spot on the memorabilia-laden shelves behind yet another wet bar.

Brett popped up from behind the lacquered bar, eyes wide, red hair mussed, and fists full of cigars. "I'm investigating."

Naya flinched and released a shaky breath as she tried to smooth down the curls let loose by rain and sweat. "How will tearing apart this game room help us find Taylor?"

Étienne approached, the scent of pine and sandalwood revealing his presence before she even felt him at her side. "He has been doing this in every room."

She bristled when he entwined his fingers with hers.

"You'll thank me when I find something useful." Brett rounded the bar, dropping the cigars in a pile on the floor. "Think about it. Every murder has been with a different weapon: impaled on a mermaid, crushed by a chandelier, shot with a—"

"Derek was stabbed," Naya blurted. "And Amelia's alive. Drugged but breathing and locked inside the room."

"Amelia's alive?" Brett's mouth tipped into a crooked grin. "That's the first good news I've heard since setting foot on this garbage barge." He shook his head. "Point is, the killer's used multiple weapons. It makes sense that the next one would be right under our noses. Like in *Clue*."

Naya's palms were clammy, and she couldn't tell whether

it was from her fears about Étienne or for Taylor. "Finding this mysterious weapon should not be at the top of our list. We have to find Taylor."

Yana nodded. "No more dividing and conquering."

"I agree." Étienne's arm was around her waist now, pulling her close. His other hand was on her cheek, in her rain-dampened hair.

"I didn't realize your hair was naturally so curly." He gently traced the ringlets that fell against her temple.

Naya's cheeks were hot, and she couldn't bring herself to make eye contact with him. She'd started straightening her hair in fifth grade, with Yana's help, after Olivia Covington had stuck a pencil in Naya's curls and shouted, in front of the whole class, that birds nested in her hair.

Étienne traced Naya's jaw and lifted her chin until her eyes met his, golden and endless.

"When I return to France, I'm going to get help." He pressed his forehead to hers. "No more stealing."

Naya bit her bottom lip.

"I don't know what's wrong with me," he continued. "But I don't want to live with this urge anymore. I'm ready for it to stop. I want it to."

Often, when people needed help, when they wanted and were actively seeking help, they were left on their own to sort out their problems. But isn't that when a person most needed the support?

Naya held her breath as she stared up at Étienne. If he continued to behave the same, continued to steal, she wouldn't stick around, but she wouldn't abandon someone in need. It wasn't in her nature. This also wasn't the time to take him to task. They had more important things to worry about.

She tucked his hair behind his ear and smoothed her palm along his stubbled cheek. "You'll have to prove to me that I can forgive you."

Yesterday, she wouldn't have headed down the path of forgiveness this easily, but losing so many people so quickly had changed her.

"I will. I promise I will. I love you, Naya." He whispered more in French, and then his lips were on hers.

Naya was lost in his kiss, in his warm body wrapped around hers, shielding, protecting, loving. His tongue glossed her lips, and she parted them, letting him explore. The soft caress of his tongue and his strong hands against her back were gentle yet demanding.

A moan escaped her lips, and he captured it with a growl of his own. He deepened their kiss, flooding her with heat.

"Hey, lovebirds!" Brett shouted.

Étienne released her, and she took a step back, breathing deeply, coming up for air.

"Hate to interrupt." Brett tilted his head. "What am I saying? *Love* to break up a make-out sesh since I was not invited to partake."

Yana rolled her eyes. "We—"

Brett interrupted with an exaggerated throat clear and took a box from Yana's hands. "*I* found something."

Gabe stepped to the side, offering Naya and Étienne a place right in front of Brett, who stood on the opposite side of the wet bar like a mixologist.

Brett pushed a shoebox-sized display case across the lacquered bar top. "Please hold your applause until the end of the show."

Naya smoothed her fingers along the polished wood case

and stared past her reflection in the glass lid at the two rows of pristine baseball cards.

Étienne brushed the hair from his eyes and squinted down at the case. "What are we supposed to see? I don't watch American baseball."

"Open it," Brett instructed.

Naya fumbled with the gold latch before unhooking it and lifting the lid. The baseball cards on display rose with the lid, attached to the glass with a barely there line of adhesive.

Cautiously, Naya flipped through the documents—Social Security cards, passports, photos, printed and handwritten letters—that filled the box.

"I don't get it." She lifted her head. "How is any of this a clue about the murders?"

"The will, Naya! The will!" Brett was practically hopping up and down.

"Yes. Most people have one. At least, most people with assets," she amended. Which didn't include her. At least, not yet. "Your point?"

With a weary sigh, Brett shook his head. "Your film education is so lacking that *I'm* embarrassed."

"Non," Étienne said, coming up behind Naya and putting an arm around her. "Naya makes me watch a different rom-com with her every single weekend. I can *almost* tell all the tall, charming, athletic romantic leads apart now."

"They sound kinda like me," Gabe said from the back wall, where he was fiddling with a framed signed baseball jersey.

"He said romantic lead, not D-list horror movie extra," Yana called from the billiards table.

Naya snorted. Yana smirked.

"People, focus! You're being obtuse. This is someone's floating safe," Brett said slowly, as if talking to a roomful of preschoolers. "They hid it for a reason. And in here"—he gripped the box, and Naya released the papers, letting them fall in a haphazard pile—"in all this *stuff* is a clue. Money and sex, I mean it's obvious."

When no one agreed, he explained, "Money and sex are the two main reasons people kill."

"Told you. Sex, greed, and money," Gabe said, mostly to Yana, fifteen feet away, like they'd had some private conversation.

"Yes, the holy trinity of homicide. We covered this earlier," she said, turning to Brett. "You've taught Gabe well."

"Damn right I have. And this, what happened tonight, is about money. That's why all our friends are dead. A dying woman's last will and testament on a yacht full of lifeless bodies. That's *exactly* how the movie script would be written. And thus, it's clear we're in our very own murder *mystery*."

A creak sounded as the framed baseball jersey slid twelve inches across the wall.

"You breaking decor to get my attention now?" Yana called out to Gabe.

"And I won't stop until I impress you." He flashed a grin and then turned back to the display case. He pushed the frame harder, putting some strength behind it, and the case moved even farther . . .

. . . revealing something that wasn't wood paneling, but something dark . . . opaque . . .

"What the . . . there are *stairs* behind here!" Gabe exclaimed, poking his head into the dark.

Naya's jaw dropped.

Brett leaped to his feet. "Holy shit! Did you just find a secret passage?"

"Don't go up there," Yana said, just as Gabe put his foot on the first step. "It could be dangerous."

"I told you I'd find a way to impress you," he said, going up a few more steps and disappearing into the empty space. "The stairs go straight up. This must lead to the library!"

Thump. Thump. Thump.

The four of them went silent, exchanging glances at the noise emanating from the game room.

Thump. Thump. Thump.

"Gabe! Okay. I'm impressed!" Yana hissed. "Now get your butt back down here."

Thump. Thump. Thump.

Gabe reappeared in the doorframe, a few cobwebs in his hair.

Naya's hand found Étienne's, and she squeezed.

Thump. Thump. Thump.

Slowly, they all turned to the glass wall that looked out onto the black waves, to the sound of knocking, to their future.

Naya's legs turned to slush, and she sank to the floor in a cold, shivering heap.

Taylor's body thumped against the outside of the glass. The metallic hem of her black miniskirt shimmered in the light of the room like fish scales as it floated around her, blending into the sea, claiming it as its own. Her life jacket and the thick rope tangled around her kept her head and chest above the water. But that hadn't mattered. Not in this storm.

Her blond hair was plastered to her face, only revealing a single ghostly-pale cheek and unseeing green eye.

Thump. Thump. Thump.

Naya cried out as waves crashed over Taylor, pushing her against the glass, pulling her under before she emerged again—a gothic mermaid.

Thump. Thump. Thump.

Above Naya, Brett cleared his throat, and she heard the distinct *snap* of the display case closing. "Guess she was serious about getting off the boat."

TWENTY-EIGHT

NAYA

1:07 A.M.

Naya scrambled to her feet and charged out of the game room, the others close behind. There was a tiny chance Taylor was alive, that they could save her if they could only get her out of the water.

Taylor had tied a rope to the railing to climb down into the water. The lights from the yacht they had seen were almost parallel to the *Seraphina*. Taylor must've wanted to enter the water from the side of the boat, in order to minimize the distance she'd have to swim to the other yacht. But her plan had backfired. At some point, she'd gotten caught up in the rope.

At the same time, however, the rope could be a lifeline. Naya had to hang on to that. They simply needed to find the rope and reel her back in. It shouldn't be hard.

It shouldn't be happening! the voice inside her fumed.

But that voice was pointless. This *was* happening, and

Naya would do everything in her power to make sure the rest of the people she cared about got off this boat alive.

Rain whipped her face as she ran up the stairs, out onto the deck, and sprinted to the guardrail. Naya gripped the railing and leaned over the side of the boat. The game room's white emergency lights cast an eerie glow against the black water.

"Taylor!" she screamed into the wind as she scanned the roiling waves.

"Taylor!" The cry was echoed by Étienne and then Gabe. Both squinting into the rain, yelling for their friend in a twisted game of Marco Polo.

"The rope. Have you found it?" Étienne called over the wind and rain to the others.

"Yes!" Gabe answered, and motioned to the water below.

As Yana, Gabe, and Brett ran to the stern, continuing to search for Taylor, Étienne again checked the side of the boat. He opened his mouth as if to yell and closed it just as quickly before turning to Naya. "The rope, it . . ." He glanced back overboard, and Naya followed his gaze.

The braided cable floated on the surface, writhing with the surging waves like a snake, and Taylor was—

"No!" Naya's knees buckled, and Étienne rushed to her side, catching her before she collapsed.

"The others are still searching, but there's no sign of her," he said.

Rain pattered against the deck and thunder rumbled overhead as Naya stared into his golden eyes, willing him to take back his words, to make it all okay, to wake her from this nightmare.

"Taylor was tangled in the rope, and the waves . . ." He took a deep breath and closed his eyes. When they opened, his irises seemed darker, haunted. "It is hard with seas like this to estimate how strong the ocean actually is. A life jacket can only do so much, and without the rope to pull her up . . . I don't know how she could have survived." He shook his head, and that one motion nearly broke Naya into a million pieces. "I . . . also don't believe she was alive when we saw her. That was minutes ago, and in conditions like this, every second is precious."

Naya sagged against the guardrail and let her tears fall into the water below. "She kept running off. Why didn't she ask for help?"

Étienne's hand was on her back, warm against her soaked jumpsuit. "She knew you would not have let her go."

"I wouldn't have let her go, because trying to swim for help is a terrible idea." A sob shook Naya's chest, and she closed her eyes against a fresh wave of tears. "She was so upset and grieving for Finn. I left her alone on this murder yacht. She wasn't safe." She glanced up at Étienne, the deep shadows sharpening his jawline. "None of us are safe."

There was a loud *click,* and Naya spun around to the *whoosh* of forced air. Something metal hurtled in her direction, winking in the fluorescent lights. A mixture of shock and fear widened her eyes and heightened her senses.

A spear.

Naya panicked, and her body froze. The scene around her slowed, each agonizing second ticking by with perfect clarity.

With a guttural howl, Étienne threw himself into the air in front of her, pushing her out of the way of the oncoming weapon. Her sandals slid against the wet wood, and she crashed against the deck. With a groan, she rolled onto her back.

Étienne seemed to hang in the air above her, a target stitched to the stormy night sky. The spear found a mark, piercing his stomach. Blood rained onto Naya and sprayed over the side of the boat as the spear's fishhooks tore through Étienne's body and emerged, red and glistening, out the other side.

The force of the blow threw him back. As he landed, his feet slammed into Naya's side, squeezing the air from her lungs. Étienne scrambled backward, his shoes slipping the same way Naya's had, his waving arms smacking against the guardrail with hollow *thwack*s.

She gasped for air and reached out, trying to steady him, to catch him before he fell. Her fingers scraped at his leg, his laces, and then . . . nothing.

Étienne had fallen overboard.

Lightning lit the sky and thunder crashed, swallowing Naya's cries as she pulled herself onto the railing. She hung over the side, hands groping the mist-filled air. He was out there.

An arm wrapped around her waist and yanked her backward, away from the guardrail, away from the hope of saving Étienne.

"Let me go!" she howled.

"You almost fell in after him! Étienne is—"

"Don't say it!" she cried, slamming her fists into Gabe's chest.

She'd said the same words to Taylor.

Finn is gone.

And now her boyfriend was in the ocean along with her best friend.

Another distinct *click* sounded.

This time, Naya didn't freeze. She grabbed Gabe's arm and yanked him down as that same deadly *whoosh* filled the night.

She was fast, but not fast enough. A warm spurt of blood splattered against her arm as Gabe crashed onto the deck. Naya crawled to him on shaky limbs. The spear protruded from his shoulder, and he struggled to sit up, a series of curses tearing from his trembling lips.

A sob splintered in her chest, shredding her throat with each wail.

Naya wanted to be relieved that Gabe had made it. But why did he get to live when Étienne didn't? Why did she? Why did anyone?

She scrambled to her feet. She had to get off this deck, off this damn boat. But Taylor had already proved there was nowhere to go.

Naya collapsed against the side of the yacht, a specter of herself. She would never be whole again. This trip had carved out sections of her heart and fed them to the sea. And worse, she would never get to say goodbye.

TWENTY-NINE

YANA

1:15 A.M.

Yana ran. From a distance, she saw the unthinkable: Étienne falling overboard, and then a spear hitting Gabe in the shoulder, the very same one that she had laid her cheek against not too long ago.

She didn't wait to witness the blood bloom across his T-shirt. She didn't stop to observe whether Gabe fell and brought Naya down with him.

She. Ran.

Yana sprinted down the deck, a howl climbing up her throat. Between the exertion and the emotion, she could hardly breathe. But she had to. She had to get to him.

She'd thought she felt sorrow before. The dragging of the heart, juxtaposed against the sensation of floating outside of her body.

But this. She'd never felt anything like this. Her heart was too big for her rib cage; her soul too big for her physical form. Grief filled her up like a balloon, overtaking her limbs, shooting through her veins. The difference was, a balloon artist knew when to stop pumping, while her despair had no limits, recognized no bounds. It pressed and pressed against her skin until she felt like she might burst.

Her legs burned. Her breath hitched. She should've— *would've*—collapsed by now had there been any other option.

There wasn't.

Brett appeared in the library doorway.

"Brett! Come on. Étienne fell into the ocean and Gabe's been hurt!" Yana shouted, her suspicions temporarily suspended.

He nodded and fell into step behind her. He didn't ask her where she'd been, and she returned the favor. They didn't have time. They would have to interrogate one another later.

Rain poured down on them, turning the railing slick and rendering the teakwood treacherous. Yana pounded across the deck, each step adding speed to her flight.

Naya was curled into a fetal position, sobbing so loudly that Yana could hear her above the steady drumbeat of the rain.

And Gabe. Gabe had fallen onto the deck, and as Yana watched, he wrapped his hands around the protruding part of the spear and *yanked it out*. He then ripped off his T-shirt and pressed it against the wound.

Yana's knees gave out, and she banged into the teakwood. She wanted to curl up next to Naya, squeeze her eyes shut, and make the nightmare go away.

But that wasn't an option. People thought she was icy, unfeeling. That she could brush her emotions aside and do what needed to be done.

But Yana's efficiency had never stemmed from not hurting—or not hurting deeply enough.

It was, and had always been, about survival.

She crawled as quickly as she could toward Gabe. His body thrashed relentlessly, as though he was in pain and unable to find a comfortable position. His skin was pale and feverish to the touch. His eyes were closed and he breathed in quick, shallow gasps, nearly panting.

His blood leaked through the T-shirt.

It spilled down his arm and dripped onto the deck.

Not good.

Not good, not good, not good.

Yana bunched up the bottom of his shirt and held it against the wound, applying as much pressure as she could. The fear drained away and cold calculation took over. He probably shouldn't be moved, but he also couldn't stay out on the deck, exposed to the whims of a killer. In addition, the yacht was rocking in the choppy waters. Any moment now, they could be thrown overboard like Étienne. Besides, they had to stanch the bleeding, and that wasn't going to happen out here in the elements.

She tossed her wet hair off her face, thinking hard. This process would be more difficult than rolling Derek. Not only did they have to get Gabe inside, but they had to get him in safely. The lounge was too open; the library was littered with shards of glass and readily accessible through the sliding glass doors. Back down into the game room was the only option. But Gabe was taller than Derek, more muscular, which meant he was also heavier, and that they'd be slower.

This was definitely a three-person job.

Yana looked at Naya, lost in a world of her own anguish, and met Brett's gaze through the sheets of rain.

"We have to move him!" he yelled, apparently arriving at

the same conclusion. "I've got Gabe. He's not bleeding out on my watch. You get Naya."

Nodding, Yana inched over to her friend. Present tense, no qualifiers. Naya couldn't be anything else, not when they were in this horror show together. Not when Yana's heart ached this much for her friend's pain.

Naya had stopped wailing. Yana smoothed back her wet hair and spoke directly into her ear. "I know you're hurting, Naya. I know you're experiencing grief like you've never imagined. But we have to move Gabe. And we need your help."

No response.

Yana climbed over her so that she could look right in her face. Naya's expression was numb; her eyes, glazed. She showed no indication of having heard Yana.

Yana pressed her forehead against Naya's so that their eyes were just inches apart. "Listen to me, Naya. You want to be a doctor, right? Your purpose in life is to help people." Yana inhaled deeply. She would have to be blunt, even cruel, to get through to Naya. "Étienne is dead. Taylor is dead. There's nothing more you can do to help them. But Gabe is still alive. We can save him, but we have to act now."

Naya blinked, but that was probably more from Yana's eyelashes jabbing into hers than any state of awareness.

"Please, Naya. Please." Yana pulled back a little. Her eyes stung, but she couldn't tell if it was from tears or salt water.

"I need you." Three little words. Had Yana ever said them before, to anyone, in her eighteen years of life? "I can't do this alone, Naya. I need you. Not just for an extra set of arms to carry Gabe. But for *you*, Naya. I . . . can't do this, I can't get through this without you."

Had she ever been this vulnerable before? Had she ever

laid out her real, true, unfiltered emotions for someone else to judge? Yana assumed that the people she cared about knew how she felt about them. She was an acts-of-service kinda gal, and they had to have expected her *not* to talk about her feelings.

She didn't always say the words. Okay, fine. She *never* said the words. But they knew.

Right?

Her parents. Her brother, Ady. Naya. And now . . . maybe kinda sorta Gabe. They must know how much they meant to her. They had to understand how she loved them with everything that she had, with all that she was.

Because if they *didn't*, and if she didn't have a chance to tell them . . .

"Please." Her voice was barely audible; her vocabulary contracted. She was reduced to a single word. "Please."

Nothing.

Just as she turned away, just as she was about to give up, she glimpsed a flicker in her peripheral vision. Yes, there it was again. Naya's pupils were on the move. More than that, they focused on Yana's face. Something . . . registered. Clicked. Connected. And then, Naya nodded.

Such a simple, ordinary action. And yet it unleashed a hailstorm that rivaled the weather tormenting them. Joy, relief, love, anger, hope. Yana felt all the feelings, and one day, soon, she would translate these emotions into words.

But not now.

"Come on." Naya pushed herself up to her feet. "Let's save your boy."

THIRTY

YANA

1:33 A.M.

Her arms were about to give out. Her nerves had long since been destroyed. Sheer determination alone kept Yana moving, step by torturous step.

Gabe. She had to focus on Gabe. On saving him, on not causing him any more pain by dropping him.

Just five more steps . . . Finally. The couch.

They laid Gabe carefully on the leather cushions. The bleeding seemed to have slowed—and maybe even stopped—but he was shivering as though he had been dunked in the Atlantic Ocean.

Naya yanked the silk runner off the coffee table, and with Brett's help, tied it tightly around Gabe's bunched-up T-shirt as a tourniquet. In the meantime, Yana grabbed a couple of soft afghans and tucked them around him.

Their collective wetness would destroy the leather, not to

mention the runner and the afghans, but given the circumstances, Yana couldn't muster the proper regret.

Dead, she thought dully. *Those cows were already dead. Hope they had a nice life.*

This struck her as hilarious, and wild laughter surged up her throat. She clamped her lips shut. If she started laughing now, she feared she would never stop.

Now that her work was done, Naya fell at the end of the couch, without any real thought or purpose, as though her limbs had just . . . stopped.

Quite the opposite, Brett prowled the length of the half-submerged wall of windows. Yana barely recognized him. Nervous energy pulsed off him, as though he was ready to pounce on any prey—be it spider, mouse . . . or serial killer.

They had begun this adventure with eight inductees, one French stowaway, one chaperone, a captain, and nine crew members.

Four of the inductees remained, with one of their friends and the entire crew incapacitated.

How many more would die? How many would arrive in Bermuda alive?

Yana wrapped her arms tightly around herself. She should really go check on Amelia and the crew to see if any of them had woken up. But she was so tired, exhausted to the marrow of each bone. She needed to rest. Just for a few minutes, until she recovered her drive once again.

Following Naya's lead, Yana sank to the floor in front of the couch, next to Gabe's head. But even though her limbs had stopped working, her thoughts continued to spin. One by one, the evilest person imaginable had taken them out.

One by one, the murderer had slowly but surely narrowed down the list of suspects.

That either meant one of the crew had a vendetta against kids whom they believed to all be rich and spoiled or . . . or the killer was one of the five remaining inductees.

Amelia could've woken up, Yana supposed. Naya had locked her inside the cabin, but that only prevented someone from entering. It didn't stop someone from unlocking the door and leaving. But that would mean Amelia had drugged herself, which made absolutely no sense. Why would she render herself so vulnerable? Besides, she couldn't have set off the firecracker if she was unconscious. It was also unlikely that she had stabbed Derek and then somehow wedged herself under his body.

No. Yana could safely rule out Amelia. The image of the slender girl wielding a hunting knife, speargun, or ax just did not compute.

The ax.

Yana's eyes widened, and she straightened up, her breath coming faster. Where was the ax? Last time she had thought about the weapon, the guys had been going to the library to retrieve it. But she hadn't seen it in the game room, and there had been no further mention of it.

She cast a furtive glance at Brett, who continued to pace. She didn't want to suspect him, especially after their arduous ordeal of transporting Gabe, with the varsity swimmer doing the bulk of the work. He wouldn't deliberately injure his best friend. Or would he? Plenty of true crime podcasts revealed that perpetrators had been close to their victims. Did Brett have any reason to betray Gabe? Or maybe Gabe had never been the target and was merely an unexpected casualty. The spear had been headed straight toward Naya. If she hadn't ducked, it would be Naya who was hurt, not Gabe.

Yana swallowed hard as Brett's actions began to line up like dominos in her head. Brett, whose tension with Everly had been palpable. Brett, who had snooped around the dead girl's body and could have destroyed evidence. Brett, who had snuck a Slender Man mask on board. Brett, who had brought two life vests instead of three to the library. And, last but not least, Brett, who had walked out of the library when they were supposed to be searching for Taylor outside.

What had he been doing, if he hadn't been aiming a speargun from one of the windows?

And then there was the good ole process of elimination. She could rule out Naya and Gabe, as they could hardly have been controlling the trigger of the speargun. (Unless spearguns had timed releases? Even so, it was highly unlikely that either of them could've orchestrated the other's position that precisely.)

That left Brett.

Liquid ice filled her veins. Yana had never been this cold, not even when she had been in the pouring rain. Not even when she wasn't sure if they could get Gabe safely inside. She had to be careful here. She couldn't let on that she suspected Brett.

"What—no jokes, Brett?" she asked, testing him.

"No," Brett snapped, his gaze trained directly ahead.

"That's how you know the world is finally ending: Brett Sullivan can't manage a single inappropriate comment." She tried again to garner a reaction, but he ignored her and continued prowling.

Before she could decide how to proceed, Gabe said weakly, "Yana."

She turned, checking his wound, checking the bleeding, checking . . . him. Even as she kept a wary eye on his "best friend."

"How are you feeling?" She laid the back of her hand against his forehead. Warm, but at least he had stopped shivering.

"It's so unfair," he said, closing his eyes.

"I know. I'm sorry." She feathered her hand over his forehead. Who knew that a little bodily injury was what it took for her to turn soft?

Gabe opened his eyes again. "No, I meant that it's unfair that I'm shirtless and you're wearing all those clothes."

Yana's lips twitched, a ray of humor shooting through her anxiety and fear. Even after a spear to the shoulder, he was still flirting. "How about we just try to make it off this boat, huh?"

"It was worth a try." He attempted a grin, but even that small movement made him grimace. Sweat glistened on his forehead, and his muscles clenched, as though he was fighting a wave of pain.

Yana's heart broke.

"You rest." She shot another glance at Brett and then brushed a kiss on Gabe's forehead. "You sleep, and you heal." When his eyes closed, she placed her lips on one lid and then the other. "And when you wake up, I'll be here." She kissed both his cheeks. And then she placed her mouth gently on his. Their contact was brief, but searing. The kiss was sweet, but it made Yana ache down to her toes.

She eased back, before her tears dripped onto his face.

Before Brett took advantage of her distraction and pounced. Gabe's lips curved, and his breath evened out. Soon, his chest rose and fell as though there was never a spear in it.

"You'd better wake up, damn it," Yana said to his sleeping form.

She glanced up to see Naya watching her from across the couch, an indecipherable expression on her face. Behind her, Brett continued to stalk the glass wall, pausing every few steps to kick something—a trash can, a billiard ball, even the wall itself.

"That's how my mom felt," Naya said softly. "Her biggest regret was not giving my dad one last kiss before he died."

This was the first time she'd said anything about her dad to Yana after he passed. Yana wanted to engage with her. She wanted to tell her how sorry she was about her dad's passing. She wanted to ask Naya if she'd received the letter that Yana had placed in her locker, the letter in which she'd written down every memory she had of Naya's dad. The first time she had seen him, when he'd dropped off Naya's birthday treats in kindergarten, a tall and broad man carrying a box of cupcakes with rainbow sprinkles under his arm. The nicknames she and Naya's dad had for each other—she called him Daddy-Dad after hearing Naya say it once in a goofy fit, and he called her Yana-Yan. The times he and Naya sang together, his low bass and her high soprano blending harmoniously, while Yana listened, her eyes closed.

But Yana couldn't ask any of those things. Because there was a potential killer in the room.

As if hearing her thoughts, Brett stopped walking and spun around abruptly to face them. "I have to pee."

"Good idea." Naya got to her feet. "We'll go with you."

"Please," Brett said, his tone haughty. "You're traumatizing me."

Panic coursed through Yana. She couldn't let Brett out of her sight. She had to know exactly what he was up to. "You should've gone earlier. We have to stick together. And we can't leave Gabe."

"Would you rather I pee on the floor?" Brett asked wryly. "You can watch the door! What kind of mischief could I possibly get up to in the bathroom?"

"Lots." Yana stood up, too. "I found one of Amelia's failed exams that Everly was using against her in a bathroom."

Brett arched an eyebrow. "Snooping again, were we?"

Oh no. This was not the route she should've taken with Brett.

"At least she's not about to bite someone's head off," Naya spoke up, defending Yana. "It's like I don't even know you."

He rounded on her. "If anyone is sus here, it's you."

"Me?" She backed up a few steps. "Are you insinuating that I killed my best friend and boyfriend?"

"You ducked at the *exact* right moment, so the spear hit Gabe," he said harshly. "It was timed perfectly, almost like a dance. Almost as though you were working with an accomplice. I saw it through the sliding glass doors."

"Give me a break," Naya huffed. "I've always had quick instincts. Just ask Yana."

"Who you just so happened to reconcile with tonight . . . ," Brett drawled.

Yana held up both her hands, frantically trying to figure out how to diffuse the escalating situation. "And you think *I'm* the supposed accomplice?"

"You have a knife in your pocket," he said flatly. "I felt

it when you brushed past me on the deck. When were you going to tell me, partner?"

Too late. Situation escalated and spiraling rapidly out of control.

"In fact, you've been sneaking around this entire time," Brett continued. "You were the one who insisted we stay together. Yet you peeled off to break into Everly's room. Did you think Gabe wouldn't tell me?"

Yana squirmed. Naya was casting doubtful looks in her direction. She *had* to say something.

"The two of you have been shrugging off the micro-aggressions for years," he continued. "Maybe enough was enough. Maybe you had every intention of teaching a bunch of privileged white kids a lesson."

Yana attempted a laugh, but it sounded as hollow as the baseball-card trick box, even to her. "Come on, Brett. You're overreacting."

"Am I?" He whipped his gaze from one girl to the other. "There's a reason you two don't want me to leave, and it's not for *my* safety. Clearly, one or both of you are behind this. And I'm not going to sit here and make it easy for you."

He sprinted for the door.

No! He'd twisted the facts. Even worse, he was gone.

Yana took a step forward. "He's lying, Naya. It was him. It's been him this whole time and he just wants to pit us against each other—"

"Is it true?" Naya groped wildly behind her, picked up a Tiffany lamp and smashed it to the floor, then armed herself with a shard of cobalt-blue glass. "Did you break into Everly's room?"

Yana *should've* told Naya about the cheating scandal.

About what she'd found on Everly's laptop. That would've been enough to secure the girl's trust. But there hadn't been time! She should've found an opening, some way somehow. That was her mistake. A miscalculation. One that might determine tonight's outcome.

"Put down the glass, Naya. I'm the only one you can trust. Remember?"

"Then give me the knife," Naya demanded.

"What?" Yana blinked rapidly. Naya had just armed herself. She couldn't give up the only weapon she had. "No."

"No sudden moves." Naya raised the shard over her head, ready to strike. She should've looked ridiculous, a pretty girl gripping the decorative glass so tightly that blood dripped down her arm.

Instead, she just appeared deadly.

Yana ran from her room, the knife handle slamming against her hip.

It wasn't her fault. Every action that she had taken had been forced upon her.

In this moment, and the events that had preceded it, she'd had no choice.

THIRTY-ONE

NAYA

2:04 A.M.

Naya's palm ached from being sliced by the glass, but she didn't loosen her grip. Instead, she clutched it even tighter and ran. Her legs burned as she bolted up the stairs, desperate to increase the distance between herself and Yana and the secrets that had plagued them since they'd set foot on this yacht.

Her sandals slapped against the wet deck as she sprinted toward safety. The irony wasn't lost on her. Which room was safe when the entire boat was a crime scene?

Amelia's.

That's where she would go. She'd held on to the coil of keys. She would head back downstairs and lock herself in with Amelia. At least then she wouldn't be alone.

Naya stopped, her breaths coming in ragged gulps and her soaking wet curls whipping her cheeks as she spun around, trying to get her bearings and find the stairwell. Everything looked the same at night in the white glow of the emergency lights.

Why hadn't she studied Everly's ridiculous map more closely before the wind had ripped it away? Why had she even come on this trip? This prestige the Yates Society offered, the opportunities, and even her spot at Johns Hopkins, no longer seemed important.

Panic swirled her thoughts, and a sob clogged her throat.

"No!" she spat into the biting winds, and squeezed the shard of glass.

This wasn't how she was going out. She wouldn't run around aimlessly, crying about her misfortune. She was made of stronger stuff; born of a people who'd struggled far more than she had. Naya would rely on the line of strong women who'd come before her and the disaster response training she'd undergone. This was a disaster—a medical emergency. This is where Naya thrived.

The hairs on the back of her neck rose. She felt something—*someone*—behind her.

Lightning cracked overhead, and she spun around. Thunder boomed as Naya's gaze narrowed on the silhouette ahead.

Yana.

It had to be.

Naya's hand pulsed around the shard of glass as she raced toward the girl who'd caused all of this. It would end here. It would end tonight.

Another flash of lightning illuminated the shadows. Yana was gone, but there was a shadow in her place—a mound on the deck, stretched out like a . . . *body?*

Naya sprinted forward, her long strides eating up the last several feet that separated her from the person sprawled on the floor, something protruding from their chest.

Lightning lit the sky, lit the scene in front of her, and thunder boomed through the night. Her resolve wavered, and the glass fell from her fingers, landing on the deck with a dull clatter that she barely heard over the pulse surging in her ears.

An ax skewered Brett's torso, its sharp metal blade buried in his blood-soaked T-shirt.

Yana had done this—murdered him just like the others.

The wind changed direction, bringing with it the coppery scent of blood and a putrid stench that made her stomach clench.

The bodies.

She pressed the back of her hand to her mouth and bit down hard. The smell came from the murdered corpses on nearly every level of the megayacht.

And blood. There was so much blood. From the handle of the ax to the splatter across the once-pristine chaise longues. From her bloody palms to the pool of crimson that stained the teak deck.

Naya swayed as if the *Seraphina* were tipping, sinking, drowning them. Black patches dotted her vision and acid surged up her throat, burning the back of her tongue as she sank to her knees.

Why did Yana do this? Why did she kill these people?

Did she harbor a deep resentment from all those years that she had been teased and bullied? Naya had thought she had risen above that. Yana had found a group of friends on the school paper. She was on her way to a highly success-ful career. Hell, she'd even won the coveted internship over Everly. Apparently, it hadn't been enough. The hate must've festered in her belly, turned acidic. She must've held the rage inside—coddled it, allowed it to grow—until she had a chance to unleash it. Until . . . today.

Droplets pelted Naya's face, and she blinked through the swirl of rain and tears.

It didn't actually matter why. Not now. Not when she and Yana were on this boat. She needed to stop her.

Naya stared down at Brett, his vacant eyes unblinking against the steady rainfall. She would do this for him, for Taylor, for Étienne. For everyone.

She took a sip of air, gagging at the sour rot of flesh now *inside* her.

Get it together, she ordered herself, swiping the punish-ing raindrops from her eyes. *This is your new reality.* And in it, she would need something more than a shard of glass to protect herself.

She crawled closer to the body. Clenching her teeth, she wrapped her hands around the ax handle slick with rain and blood. Her arms flexed. Her muscles bunched. And then she yanked with every last cell in her being.

The ax dislodged with a final gush of scarlet, and she fell backward, banging her head against the deck. Lightning flashed just as bursts of pain exploded in her eyes—but Naya was okay.

It was interesting that it had come down to the two of them—Naya and Yana—made the same by their otherness in a predominantly white town. As children, they'd found safety in the friendship that had grown into a sisterhood. They had always made each other better. The two, more alike than any of Naya's friends had been since, had held the pieces of each other in more ways than just the letters of their names. But that was at an end.

How could she have missed the clues? They were all there. She had just failed to see them. The hunting knife with Yana's fingerprints on it. The keys that she had "borrowed" from Étienne. It was so damn convenient. More importantly, Yana had been opportunely absent each time someone was killed. Chilling by herself while the others were at the dance party. Rushing in the door late when Naya had discovered both Finn and the intertwined couple. She'd even been out of sight when Étienne and Gabe were speared.

The more Naya thought about it, the more she felt no doubt: Yana was a cold-blooded killer, fathoms from the friend she had once cherished.

"It's like you said, this is a gory murder mystery," she murmured to Brett, his body splayed across the deck like an offering. "I hope that at least she gave you one hell of a speech."

Naya patted his hand. Her fingers grazed plastic and she paused. She peered at Brett's pale fingers, slack around a thin black and silver rectangle. She picked it up and ran her thumb over the Record, Stop, and Play buttons on it. Old-school.

More questions sprang to mind, but they would have to wait.

Ax in hand, Naya got to her feet and tucked the recorder into her pocket. She was tired of fearing for her life. It was Yana Bunpraserit who needed to worry now. Naya was coming, and it was her ex–best friend's turn to be scared.

THIRTY-TWO

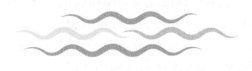

NAYA

2:17 A.M.

Once more, Naya's sixth sense tingled against the back of her neck. Yana—the murderer—had returned to the scene of her crime.

Naya's hands ached as she squeezed the ax handle and glanced over her shoulder at the one person who stood between her and the rest of her life. At least she hadn't had to go far to find her.

"Oh my God, Brett!" Yana's hands flew to her throat.

"Don't look so surprised." If Naya wasn't heartbroken, she would have laughed. Who did Yana think she was fooling? "It's just us. You don't have to pretend anymore."

"Pretend?" Yana cocked her head. Her mouth opened as if to speak, to tell more lies, but instead she remained silent.

It was probably for the best. The more they talked, the more Yana played at being the girl she'd known five years ago, the weaker Naya's resolve.

Naya fidgeted with the ax. Swinging it at a person was much different from throwing it at a target.

Yana's eyes widened, and she took a cautious step back. "You don't have to do this, Naya."

This time, Naya couldn't control her laughter. Chuckles surged up her throat and popped on her lips. She inhaled sharply, struggling to get her nerves and herself under control.

"You haven't left me many choices," she said as calmly as she could given that this fantasy cruise had turned into a nightmarish bloodbath.

Yana held up one hand and slowly inched the other toward her pocket. "We can talk about this."

Naya's gaze focused on Yana's dress. One side drooped. She still had the knife.

Naya squeezed the handle, settling the ax against her shoulder like a bat. She'd played softball once with Taylor and their group. Sure, this wasn't a charity event, and Yana was a far cry from the purple Alzheimer's Awareness softball she had hit, but Naya had knocked that ball clear to left field. If Yana wasn't careful, she'd do it again. To her head.

"What would make you think I want to talk to you? You killed my friends!" Naya watched Yana's hand get closer and closer to dipping into her pocket. She had to do something before Yana got to the knife.

Her hands shook, and the ax bounced against her shoulder. Naya would protect herself, but she wasn't a murderer. She wanted to *save* lives. There had to be another way to end this.

Naya swallowed. "Is that what you said to Brett before you killed him—that you wanted to talk? Did you pretend to be his friend just like you did with me?"

Yana shook her head, her dark hair clinging to her rain-drenched face.

"You needed Brett and Gabe and me to be on your side so we wouldn't suspect you." Tears stung Naya's eyes. "You made me believe we could be friends again and then you killed my real ones."

They stood in silence. The rain gently pattered against the deck as Naya calculated her next move, and Yana, no doubt, her next manipulation.

Yana was the first to break the silence. "I thought you were just spiraling before. You can't really think *I* did this."

Naya shook her curls from her face and leveled her gaze on her former friend. "During each murder you were mysteriously gone, and now we're the only two left. Besides Gabe and Amelia. But it's pretty clear why you would want to leave Gabe alive. Unless you're somehow in this together, and his conveniently nonlethal injury is part of your grand plan."

"We weren't together the whole time, Naya," Yana threw back, her hand hovering half in, half out of her pocket. "Don't forget, he and I didn't board this yacht as friends, either."

Naya's grip on the ax tightened. "And it's obvious we still aren't."

Yana took a step closer, motioning toward Brett. "You're the one I just watched take an ax from a guy's stomach."

"A guy you murdered!"

"Naya—"

"No! No more lies."

A sob quaked in Naya's chest, but she forced it down. Sadness was of no use. Right now, she needed anger.

"My best friend and first love are dead because of you,"

she seethed. "I won't spend the next few hours cowering in some corner, waiting for you to find me. This ends now."

Her hands slid to the end of the handle, and she raised the ax overhead ready to throw as Yana withdrew her hand from her pocket and held the knife even with Naya's gut.

"Naya, please . . ."

She didn't wait for Yana to finish. Naya charged, a vicious howl warring with the rumbling thunder.

Still clutching the knife, Yana bent at the waist, dipped one shoulder, and surged forward. She crashed into Naya, and they fell in a heap onto the deck.

Black specks dotted Naya's vision and she struggled to take a full breath lying beneath Yana. Grunting, Naya drew her knees to her chest and kicked out, pushing Yana off her.

This time, Naya wouldn't hesitate and give Yana a chance to charge. The ax was bigger than the one she'd thrown before, but she still knew how to do it. She would hurl it at her target and watch it soar end over end until it struck Yana.

Naya rolled onto her stomach and felt around for the ax. Her pulse hammered in her ears, and each beat of her heart quaked through her limbs.

Where is it? Where is it?

Frantically, she groped in the dark and came up empty-handed. The ax was nowhere to be found.

Yana groaned, rubbing the back of her head as she got to her feet. She teetered, leaning one way and then the other as if drunk before blinking and lowering her gaze to Naya.

Naya scrambled to her knees and leaned forward, fanning out her arms and sweeping them across the deck in a final attempt to locate the ax. The blade could take off her fingers, her hand, but it didn't matter as long as she found the weapon.

Lightning illuminated the deck and glinted off the knife's steel blade.

That would do. Yana saw it too, and they both dove for the weapon.

Naya's fingertips skimmed the handle before Yana batted the knife away. It spun across the rain-slick deck like a glass bottle before glancing off a dark tennis shoe and skipping overboard into the dark Atlantic.

The two froze, and Naya's gaze followed the baggy black sweatpants up to the Yates Society sweatshirt that had been given to each of them upon their arrival. The figure was wearing a Slender Man mask, obscuring their face, and had put up the hood of the sweatshirt and pulled the drawstrings tight. They stepped back into the shadows, water splashing up from the deck as they turned from Naya and Yana and ran.

THIRTY-THREE

YANA

2:34 A.M.

They hobbled back to the game room, their arms around each other's waists, Naya dragging behind them the ax they finally located in the hot tub, blade down, mutual suspicion abandoned. It was unclear who carried whom. At different points, both Yana and Naya stumbled and tripped. Only the support of the other kept them from tumbling to the floor and accidentally killing themselves with the ax.

What a way that would be to go. The reporters would rub their hands with glee. *Serial Killer Hits Luxury Yacht (and One Clumsy Teen Axes Herself in the Back)*.

At long last, the game room and its partially submerged windows greeted them. Gabe remained on the couch, sleeping.

Yana pressed a hand against her mouth, keeping the wild laughter inside. She had to hold it together.

"We have to barricade the door," someone said. It took

Yana a moment to recognize the low, matter-of-fact voice as hers.

"On it." Naya got behind the billiards table and pushed. Good thing it was set on wheels.

Yana reached for the closest piece of furniture—an oversized, sleek leather armchair—and dragged it to the door. So long as she moved, she didn't think. So long as she shoved and pulled and heaved, she didn't feel any pain. Maybe her body had decided that pushing herself *past* her limits was the new normal. Or maybe she had already died, and her corporeal self was incapable of feeling any sensation.

They soon had a jumble of furniture piled six feet deep against both the door and the secret passage that led to the library. That would keep the masked figure at bay, at least for a while. And if their enemy tried to shove their way in, the movement of the furniture would give them advance warning.

"Damn, I hope I don't have to pee," Naya remarked.

Yana tried to laugh—she *thought* she was laughing—but it came out as a wail.

They'd have to talk about the masked figure, whoever it was. Amelia, after all? One of the crew? Were they back to a mysterious stowaway? Yana no longer had any idea. All of her theories had gone out the window. And now she was coming apart at the seams.

She hadn't cried this entire time. A couple of tears when she pleaded with Naya on the deck. But she hadn't given herself permission to let down her walls. Now, *permission* had no meaning. It had been swept away, along with the last brick of her inhibition, the last mortar of her self-preservation.

The tears finally came, flooding her. At the moment, they were more dangerous than any killer, more threatening than the roiling ocean.

Her breath came faster and faster. Her stomach clenched. Acid surged up her throat.

She had to stop. She had to employ her techniques, get her breathing under control, or she would throw up.

Emergency. Emergency. Emergency, her brain blared, but her body was no longer listening. It had gotten used to the never-ending crises. No will to resist the panic remained. Yana ran to the small wicker wastebasket and vomited. With nothing left in her stomach, only yellow bile came up.

"Yana. Focus on my voice, okay? We're going to breathe together. Slooowly. Inhale, one, two, three, four. Exhale, one, two, three, four."

Cool hands helped Yana ease to a sitting position and then gripped both of her hands. Her queasy stomach started to relax. She concentrated on Naya's voice, she followed her instructions. And she breathed.

From previous experience, Yana knew she would continue to feel nauseated for hours. But the anxiety attack had passed. And Naya had remembered how to help her. *Thank you* seemed too banal a phrase, but she had to say it anyway.

"Thanks," she croaked.

"Anytime." Naya grabbed two bottles of water from the small fridge and tossed one to Yana.

Yana caught it neatly, but instead of unscrewing the cap, she just turned the plastic bottle around and around in her hands.

"You're supposed to drink it," Naya said gently. "Hydration, good."

"I thought you were the killer," Yana said, so softly she wasn't sure if Naya could hear her. "You were covered in blood. Brett's blood. I watched you take the ax out of his body, and I thought it was down to you and me. And I thought . . . I thought . . . I would have to kill you in order to survive." Yana's face crumpled. The knowledge broke something inside her. The last vestiges of her youth, perhaps. All she knew was that moment changed her, irrevocably.

"Same. I was getting ready to take you out." Naya sat in front of her, cross-legged. Blood streaked her cheeks, her arms, her legs, like war paint but without the symmetry or design. Her yellow jumpsuit was ripped and stained, and she sported broken nails, half a dozen scratches, and one enormous bruise blossoming on her elbow. Gone was the light floral perfume she'd spritzed herself with earlier; in its place was the scent of sweat and blood.

"I thought *you* had just finished off Brett and that you were coming back for me," Naya continued. "I was preparing for my death or yours."

"I didn't do it, you know," Yana said. "I didn't kill *or* drug anyone."

Truth. No more obfuscating the facts or divulging select information. No more secrets—especially with her oldest and dearest friend.

"I swear I'm not working with the killer, either," Naya said. "And I believe you."

She twisted the cap off Yana's water bottle and handed it to her. Obediently, Yana drank.

"I shouldn't have doubted you," Naya continued. "I should've trusted there was an explanation for your disappearances. I should've believed *me*, my gut, telling me you hadn't changed, at least not fundamentally." She dipped her head. "Everything just happened so fast. I was so scared. I'm sorry I thought you could be a serial killer."

"You don't have to apologize!" Yana exclaimed. "I also doubted you. And, er . . ." She cleared her throat. *No more secrets,* she reminded herself. Life was too short to hide so much of herself. "I *was* on a secret mission."

"I knew it! You were trying to find out what brand of underwear Gabe wears," Naya said, a weak attempt at humor.

"What? No!" Yana finally laughed. "My mission has nothing to do with Gabe. Besides"—she made herself wink—"maybe I already know."

Naya's eyes widened to the size of the billiard balls.

"Kidding, kidding," Yana added quickly. "I was investigating a cheating ring."

"I know," Naya blurted out. Her cheeks were still flushed, but her gaze was steady and direct. "I was the one who sent you the text after I heard Mrs. Stewart tell Taylor that you had been invited to join the society. They asked me to join their cheating ring, you know. I refused."

Yana's jaw dropped. "That was you? But I thought you *liked* them. Why would you turn them in? They were your friends."

"Eh, not really." Naya shrugged. "I mean, Taylor was my best friend. She could be a lot of fun to be around. Not trying to talk ill of the dead, but the others—well. They never made me feel good about myself, you know?"

Yana nodded. She did know. That's why she'd always steered clear. Their antics cast her as less than. Not white, not rich. Not worthy of their attention.

"Except for Étienne, of course. And Gabe," Naya teased. "He's okay or whatever."

"Just okay?"

"I mean, he's no Étienne obviously." Naya clamped her mouth shut, tears swamping her eyes.

"Hey." Yana moved over to sit next to her and wrapped an arm around her shoulders. "You'll get through this."

Naya pulled her knees to her chest, burying her face against the bony knobs. Yana stroked her hair, and they sat like that for a few minutes. Silent but for Gabe's light snores and the waves crashing against the windows. Safe but for the killer roaming the yacht, plotting their demise.

"Yana." Presently, Naya lifted her head. "I don't care who the killer is. I don't want to be strong anymore."

"Me neither," Yana confessed in a rush. She looked at her watch. "It's almost three. We've got three more hours until we dock. You wanna hole up in here like sewer rats until we arrive in Bermuda? Arm ourselves and watch the furniture to make sure it doesn't move. Then, when we're close enough to shore, we'll jump off the yacht and swim for it?"

"That depends." A smile ghosted over Naya's lips. "Are we *cute* sewer rats?"

"The cutest," Yana said—and prayed that when this nightmare ended, they would also be the most alive.

THIRTY-FOUR

NAYA

3:06 P.M.

They were safe. At least, for the moment. Only time would tell if they made it off the yacht alive. And what would happen to Gabe when they arrived in Bermuda and she and Yana swam to safety? Would the killer chase them, or would they use the opportunity to take out Gabe?

Naya put the questions aside. For now, she would focus on being here, staying *alive* with Yana. Naya leaned into her friend, loosely holding the ax, their hips pressed against each other's.

"Leave me alone!" Taylor's voice sounded like a siren, vibrating against Naya's leg.

Naya scrambled backward, the ax sliding against the floor and her heart lurching into her throat.

"Naya?" Yana's wide-eyed gaze asked the same question Naya had on the tip of her tongue. She gripped the billiards cue tighter.

With a shaking hand, Naya smoothed her fingers over the device in her pocket.

"Leave me alone!" The cry from beyond the grave made Naya's stomach clench.

She reached into her pocket and pulled out the recorder she'd taken from Brett. So much had happened between now and then, she'd forgotten about it. Naya held it out and pressed Play.

"Leave me alone!"

Yana's throat tightened with a swallow. "Where did you find that?" she asked, holding out her hand to inspect the recorder more closely.

"On Brett. His . . . body." Naya set the device on Yana's upturned palm. "Did you know that he had it, or why? You were working together, right?"

"No, no, and sort of, but . . ." Yana turned the recorder over as she shook her head. "Why would Taylor be on it?"

"Press Play again."

Naya braced herself to hear the echo of her friend. She hadn't thought about what it would be like when she finally got home—*if* she got home. There would be so many reminders of what she'd lost. She'd be trapped by memories, like Taylor's voice, of being in this time of horror. A knot of emotion formed in Naya's throat. She couldn't think about it now. Not while they remained on the boat. Not when they'd found another piece of the puzzle.

"Leave me alone!"

Naya shivered, and Yana jabbed the Stop button. The cascade of chills that ran through her were for more than just the eerie reminder of the loss of her friend. There was something recognizable about it, something familiar.

"I've heard that before."

"Of course you have. She is—*was* your friend." Yana's brow knit. "But who was she shouting at?"

"Brett picked up something off the floor when Taylor rushed past us in the life vest," Naya blurted out. "He said it was his cell phone, but what if it was this recorder all along? It must've fallen out of Taylor's pocket."

She sprang to her feet and rushed to the couch, sinking down next to Gabe. "Hey!" she whispered urgently, shaking his uninjured shoulder.

Yana shot a nervous look over her shoulder. The furniture hadn't moved an inch. No one was trying to get through the barricade. She joined Naya at the couch, resting her cold hand on top of Naya's. "He needs to rest. We're lucky he's even alive."

"He needs to wake up or we might not be alive for long."

Yana frowned. "I'm not following."

Naya stood and began to pace. "After we all went down to get on the speedboat we were towing and drive it to that ship in the distance—"

"But the tender wasn't there."

"Right, and then Taylor freaked out." Naya paused her pacing and shrugged. "Well, *continued* to freak out even more and then ran away."

"And you went after her," Yana supplied.

"I went to our room. When I knocked, I heard Taylor say, 'Leave me alone.'" Naya pointed to the recorder. "I didn't actually *see* her, but Gabe did. At least, he said he did."

"I didn't." Gabe's voice was scratchy and dry, and Yana found her water bottle and held it to his lips. He took a few small sips and offered her a weak smile. "Thanks."

She pushed his hair from his sweaty brow and trailed her fingers along his cheek. "Don't mention it."

A small blush pinkened Yana's cheeks as she pulled away from Gabe. She darted a gaze at the two barricaded entrances once more. No sign of an impending break-in.

"So," Naya continued, blinking all traces of tears from her eyes, "you didn't actually see Taylor in our room before we heard the shot?"

Gabe shook his head, the movement making him wince and inhale sharply. "I heard her," he said through clenched teeth.

"Leave me alone!"

Naya stiffened as Yana once again played the recording.

"That's exactly it, but"—sweat beaded on Gabe's furrowed brow—"it was a recording?"

Naya's knees nearly buckled, and she leaned against the pool table to keep from crumbling. "Taylor wasn't ever in the room."

"She used this to make us think she was." Yana stared down at the device like it held all the answers. Or maybe it was just that she, like Naya, wished it did. "But what was she trying to cover up?"

Naya resumed pacing from the couch to the pool table and back again, fueled by the questions coursing within her, roaring like a pulse between her ears.

"The tender's gone. Taylor runs away," Naya said, ticking the points off on her fingers. "Gabe and I both hear what we think is Taylor in the room. Someone sets off a firecracker that leads all of us—"

"Minus Taylor," Yana added.

Naya nodded. "Minus Taylor to Derek's room, where we find him dead and Amelia unconscious."

"So, Taylor killed him?" Gabe asked through chattering teeth.

"I'm not sure," Naya said, sharing a look with Yana.

"Wait, wait, wait." For a moment, Gabe seemed like he was going to attempt to sit up before thinking better of it. "I thought . . ." He paused and let out a slow, quaking breath before continuing. "I thought that's where you were going with this."

Yana offered Gabe another drink and dabbed his sallow, sweat-streaked cheeks with the blanket drawn up over his shoulders. "Derek had rigor mortis when we found him," she explained. "He'd been dead for a couple hours."

"Let me get this straight." Gabe swallowed and closed his eyes against another wave of pain. "Taylor made Naya and me think she was in her room so she had time to sneak to the already dead Derek where she set off the firecracker for no reason?"

"To distract us," Yana said with a curt nod.

"Like a magician," Naya added.

"If you're looking over here"—Yana wedged the water bottle between her knees and wiggled the fingers on one hand—"you're not looking at the real trick over there." She held up her other hand and waved.

"Which was what?" Gabe clenched his teeth as he tried to shrug. "Using a rope to climb overboard, getting tangled up in the same rope, and then drowning?"

Naya stopped pacing. The recording was meaningful. Brett had literally been clutching it in his hand when he'd died. And she'd been building toward a revelation. At least, she'd thought so.

Yana stood, the same anxious energy that Naya felt etched

on her face. "Does this mean Taylor was working with Amelia? That might make sense. Amelia would've needed an accomplice if she was going to render herself unconscious."

"Maybe," Naya said slowly. "But Taylor didn't think much of Amelia. The girl was book smart, but Taylor always said that she wouldn't survive an hour during a zombie apocalypse. What reason would those two have to work together?"

"We're missing something," Yana said. "A clue that will crack this whole thing wide open."

"You sound like Brett." Gabe's voice was barely a whisper.

"Gabe, he's . . ." Yana pressed her fingers to her lips.

"I know." The shadows under his eyes seemed to darken as he glanced up at her. "I figured since he's not with you and Naya . . ."

Naya stared down at the crusted blood on her hands and the stains on her once-yellow jumpsuit, and she envisioned Brett, now lifeless on the deck.

The three of them fell silent. The thunder had ceased and the water no longer pummeled the wall of glass.

Gabe was the first to speak, clearing his throat to ask, "What would Brett say if he was with us now?"

Naya's gaze met Yana's.

"Money, sex, and greed," they said in unison.

They shared another glance, and with it a language between sisters. Without words, they raced to the bar.

"Gabe, keep an eye on the door," Yana instructed. "Let us know if that furniture moves even a millimeter."

Yana opened the display box that held much more than old baseball cards.

Together, she and Yana dumped out the box's contents. Passports, pictures, letters, and Seraphina's legal documents slid across the shiny bar top. Yana dove for a photo and a few papers, snatching them before they spilled onto the floor, as Naya grabbed the legal documents.

For a few minutes, they quietly sifted through the papers, examining photos and documents before placing them in their appropriate pile, each knowing the other would sound the alarm if she found anything of merit.

Enough time had passed that Naya started to think that following the advice of a deceased friend who had garnered his investigative knowledge from a multitude of streaming services was a terrible idea when she sucked in a breath and thrust Seraphina's final will and testament into Yana's hands.

"We saw this already."

Naya plucked it from Yana's grasp and flipped through the first few pages with a frenzy that belied their all-nighter status. "But we didn't really study it," she said, finding the right page and handing Yana the addendum to the will.

From: The desk of Seraphina Yates

To: The law offices of Moore and Elder

There has been a change. Instead of listing my grandchild by name, please update to include all my biological grandchildren.

"*All* of her grandchildren . . . ," Naya whispered more to herself than to Yana.

"Someone must have come out of the woodwork with a

legitimate claim to the Yates fortune. And check this out!" Yana turned more pages. "This is Seraphina's trust. She made the same change here."

There it was again—the matriarch of the Yates' riches instructing her lawyers to update the documents that dictated exactly how her money was to be distributed.

Naya ran her fingers along the seal at the bottom of the page. The updated trust had been signed, dated, and notarized only a month before.

She turned to Yana. "Are you thinking what I'm thinking?"

Yana glanced down at the papers, then back up at Naya. "Money, sex, and greed."

"What's happening over there? The speargun didn't kill me, but the suspense might." Gabe's voice and a series of wet coughs struck Naya like a jolt of electricity, and she dropped the pages.

"Everly is a Yates," Yana began. "But she wasn't the only one."

"We just found out," Naya said, picking up where Yana left off. "So did Ev."

Gabe's brow furrowed with confusion.

"Think about it," she continued. "If Everly had known her whole life that she was a Yates, we never would have heard the end of it. She would have lorded it over us every chance she got, but she didn't."

Yana picked up the will and trust and waved them in the air. "This proves Seraphina Yates only found out that she had more than one progeny a month ago. That's why Everly was killed."

The deep crease hadn't left Gabe's forehead. "What does that have to do with Taylor and Amelia and everything else that's happened?"

Naya's gaze drifted to the display case with the auto-graphed baseball jersey—and the set of stairs that Gabe had uncovered behind it. "If either Amelia or Taylor were the other progeny, they'd have a lot to gain by getting rid of Everly. A whole half of an inheritance, in fact."

Yana nodded. "There's one room on this megayacht that has files on each of us."

"The library's right above, through the secret passageway! And that's where the locked cabinets are."

"That's one wild theory," Gabe said.

Naya shrugged. "It's the one that makes the most sense so far. You don't kill this many people because someone cheated on a test or a partner."

"But you would for. . . ." Yana stopped and checked the papers once more. "Two and a half billion dollars."

Naya moved to the black space and stuck her head in-side. A rickety spiral staircase wound up to the next level. A thick layer of dust coated each step Gabe hadn't reached, and spiderwebs trailed off the railings like bits of lace.

She sneezed as she came back into the room. "If we're lucky, we'll only encounter a spider or two on our way up."

"Lucky?" Yana asked incredulously.

"Would you rather face off with the killer?"

Yana tilted her head as though she was actually contem-plating the question, and Naya suddenly remembered her childhood phobia of eight-legged insects. "Can I think about it?" Yana asked.

"Nope, no time. If Brett was right, and it seems like he has been so far, Taylor's and Amelia's and Everly's informa-tion is up there." Naya pointed to the staircase. "The answers we've been searching for are in those files."

"You can't go up there," Gabe interjected. Naya hadn't thought it was possible, but his face went even paler. "Why do we have to verify who the progeny is? We'll find out soon enough when she bursts in here."

"We have to know exactly who—and what—we're up against," Yana said, tucking the documents under Gabe's pillow for safekeeping. "Besides, don't you want justice for your friends?"

"I'd rather you stay alive," Gabe muttered.

Naya wound her hair into a bun and stuck a pencil through it, as though preparing for battle. "It's a straight shot between here and the library. We'll go up, grab the files, and come right back."

"No, Yana—" Gabe let out a hiss of pain as he reached for Yana's arm to keep her from following Naya.

"Hey," she said gently. "You were willing to do anything to impress me, remember? Now it's time for me to impress you."

Naya turned her back to them, holding back tears. There would be time to mourn Étienne later. She had to keep it together and get off this boat alive.

While Gabe and Yana talked, Naya grabbed the ax by the door where she had dropped it when they had stumbled back into the game room. She wished it were a little—okay, a lot—less bloody, but this was not the time to be squeamish.

"Ready?" she asked, heading back to the hidden stairway.

"Yeah." Yana reached Naya's side, a pool cue in hand. "Let's go."

THIRTY-FIVE

NAYA

3:43 A.M.

Naya clung to the ax as she and Yana crept up the winding staircase like thieves. Thank goodness she had Yana. No matter how confident Naya had sounded when talking to Gabe, not knowing for sure where the killer lurked had her on edge.

She reached the top of the stairs and stopped in front of a large rectangular panel. This must be the entrance to the library. "How many cameras do you think are in there?"

"Gabe destroyed them," Yana said, pool cue raised, ready to strike. "He was on a bit of a rampage earlier. But we still have to do this fast."

"Smash and grab and back to safety. Got it." Naya pushed firmly against the rectangular panel. Nothing.

"Let me help you," Yana said, positioning herself next to Naya on the narrow platform. "It's just like rolling Derek. One . . . two . . . three . . . *push*!"

The panel flew open and the two of them tumbled into the room and onto the library's tapestry rug. Naya glanced up just as the portrait panel swung closed, and met Seraphina's serene eyes.

"The secret passage is behind Seraphina's portrait!" Naya exclaimed. She sucked in a breath, as her eyes focused on the room. "I'd almost forgotten." She pressed the back of her hand to her nose, fighting back the sour scent of blood and bile.

Yana put her hand on Naya's shoulder as they stared at the destroyed chandelier and Finn's body beneath it.

"How could I not remember this? Him?" Naya whispered.

"You didn't forget. Your focus is on trying to stay alive."

Naya swallowed and brought the ax up in front of her. "Stay alive. Find the files and stay alive."

She averted her gaze from Finn and skirted the chandelier that pinned him down, heading straight to the row of charcoal-black filing cabinets.

Naya scanned the silver nameplates in the upper left-hand corner of the cabinets. Engraved in each was a set of letters: A–E, F–K, L–P, Q–Z.

Amelia Brown, Everly Fuller, and Taylor Stewart. Naya had three cabinets to break into, three safes to crack, and she would start with Q–Z.

She positioned herself in front of the second cabinet and lifted the ax. A question wriggled in her mind. None of the girls had the last name Yates. She supposed that was to be expected if Seraphina and her husband had given their children his last name. With how secretive the family and everyone they employed were, no one really knew who Seraphina's husband had been. The mystery and allure made them the ultimate secret society.

"Want me to do it?" Yana asked, snapping Naya out of her musings.

"I got it," she said, and swung the ax.

The blade connected with the cabinet with a sharp *thwack* that sent it bouncing off the stained wood. The impact reverberated up the handle, stinging Naya's palms and sending tremors of pain up her arms.

"Merde." She gritted her teeth against the pain not only from the ax but also the thought of Étienne. A rush of heat surged through her cheeks. She clenched the ax handle, anger roiling in her gut. It was a good thing she needed to destroy these cabinets.

"I finally find a guy who doesn't see me as some exotic, mixed-girl trophy."

She swung again, and the blade connected, sinking into the wood.

"A guy I love and who loves me."

Another swing, another crack of wood.

"And he's murdered on a yacht I sacrificed everything to be on. And for what?"

A final swing and the cabinet splintered. Without missing a beat, she moved to the next one.

"When will the universe stop taking?"

Crack. Crack. Crack.

"How much do I have to give up? My identity wasn't enough?"

Naya dropped the ax and tore away the fractured wood. It jabbed into her injured palm and bit at her fingers, but she kept going, determined to get to the files, to get to the truth and a plan to fight back.

Next to her, Yana picked up the ax. It cut through the air and sliced through the untouched L–P cabinet. When she was finished, she moved to the first cabinet, A–E, and broke into it as well.

Yana wiped the sweat from her brow and set the ax on the pile of rubble. "Don't you want your file?" she asked, tearing away the last pieces of the front of the cabinet, revealing more olive-green file folders.

"Hard pass. I don't need to know what these people really think of me."

"Well, I'm getting both of ours. You'll thank me later."

"Curiosity killed the cat, Yana." Naya pulled out the drawer and thumbed through the folders until she found *Stewart, Taylor.*

"Good thing I'm an investigative journalist. We're more like hounds." Yana lifted Naya's folder from the destroyed cabinet and set it, along with hers, Amelia's, and Everly's, on top of Taylor's.

Naya frowned down at the green folders. Judging by their weight, the society had collected quite a bit of information on each of them. There had to be something in the files that would come in handy.

Yana picked up the ax and propped it against her shoulder. "We should get back before Gabe thinks he has to come find us."

"Find *you,*" Naya corrected as she trailed after Yana back to the larger-than-life portrait of Seraphina on the panel through which they had emerged. "I could dissolve into a puddle of Jell-O and he wouldn't notice."

Even in the dim light, Naya saw Yana's cheeks turn pink.

"Oh, whatever. Just try not to liquify until after we go through the files."

~

Thankfully, Naya and Yana made it back to the game room before Gabe could get up. Both girls now sat on the floor next to the couch, poring over the most important files they'd collected: Amelia's, Everly's, and Taylor's.

Naya read through the copies of Taylor's transcripts, from middle school through high school. The pages were littered with As. A long line of them stretched out like a scream.

How many of these did she actually earn?

Yana threw up her hands. "I haven't found anything that says Everly is the least bit connected to the Yates family. There's a copy of a birth certificate that clearly says she's a Fuller, not to mention an ancestry printout that does not list the Yates anywhere on a family tree."

"You know," Naya said suddenly, "Everly never actually said she was a Yates. She only let us assume that after Taylor suggested it."

Yana blinked as the implication settled in. "It's just like Everly to bask in the glory whether or not she deserved it."

The girls glanced at each other before picking up the remaining folders to sift through.

"Whatever you do needs to happen fast. This is taking too long." Gabe let out a breath. "What do you think our masked stalker is doing? Kicking up their feet in the wheel-house, attempting to watch us on the security monitors?"

Yana shrugged. "Or maybe she's cleaning up the mess that she made with all the bodies before we dock in Bermuda."

"Like I said," Gabe began, "we need to hurry."

Naya agreed. She reached for the closest unopened file and passed it over her shoulder to him, the thought of the killer prowling the yacht making her hands shake.

A grunt of pain left Gabe, and the file fell back over Naya's shoulder, its contents spilling onto the floor.

Yana jumped to her feet and was at his side in an instant. "This is what I was talking about." Her voice was stern but held no anger. Yana was beginning to care for Gabe the way Naya had for Étienne.

Tears pricked her eyes. She just needed to hold them off until they were all safe.

Naya sifted through the mess of papers.

Don't cry. Don't cry, she told herself as she haphazardly swept the documents back into the folder. Her fingers slid across a glossy photo. She'd emptied the contents of Taylor's folder, and while she hadn't read over every document, she knew it didn't contain any pictures outside of black-and-white copies of photo IDs.

Naya blinked down at the photo.

The colors were vivid. A crisp, cloudless blue sky and a flat verdant lawn that seemed to flow into the slice of ocean that peeked from behind a magnificent gray Colonial. It was perfect—like a picture that came with a new frame—complete with a family of four.

Naya couldn't take her eyes off the youngest man's face. Couldn't make her mind comprehend what she saw. She touched the round tip of her nose. The same nose she'd gotten from her father. The same nose she now looked at in the photo.

Yana picked up the disheveled, half-spilled file and sank

down on the floor next to Naya. "This is yours—Morgan, Naya—this is your file."

"And that's my dad," Naya croaked, unable to tear her gaze away. It all made sense now—she did look like the portrait of a young Seraphina Yates. She hadn't imagined it. "And there's Taylor's."

She pointed at the man next to the younger version of her father, their arms slung over each other's shoulders, grins lighting their faces. They didn't look alike, not really. Yes, they were the same height, both tall and in shape. But seeing the family of four together, it was clear that they each favored a parent—Taylor's dad was their father's twin, while Naya's resembled their mom.

"Hang on. Then your dad and Taylor's dad . . ." The unspoken words hung in the air.

Naya's eyes welled with fresh tears. This time, she couldn't hold them back. She blinked, and they spilled down her cheeks. "Our dads weren't on that helicopter just as pilot and student. They were brothers."

Why had her parents withheld that very pertinent information from her? Why had they chosen to struggle instead of living an easy life as a Yates descendant? Why, even after her father's death, had her mom kept his secret?

Naya clutched her chest, afraid that her heart would beat out of her ribs and fall to the floor.

"Whoa, whoa, whoa. What's going on?" A cry rang out as Gabe tried to sit up to get a better view of what they'd discovered.

Startled, Naya dropped the photo. It twirled in the air, landing face down in her lap.

Naya's mouth moved as though she were speaking, but it took Yana's hand on hers for her to realize she hadn't made a sound. She swallowed, tracing the names scrawled on the back of the photo in the same looping script as on the will and trust.

Richard Stewart and Seraphina Yates with sons Robert and Theodore. Yates family summer house, Martha's Vineyard.

Yana lifted herself back onto the couch and smoothed her hand against Gabe's sweaty forehead. "Rest."

"I can't," he whispered. "Naya's dad and Taylor's dad were brothers?" He settled back against the sweat-drenched pillow.

Naya swiped the tears from her cheeks and collected the photo of her father and his family. "Apparently. That's my dad." Her voice and hand trembled as she passed the photo to Gabe. "And that's their mom, Seraphina Yates."

Gabe squinted at the photo, his clammy fingers leaving smudge marks on its glossy surface. "Are you sure?"

"I'm sure I know what my dad looks like. Plus, it says on the back, *sons Robert and Theodore.*"

Yana pointed to Seraphina's note on the other side of the photo, adding, "Naya's dad's name was Robert."

Gabe handed the picture to Yana before taking a deep breath and meeting Naya's gaze. "I remember when your dad died," he said slowly. "My nana died around the same time. . . ."

Yana ran her finger over the image of Robert, her eyes sparkling with tears. Except at his funeral, the only other person Naya had seen cry over the loss of her father was her mom. After years of sadness, Naya had become numb to her mother's grief. Then, her mother had found Marcus. *They'd* found

281

Marcus. Naya would always miss her father, but having Marcus in her heart made it hurt a little less. Now, seeing Yana mourn her dad made it hurt all over again.

Yana sniffled and cleared her throat. "I need Taylor's file," she said, grabbing the handful of Taylor Stewart's paperwork Naya had yet to read through. She flipped through the pages and then surged to her feet, the papers containing Taylor's information floating to the floor like ash.

Yana held up Taylor's birth certificate with Theodore's name printed on it. "Taylor's the heiress."

With the changes of Seraphina's will and trust from her grand*child* to her grand*children*, Taylor had every reason to want Naya gone, and without a corpse there would be no way to prove she'd actually drowned.

Still, one question bubbled up from the hundred within Naya's brain—

Why did everyone else have to die?

Naya pushed it aside and pawed through her own documents, throwing out her grades and lists of academic achievements, a transcript of the interview she'd had with a member of the Yates Society before receiving the scholarship, and her SAT scores. Her fingers halted on a stapled bunch of papers. A copy of her learner's permit stared up at her. She flipped through the pages: Social Security card, school ID, passport, school photos, birth certificate—

Her heart froze in her chest as she studied the document she'd never seen before. She'd figured her mom had lost it. She'd been born in a different state as *Naya Rose Stewart*.

"I found it." Naya didn't recognize her own voice as she numbly flipped the page and surveyed the last two items. Ahead of her first birthday, her parents, Rose Amara Stewart and Robert Morgan Stewart had petitioned to change her name. Before they left Colorado, before they returned to Oklahoma, her parents had changed their surnames to Naya's mother's maiden name. Naya *Stewart* became Naya Morgan.

Naya held the papers out to her oldest friend, the one she'd need now more than ever if she hoped to stay alive long enough to break free from the web of deceit that clung to her family. "I'm the progeny. I'm a Yates."

THIRTY-SIX

YANA

5:03 A.M.

An hour later, Yana still couldn't believe their discovery.

Naya was a Yates. So was Taylor.

Since Amelia's file was devoid of any evidence that she was also a progeny, it was unlikely she was working with Taylor. She was probably still passed out inside the locked cabin where Yana and Naya had left her.

Yet there was a killer out there, dressed in black. And that meant only one thing: Taylor was alive. Somehow, she had faked her own death in order to throw them off. Neither Yana nor Brett had thought of this possibility. But maybe they should've. Out of all the deaths, only Taylor's appeared to be an accident, getting tangled in the rope as she descended into the ocean. What were the odds that an accidental death would occur in the midst of a murder spree? Very, very slim.

The revelations were enough to make Yana's head explode.

If and when they made it to safety, the police would be very interested in these files. But for the time being, their plan remained the same: sit tight until the yacht docked and try to survive.

Naya sat cross-legged on the shorter section of the L-shaped couch, deep in thought, one hand lying lightly on the ax handle. Yana had settled herself on the rug in front of Gabe, the pool cue balanced on her knees. In sleep, Gabe had tangled his fingers in her hair, as though to keep her near.

Yana straightened, gently dislodging Gabe's hand. The storm had ceased. The water no longer pummeled the windows, and the yacht bobbed peacefully in the ocean. The sky had lightened from an opaque black to a translucent navy. Many shades would remain until the sun rose in the sky, but the changing colors should've brought optimism. The docking hour approached quickly now.

Instead, the sky screamed apprehension. It was a little *too* calm. Too uneventful. Yana doubted that Taylor was also counting down the clock. The girl had drugged a crew and murdered at least five people. She would not leave her final act to chance.

A fish swam right up to the submerged windows, its cheeks puffing. Its iridescent scales might have been tinged purple. As Yana moved closer to investigate, the fish darted away.

Yana paused. Wait a minute. The fish *darted* away? But they were in the ocean, not an aquarium. No way could the fish's speed rival the yacht's . . .

. . . unless the yacht had stopped moving.

"Holy crap!" she exclaimed out loud. *That* was what had gotten her attention—the sudden drop in speed.

Naya startled. "What? What is it?" She raised the ax over her head, ready to strike.

"Whoa there, Jason Voorhees." Yana held up her hands. "The boat has stopped."

"What do you mean, *stopped*?" Naya frowned. "Can yachts do that?"

"If they drop anchor, sure."

"But that would mean—" Naya broke off, horrified.

"Yeah," Yana said grimly. "Your bestie's not letting us wait this one out. She's gearing up for a fight."

A few minutes later, Yana planted a final kiss on Gabe's cheek. Well, she also kissed his other cheek. And his forehead. And his lips—twice. She couldn't help it! There was no telling when she'd ever have the opportunity again.

"I should've gotten injured earlier," Gabe said, smiling through his ragged breathing.

"We'll be back for you," she said solemnly. "I promise."

"Um." Naya balanced the ax casually on her shoulder. "Not to interrupt again, but this could go on forever. And we don't have forever."

If they squinted, they could just make out an island in the distance, something that hadn't been possible a few hours ago. That's why Taylor dropped anchor, according to Gabe, who guessed that they might actually be close enough to reach land on a Jet Ski. And if not land, surely there would be causal boaters exploring the waters around Bermuda who would be able to help.

"Right." Yana was quite proud that she tore herself away from Gabe with only one final glance.

"I'll wait here," Gabe said.

"You don't have much choice."

"For you, Yana? I'll wait until my very last breath."

It was an echo from his earlier statement, in the library, when he was describing his persistence. It was a joke then, and it *should've* been a joke now. But too many dead bodies littered the ship. The words hit too close to the truth.

Yana turned before he could see the sheen in her eyes. She wouldn't say goodbye, damn it. Because this *wasn't* goodbye.

She and Naya crept back up the secret staircase and into the library. With any luck, Taylor had no idea that the passage existed. The barricade they had built against the game room door would hold.

Gabe would be safe.

Yana had to believe that. Taylor clearly didn't want Gabe. Her focus was on Naya. No doubt the rich girl would kill him, though, if she stumbled upon him. But in the last few hours, the wall of furniture had yet to budge. Taylor hadn't tried to seek them out. Yana would just have to hope and pray that remained the case.

"No emergency lights," Naya hissed in the near darkness as they exited the library. "That means she can't see us even if any cameras are functioning." Gabe thought he had destroyed them all, but they couldn't be certain.

The element of surprise was key. They needed time to wrestle the Jet Ski into the water and head toward shore, and help. It would be better if Taylor never realized they had left.

The girls groped their way to the beach club. The emergency lights had malfunctioned here as well, but they could see due to the open wall and the gradually brightening sky.

Yana's gaze bounced around the room, performing a quick inventory. A Jet Ski in the far corner. A camera in the ceiling, unfortunately too high for them to reach. The deflated inflatable slide littered the center of the room. Last night's storm had likely shifted it from its original position against the wall . . . a wall that was now revealed to hold an orange flare gun between a conspicuously empty hook and a long cord that had been cut at both ends.

"Why didn't you reveal yourself to us before?" she murmured as she picked up the flare gun. "We could've used your flame to signal that vessel."

There was no use for regrets, however. . . . especially because the weapon could aid them now. With the flare gun in her hands, Yana spun around so that she faced the entrance. She wasn't exactly sure how effective the flare gun would be when it came to self-defense. But flames had to be a credible threat, especially up close. Right?

The camera was functioning. If Taylor was watching the surveillance monitors from the wheelhouse, which was what Yana and Naya suspected, she would know exactly where they were and what they were doing. They had to be prepared for the worst.

"I'll guard the door," she told Naya. "You check out the Jet Ski."

Nodding, Naya walked briskly to the back corner, ax in hand. Yana's hands trembled; her breath shook. Adrenaline and hope pumped through her body. This was it. If their plan worked, they were getting off this yacht. They would be one step closer to saving Gabe and Amelia, to stopping Taylor. . . .

"We have a problem." Naya's grim voice punctured a hole in Yana's optimism.

"What's that?" Yana asked, ice gripping her core.

"The keys to the Jet Ski. They're missing. Taylor must've taken them."

THIRTY-SEVEN

NAYA

5:28 A.M.

Naya's heart sank and the hope that had propelled her forward died. Worse than that, it was now a weight holding her in place. She glanced at Yana, her friend's face pale in twilight's light-blue glow, crusted blood smudging her cheeks.

"The keys aren't anywhere. We're stuck." Naya sank onto the Jet Ski's vinyl seat and stared out at Bermuda, a mound of green and beige in the distance. She held out her hand, and her fingertips grazed the tips of the verdant vegetation. She had as much likelihood of actually reaching the island as she did the moon.

"There has to be something we can do," Yana said, her grip tight on the flare gun. In her rumpled, torn dress, she looked like a survivor. Naya supposed she was one. They both were. For now.

"Look around, Yana." Naya threw up her hands, motioning to the items in the beach club. "How are bodyboards, a deflated waterslide, and a flare gun going to get us to Bermuda?"

"You forgot the scuba gear in that corner." Yana pointed to the two buoyancy control vests, wet suits, regulators, and oxygen tanks.

Once more, hope swelled within Naya before popping like a balloon. Yes, she could scuba dive, and yes, she could use the gear to slip into the water and disappear from Taylor's murderous plot, but she couldn't remember the last time she had seen Yana swim, much less dive. Plus, even if she did decide to go by herself, there was no way she could make it all the way to the island. They needed the Jet Ski, or the tender, or anything with power.

When Naya didn't reply, Yana sighed, "I'm trying to stay positive."

"I know. I'm sorry. I just . . ." Naya kicked a bag of snorkel sets, her voice trailing off as the bag slid to the floor, uncovering a neon yellow water toy exactly like the one Taylor had at her lake house. Her former friend had called it a "mini Jet Ski," and as long as the Seabob was charged, it didn't need a key.

"I get it," Yana continued. "There are a lot of reasons to feel like we're doomed, but that energy won't help us. We need to come up with another plan."

"Yana . . ."

"What if we—" Yana wrinkled her nose and tapped her chin. "No, I guess that won't work."

"Yana . . ." Naya glanced up at the camera in the corner of the room above the scuba gear and turned so her back was to it.

"But what about—"

"Yana!"

She jumped and lifted the flare gun, ready for action.

Naya motioned for Yana to join her on the Jet Ski. "I know exactly what we should do."

~

Naya grunted as she and Yana carried the heavy water sled over the scuba gear they'd already moved into place on the platform. A couple of minutes ago, they had sent a flare up into the dawn sky, with a silent plea that it would be seen. That help would come. But they also needed to take action. They could no longer wait; Taylor might attack at any moment. Besides, what this long, hellish night had taught them was they couldn't expect aid from anyone else. They had to rely on themselves.

They set the Seabob in the water and Yana secured the bungee to one of the yacht's tie-offs as Naya stared out at the ocean, beyond aware of the camera watching them.

It was more beautiful with each minute of the sunrise. She just wished she had the luxury to appreciate it.

Naya cleared her throat and kicked off her sandals as she joined Yana on the platform next to the scuba gear. "As long as I don't take too long, Amelia will be fine. But Gabe, you have to protect him. Your future relationship status depends on it," she said, trying to inject a bit of levity into what might be their final conversation as she set the oxygen tank upright, slid the buoyancy control device over it, and secured the tank straps.

"Well, if my relationship status is at stake . . . ," Yana attempted to joke back. But the joke flopped as much as the regulator hose that dangled against her arm as she handed it to Naya.

With practiced ease, Naya removed the dust cap and attached the regulator to the oxygen tank before snapping the low-pressure inflator to the buoyancy control vest and putting her alternate air source within reach. Getting certified and going on murky Oklahoma lake dives with Taylor had been worth it. Naya double-checked her work. In order to save herself, Yana, Gabe, and Amelia, everything had to be perfect.

Yana swiped at a crusted stain on her dress and adjusted her ponytail. Who knew a little black dress could survive so much? "You know, I'm pretty sure Gabe would be lost without me."

Naya threw her arms around Yana. "I'm sure I would be lost without you." Her throat clogged with emotion, but she pushed through. This might be her last chance to tell Yana everything. "I never should have turned my back on you. Not to be popular. You were like my sister. You *are* and always have been. I love you, Yana."

Yana's shoulders shook, and she hiccuped back a sob. "I—I love you too, Naya."

They stood there for a moment, neither friend wanting to let go, neither friend wanting to say goodbye. They had a lot to catch up on, but time apart was nothing to a bond like this—a sisterhood.

"You should go," Yana said, giving Naya a final squeeze. "One of us has to get help."

Naya bent to pick up her vest and oxygen tank. "I refuse to say the g-word. No *goodbyes* coming from these lips."

Yana smiled and held out Naya's diving mask. "Well, now I have to survive. That superstition practically ensures it."

Naya slung a waterproof bag across her body, strapped herself in, and pulled the mask down over her face. "Thems the rules." She turned, and without looking back, jumped into the water and plunged into darkness.

THIRTY-EIGHT

YANA

5:45 A.M.

Yana stepped onto the main deck, gripping the ax. The teak floor had been scrubbed clean. The hot tub bubbled merrily, the water once again clear. Even the mermaid figurehead lifted her head proudly, devoid of blood, pointing toward land. Toward safety.

No Everly hanging from the spike of the crown. No Brett splayed in the center of the deck.

Yana supposed whatever story Taylor planned for the authorities would be more believable the less evidence there was. Taylor had been a busy—and very strong—girl. It had taken three of them to move Gabe. But their nemesis wouldn't have been concerned about further injuring the bodies. If she had been able to wedge a dolly below them, she could've carted them to the side of the yacht and rolled them under the guardrail and overboard.

No wonder she hadn't had time to try to find them.

Swallowing hard, Yana crept to the spot where Brett's body had once lain. Was it her imagination, or could she smell blood cutting through the lemony scent of the cleaning supplies? The wind whistled past her ears, and over the whoosh she heard a bird sing out to its friend.

Day was approaching. Finally.

She turned toward the wheelhouse, spreading her arms wide. Even if no functioning cameras remained, she should be visible to Taylor.

"Come out, Taylor!" Yana yelled, banking on the fact that Taylor was waiting, watching from above. This was Yana's opening salvo, the shot that would begin the ending of this war. "It's just you and me."

This deck was where everything had started—the place where every person on this yacht had gathered, for the safety meeting, for Derek's catastrophic toast. And this would be where it ended.

Naya was gone, Gabe indisposed. The crew and Amelia most certainly remained drugged and unconscious.

Yana was the last person standing. No one was going to wake up and rescue her. If she wanted to be saved, she would have to be her own hero.

"Naya took off," she called out. Taylor had to be within earshot by now. "She abandoned me, once again. She left me here to die! I've got no loyalty to her. I haven't had any for a very long time."

Yana wore a life vest—two in fact, one layered on top of the other. The very same ones that Brett and Gabe had left in the beach club when they'd discovered the line to the tender had been cut. No slasher-proof vests, these. But some protection was better than none.

She took a deep breath. "I know why you want to kill Naya. I even agree with you. Why should *Naya* get half of Seraphina's inheritance? She doesn't even know your grandmother!"

The column of Yana's throat *burned*, as though she had swallowed seawater. But she would not puke now. She refused. "In fact, I'll even help you. You've got the keys to the Jet Ski; I know which direction Naya was heading. We can go after her. If we get to her before she reaches the island, we can end this. The whole inheritance can be yours. You wouldn't even have to worry about me telling because I'd be guilty, too."

Was her speech working? Was Taylor even listening?

Doubt flooded Yana. Maybe they had been wrong. Maybe Taylor *had* been swept out to sea, and Yana was standing here, talking to herself. Hell, maybe the killer was still on board— a crew member, after all—and they were utterly uninterested in anything Yana had to bargain with. Maybe, after numerous trips catering to a bunch of wealthy, spoiled people, they had flipped. Maybe they would kill her on the spot, thinking she was like the others.

A bird swooped low overhead, and the yacht rocked, as though it were hit by an extremely strong current. Yana's stomach rumbled and more acid rushed up her throat. She was going to be sick at any moment.

The headlines would be epic, even though the true story would never be uncovered. *Teen Girl's Puke Allows Killer Slippery Escape.*

"Not much of a negotiator, are you?" Taylor strode onto the deck, and Yana's heartbeat kicked into high gear.

Her enemy wore head-to-toe black—black sweatpants,

black hooded sweatshirt, black gloves, black tennis shoes. She'd removed the mask. More importantly, she was pointing a speargun directly at Yana's chest, the arrow loaded and ready to fly. "I would've given you one mil, two mil, easy."

Yana lifted her chin. "I've never cared much about money."

"That's rich. Pun intended." Taylor laughed scathingly. "You don't care about money because you've never *had* it."

"Maybe," Yana conceded. "I only need enough to lead a comfortable life. I wouldn't know what to do with the excess."

"Believe me, *I* do. Someone's got to live a life of luxury." Taylor began to circle Yana, the speargun remaining at chest level. Her arm would get tired sometime. She couldn't hold it like that forever. Yana just had to keep her talking.

"What do you say? How about you and me go after Naya?" Yana flashed a bright, fake smile. "I'll even take the two million, if you're offering."

"No," Taylor said flatly. "Put down the ax."

Yana's mind whirled. No way did she want to part with her only weapon. But at this distance, her ax couldn't take on Taylor's speargun. The arrow would pierce her chest before Yana could ready her throw.

"We have to stop Naya," Yana said quickly. "If she reaches land, she'll contact the authorities—"

"So what? By then, you'll be dead. It will be my word against hers, you lonely, jealous, ragey outcast, you." Taylor continued to stalk around Yana. "I was so pissed about Everly giving you that late invitation to the society. But then I realized I could use it to my advantage and pin the murders on you. It's too bad the knife with your fingerprints flew overboard, but there's also the Rohypnol I hid in your bag."

"Nope." Satisfaction coursed through Yana. "I found the Rohypnol and I hid it in a different location."

Taylor blinked a few times, rattled, but then she pushed on. "You already fit the part. It's not such a stretch that you came onto this yacht to seek revenge against the people whom you've envied your entire life. My mom will back me up, everyone at the society. Hell, our entire high school will readily confirm that you've always been an unstable, pukey pathetic loser."

The panic burned, hot and desperate, in Yana's throat. "They'll never believe you."

"People will believe anything if you pay them enough." Taylor tossed back her hair. "I'm the heir to the Yates fortune. Naya is a nobody, no matter what her birth certificate might say. Now put. Down. That. Ax."

Yana held one hand up and slowly bent, placing the ax on the deck.

"Kick it over here."

With the weakest effort possible, Yana sent the ax a few feet away from her—and a half a deck away from Taylor. Before Taylor could protest, Yana held up both hands and backed away. "I'm not your enemy."

"Aren't you?" Taylor's nostrils flared. "Ever since you stepped foot on this yacht, you've been snooping around, trying to find evidence to bring down me and my friends. I read your little notebook. You suspected all of us. Is that any way to treat your society sisters?"

So that's where her notebook went. Sure, it was a small transgression, compared to Taylor's other major life violations. But it was yet another layer of pain. "It beats killing them," Yana said, struggling to sound casual. "Is that how you treat your friends? Glad I never got close enough to enjoy the privilege."

"Shut up!" Taylor shrieked, her eyes wild. "I didn't want to kill all of them. In an ideal scenario, only Naya would have died under mysterious circumstances." She panted, as though her windpipe were blocked by remorse. (Guilt? Grief? Regret? What sorts of emotions did serial murderers feel?) "The others were . . . casualties. They left me no choice but to kill them."

So, she thought both Gabe and Amelia were dead? Relief flowed through Yana. Maybe that meant Taylor wouldn't go after them. Maybe they would have a chance to survive, no matter what happened to her and Naya.

Taylor's arm trembled. Yana's chance would be coming soon. "If anything, all of these deaths are Naya's fault. If she had just died when I tried to suffocate her with the curtain, before Everly's big meeting, none of this would have happened."

Yana inched forward, closer to the ax, while she locked her gaze on Taylor's face. "I'm sure you had a very good reason for what you did," she said soothingly.

"I did!" Taylor exclaimed. The speargun lowered an inch.

This was what Taylor needed. A cheerleader by her side, an audience to witness her cleverness. It must've killed her these last few hours, making these big moves without anyone around to admire them.

"You were brilliant, really," Yana said. "You had us terrified and completely baffled. We couldn't imagine *why* anyone would kill all those people."

Taylor's lips curved. She shifted the speargun from her right hand to her left, shaking out her tired arm—which meant that she was a little more relaxed. Taylor *wanted* to talk about her exploits. Yana just had to give her an opening.

"Could you explain?" Yana asked. "The journalist in me is dying to understand your story. And if you're going to kill me anyways, then it won't matter."

Taylor lowered her arm, so that the weapon was pointed at a forty-five-degree angle. Either she was less proficient with her left hand, or she was distracted. Hopefully both.

"It started with Naya and spiraled outward from there," Taylor confided. "Mom and I saw a copy of Grandma Seraphina's will the morning of prom. She had long since promised her estate to me—her only surviving heir—and when Mom saw the new wording, she panicked. You see, she knew a secret that no one else did, that Robert, my grandmother's estranged son, had a daughter. And that daughter was Naya."

Yana took another infinitesimal step toward the ax. The speargun lowered a few more degrees.

"I was shocked, of course," Taylor continued. "I had *no* idea Naya and I were related, much less cousins. Maybe that explains why we connected so deeply," she mused. Grief crossed her features but only for a moment. "And so, for obvious reasons, we had to get rid of her.

"Mom and I consumed a couple bottles of Dom that afternoon—we'd just lost half our fortune, after all. And then I went to prom and got even more wasted. I *might've* sorta possibly told Ev about Naya. I'm not sure. That night's such a blur." She moved her shoulders delicately. "I couldn't risk her spilling our secret. Especially when she started parading around the yacht, threatening to blab about her life-changing secret. She even wrote a post for *Rumor Has It* alluding to it! The silly girl had me editing all of her articles. It was a message to me, *threatening* me. Nobody gets away with that. The only favor she ever did me was going along with my suggestion that she was a Yates. Kept me from having to answer any pesky questions. And, Finn, well, I loved him. I really did. But I think he overheard Ev and me whispering at prom, and he was acting so weird after her death."

She shook her head. "I wished he hadn't said that bit about how Everly was killed because she had a big secret. That proved he couldn't be trusted. I knew he only stayed with me because of my money, but that meant he should've toed the line—not allude, however subtly, to the fact that he knew about Seraphina's inheritance. That's why I killed him with the chandelier that was meant for Naya." Resignation filled her voice. "It didn't have to be that way. We were the perfect couple. He was so obedient. You know, he even got rid of the hedge clippers that I used to cut through most of the chandelier chain, just because I asked. The very same chandelier that eventually ended him. That's poetic justice for you."

Yana gaped, her attention ripped from the ax only two feet away. Not a sliver of remorse shaded Taylor's words as she talked about her dead boyfriend. "What about the others?" she asked quickly.

Taylor frowned, a crease between her brows. "Nobody else was supposed to get hurt. Mom and I agreed that Everly and Finn might have to be casualties, because of my slipup at prom. Any more than three, and this case would escalate to national news."

"Makes sense." Yana bobbed her head sarcastically. "Four deaths would've crossed the line, but three is *totally* reasonable."

Taylor ignored her. "Derek. Poor lovesick, spineless Derek.

Who knew he would turn out to be such a predator?" She shook her head in disgust. "I blackmailed him into drugging the crew, and I wasn't even worried about him keeping my secret since he had already risked his college and professional career by helping us cheat. Not to mention the fact that he became my de facto accomplice. But Creepo decided to use the date rape drug on Amelia, too. I walked in just as he was about to get cozy with her unconscious body. I had no choice but to knife him in the back."

Her eyes glittered. "You see? I'm a good person. I protect the people I love. I even loved Naya, like a dear, dear sister. I just love myself more."

Chills ran up Yana's spine. Taylor actually believed what she was saying. "And the guys?" Taylor looked off to the side, and Yana advanced an entire foot. The ax was just within reach now. She bent her knees, ever so slowly.

"Étienne and Gabe," Taylor mused. "Now, those *were* unfortunate accidents, especially since I brought Étienne along to make Naya's last moments the happiest they could be. I didn't mean to kill him. I told you, I'm a good person." She paused, as if waiting for Yana to agree. She didn't but nodded anyway.

"Of course, I had no idea Étienne got off on being such a hero, and Gabe, well"—she shrugged delicately—"not my fault he didn't have quick enough reflexes to duck."

Yana's anger flared, but she quickly reined it in. "Brett?"

Taylor sighed. "I'm most bummed about Brett. He cracked me up. But he was too keen on playing detective. Just like you." Suddenly, Taylor raised the speargun again.

Yana dove for the ax, but Taylor was quicker. Pain exploded in Yana's thigh, and she collapsed to the floor. She took a second to recover, only a second, but Taylor raced to the ax and kicked it. The ax spun across the deck . . . and lodged in the crevice between teakwood flooring and wall.

"Maybe I should've played soccer," Taylor said, pleased with herself. She marched to the ax, grasped the haft, and pulled. The wooden handle came off in her hands, the blade firmly stuck in the crevice.

A slow grin crossed her face, as though she was just realizing that the weapon was now useless. "And you." She dropped the handle and seized the speargun once more. "Maybe *you* should've minded your own business."

"I have more questions," Yana pleaded. "There's so much I don't understand."

"Enough talking," Taylor said icily. "Better pray to whichever god you worship."

Yana squeezed her eyes shut. Her mouth was bone dry, and no wonder. Sweat drenched her entire body. There wasn't a drop of moisture left to wet her lips. They'd . . . miscalculated, once again. It was a good plan, the only viable plan. Too bad it hadn't worked.

Dear pra Buddha cho, Yana prayed. *Save me. I'm not done with this life. I have so much merit left to make. I've only just learned how to let down my walls, how to allow people in. I've only just learned how to love, fully and without holding back. Please. If you save me, I will do so much good in this world. I'll—*

"Drop the weapon, Taylor. It's over."

Yana's eyes flew open. *That was fast, pra Buddha cho, thank you.* An angel stood before her, dripping wet, a flare gun pressed into Taylor's back.

Naya had returned, with a glint in her eye.

THIRTY-NINE

NAYA

5:52 A.M.

Naya could only hear the hiss of air and release of bubbles as she guided the Seabob through the crystal blue water. No more pulse in her ears or fear pricking her spine. She was cocooned in the warm waters of the Atlantic, flying behind the water sled. A sense of peace came over her knowing that this was their last shot.

Que será, será.

Naya finished her second underwater loop around the megayacht. Lazy angelfish and parrotfish scattered, their iridescent scales shimmering blue and yellow in the clear water, a small glimpse of what this trip could have been if not for her murderous newfound cousin.

She slowed the sled as she approached the beach club and adjusted the waterproof bag she'd clipped to her gear.

She didn't bother to secure the Seabob to the boat. Instead, she released it and swam the rest of the way to the platform. Slowly, she emerged from the waves and lifted her dive mask. The beach club was empty. With any luck, so too was the wheelhouse.

At this very moment, Yana would be on the main deck, luring Taylor away from her hiding space, away from the camera that looked out onto the beach club.

Still in the water, Naya set the waterproof bag that held the all-important flare gun on the platform before unclipping her gear and shrugging out of it.

Naya lifted herself out of the Atlantic and crouched next to her discarded sandals. She didn't have time to wait, didn't have time to think. She and Yana had discussed their only option; now it was time for Naya to do her part.

She grabbed the loaded flare gun's black and orange handle and crept toward the stairs that would take her to the main deck. She stayed low, nearly crawling on her hands and knees up the final steps.

Taylor's back was to Naya, her arm extended, speargun aimed at Yana.

Yana held up her hands. "I have more questions. There's so much I don't understand."

"Enough talking," Taylor ground out. "Better pray to whichever god you worship."

It was now or never.

On silent feet, Naya ran up behind Taylor and pressed the tip of the flare gun between her shoulder blades. "Drop the weapon, Taylor. It's over."

Taylor stiffened but kept the speargun pointed at Yana. *"Cousin,"* she seethed. "So nice of you to join us."

Naya dragged the plastic barrel down Taylor's back, stopping just above the waistband of her sweatpants. If she fired now, would the flame cut through Taylor's stomach the same way the spear had pierced Étienne's?

"Drop it," Naya repeated, stepping closer, digging the barrel of the flare gun into Taylor's sweatshirt.

With a hiss of pain, Taylor jerked and yanked her elbow to her side. She hadn't dropped her weapon, but at least it was no longer pointed at Yana.

"You're going to have to kill me."

Before she could think of a reason not to, Naya squeezed the trigger.

Taylor sucked in a breath and then released it in a wave of laughter. "You don't just point and shoot. There's more to it than that."

Shit.

Naya stumbled backward, her body going cold as Taylor spun around. Naya's gaze found Yana's, and a silent *I'm sorry* passed between her lips.

"Guess I'm lucky I never taught you how to shoot a flare," Taylor said, leveling the speargun at Naya.

Naya's hands shook as she tried to pull back the flare gun's hammer. It wouldn't budge, as cemented in place as the fear in her chest. "I tried to take you out quickly by suffocating you with the curtains. But you're like a cockroach, Naya. You just won't die." Taylor set her jaw, green gaze beaming. "My mother was right. You need to be shown your place."

Naya's thoughts flew to Yana, to what her friend would do, to how she'd survive.

In for four . . . She took a deep breath, her fingers searching the sides of the plastic flare gun. *Out for four* . . .

With Taylor aiming the speargun at Naya, the point of the arrow was an unblinking eye that saw through to her very soul. "Get down on your knees, dear cousin."

FORTY

YANA

5:58 A.M.

Taylor lowered the speargun until the tip pressed against Naya's forehead. "I'm sorry to see you go," she said. "You were a good friend. The best a girl could ask for."

Naya flattened her lips, refusing to respond, to return the sentiment. That apathy, to Taylor, would be worse than any insult.

Sure enough, Taylor narrowed her eyes. "Nothing to say, Naya? Don't you like your second surprise? You know. The one I mentioned at the beginning of our trip?"

Naya's eyes remained wide open. She looked directly at Yana, her gaze steady and loving. They never needed words to communicate, and even after so many years apart, the message beaming from her eyes was clear. *If these are my final moments, I'm glad we were able to reconnect.*

But goodbye didn't sit well with Yana.

"Naya is *my* best friend, damn it." She lunged forward, keeping her body low to the ground, and smashed into Taylor's calves.

They both fell, the speargun flying out of Taylor's hand as her knuckles banged against the deck. The two of them rolled, and an object shot out of Taylor's pocket, but before Yana could identify it, Taylor shoved her hand up and against Yana's jaw, pressing her face to the deck.

Yana brought up one knee, catching Taylor in the stomach. The pressure against her jaw slackened, and she scrabbled to her hands and knees. The speargun was three feet away.

She reached for it, but more than a hundred pounds crashed into her lower body, flattening her. An instant later, her head was yanked back by her hair, and pain erupted.

Yana bucked wildly, rage fueling her muscles. She managed to dislodge Taylor and flipped over so that she could launch her attack—but her enemy was rageful, too.

Pro: Taylor's anger had distracted her enough that Yana had been able to knock the speargun from her hands.

Con: This temper also made her freakishly strong.

Taylor straddled Yana, pinning her shoulders down with her forearms. She then wrapped her hands around Yana's neck and squeezed. And squeezed. And squeezed some more.

Yana clawed at Taylor's hands, but she dug her nails more firmly into Yana's skin. There was no budging those talons. Yana continued to fight, angling for a better grasp, attacking each finger at a time.

But her energy was sapping. Her vision blackened around the edges.

Must. Breathe.

She couldn't see, couldn't think. Her chest burned, and her entire being was one white-hot flash of pain.

This was it. The end of her life. Taylor had won.

A loud *pop* pierced the air, and suddenly Yana was gulping oxygen. She could only inhale tiny, shallow sips, but that was okay. That was enough.

An eternal moment passed, and then awareness returned. Her ears rang and her throat was on fire. A drop of sweat rolled down her forehead and plopped onto the teak floor.

Blood. There was blood. Lots of it.

Yana lifted her head.

Naya had crumpled to the floor, one hand curled around the speargun, sobbing and laughing. Grief and relief.

Next to them lay Taylor. Her limbs were twisted at awkward angles; blood covered her blond hair. The one eye that peeked out from all that hair was staring, empty and . . .

Dead.

The nightmare was finally over. Taylor was dead.

FORTY-ONE

YANA

8:37 A.M.

The helicopter rose from the makeshift helipad on the main deck. Yana pressed her face against the window, her headset banging against the glass. The sleek and majestic *Seraphina* got smaller and smaller, until the white vessel bore a startling resemblance to her brother's old Legos.

As she watched, the megayacht started to move, slicing through the impossibly blue waters toward Bermuda. Its decks crawled with Coast Guardsmen, paramedics, and even a couple of detectives. More police waited on land.

Cool fingers laced through Yana's, and she looked up into Naya's warm brown eyes.

"You doing okay?" she asked, that oh-so-familiar voice echoing through the headset against the dull roar of the helicopter rotors.

Yana nodded. Her throat still hurt like it had been crushed by a demon—or, excuse her, *Taylor*, which was pretty much the same thing. But the paramedics had declared her vitals stable, which was why she sat in the middle passenger row with Naya and Amelia, instead of in the back with Gabe.

She peeked over her shoulder. Gabe lay on a stretcher, with a paramedic hovering over him. Tubes of every size sprouted from his body and connected to machines. But despite the oxygen mask covering his face, and his paler-than-usual skin, he looked good.

More than good.

Gabe turned his head, as though sensing her gaze. Their eyes locked, and he smiled—or at least tried to. The oxygen mask distorted his lips and blocked off the curves of his mouth. Instead, he lifted the hand *not* attached to the IV and formed a reverse *C,* with his index finger crooked and his thumb pointing down.

Yana squinted. What was he doing?

"It's half of a heart," Naya said into her headset. "Since he can't use his other hand. Make the other half."

Twisting awkwardly in her seat, Yana formed a forward-facing *C.* Her muscles screamed, but her heart sloshed. Which, Yana decided, more or less canceled out the pain.

Gabe winked—the only other action he could comfortably perform—and Yana turned back around. Her lips felt permanently curved.

"That's the corniest thing I've ever seen." Amelia's tired voice sounded through the headset. "But after all this drama, I'll take some corn. Pass the butter."

Amelia sat on Naya's other side. More accurately, she huddled under a blanket, knees pulled up to her chest, cheek resting on knees. She had stirred just as the paramedics were moving her onto a stretcher. Like the crew, she had passed out before Everly's body had been discovered—and thus missed the entire nightmare.

News of the multiple deaths of her friends and the college boy she was sorta dating had shocked her into silence.

Naya picked up Amelia's hand, too, so that the three of them were physically linked.

"You're safe, Mel. That's what matters."

"I'm so very sorry about Étienne. Words can't say how sorry," Amelia responded.

Yana licked her parched lips. At great cost, she'd learned how to be vulnerable on this so-called celebratory cruise. If she didn't implement these lessons, then Taylor would win, albeit a small victory. Yana refused to let the haters change who she was, ever again.

"I know it's not the same," she began, well aware that Amelia was also on the channel. "But as your friend, and your true sister, I want you to know that I love you unequivocally. I've never stopped."

The tears dripped onto Naya's face now, but she managed to smile. "Same. Why do you think I packed these bulky things in my unfairly limited luggage space?"

She pulled a stack of blue-rimmed plastic from her suitcase, and Yana burst out laughing. A thousand razor blades attacked her throat, but she didn't care. Disposable vomit bags. Yana used to carry them in her backpack before she learned how to control her pukey reaction to stress. Naya had always tucked one or two in *her* bag, too, just in case.

"What on earth?" Amelia asked.

"Inside joke," Yana and Naya said in unison, and then exchanged mischievous grins.

At that moment, static crackled on their headsets as the

pilot switched onto their channel. "Hate to interrupt, but I've just received a message that a nearby yacht found a guy floating in the water, a spear in his hip. The captain says that the current washed him right up against their swim deck. The kid's got a French accent, and his name's . . . Ethan? Is that right? Any of that sound familiar?"

"Étienne!" Naya practically leaped out of her seat. "Is he alive?"

"Yes, but he's pretty banged up," the pilot said. "And of course, there's the wound to contend with. But the doc says he's going to be okay. He was airlifted to a Bermuda hospital hours ago."

Naya screamed so loudly it would've cut through the whirling of the rotors even without the headsets. As it was, Yana and Amelia—and probably the pilot—winced, as Yana's eardrums rang a second time.

Unimportant.

Yana mentally wrote the headline:

In Shocking Rescue, Love of Naya's Life Found in Atlantic Ocean, Alive!

SIX WEEKS LATER . . .

EPILOGUE

NAYA

There's nothing in the world so demoralizing as money.

Naya ran her fingers along the words branded into her late father's journal.

"I think of Robert every day." Seraphina folded her hands on top of the crisp white blanket that her nurse had wrapped around her legs. "I know him better now, through his written words"—she paused and gave a shaky nod toward the journal she'd passed to Naya—"than I ever did when he was breathing. I suppose that is what I get for abandoning my son and siding with his father. But he's gone now. They both are."

Despair settled in the room as real and tangible as the leather-bound journal Naya clutched to her chest.

Tears fell from Seraphina's blue eyes, deep and fathomless, just like Naya's father's. She reached for her handkerchief with a trembling hand, knuckles gnarled and knobby as tree roots. "I don't deserve your forgiveness, but I hope you can forgive your father for keeping so many secrets. He was trying to provide you with the protection I did not offer him."

Naya's mouth was dry, her tongue glued to its roof. She could count on one hand the number of times she'd been in Seraphina's presence since returning from her harrowing trip at sea. At home, her mother had finally been honest with her. Now, for the first time in her entire life, she knew the truth of who she was and why her father had cut ties with the Stewart name and the Yates fortune. A wealthy white man marrying a middle-class Black woman in Oklahoma twenty years ago was not an ideal narrative for the Yates. According to her mom, they'd only returned to Yatesville so Naya could be close to the maternal side of the family. With how secretive the Yates family was about their lineage and the hate and shame her paternal grandparents felt about their son's life choices, Naya's mom and dad didn't expect the truth to be uncovered.

As Naya sat next to Seraphina, her high cheekbones, round nose, and hooded eyes so much like her father's, she couldn't help but guard her heart. She didn't know if her paternal grandmother disliked her mom. She didn't know how Seraphina felt about Naya picking up the Yates torch and fortune.

In truth, Naya didn't want to know. What Seraphina Yates thought of her and the fact that her grandmother had had a sudden crisis of conscience when she'd realized she was nearing the end of her life bore no weight on the rest of Naya's.

"Thank you for the journal."

The wrinkles surrounding Seraphina's lips deepened with a smile. "And thank you for allowing me to bring your family and friends to Antibes. This will be my last summer here in France and your first. It is nice to see it so full of life."

They settled into a comfortable silence, both taking in the blues, purples, and whites of the expansive garden and the soft beige of the French limestone that yawned around the shimmering pool.

Yana and Gabe were tangled together on a chaise stretched out next to the pool under a navy-and-white-striped umbrella, while Adisorn and his boyfriend, Blake, splashed in the pool.

Someday soon, this and more will be mine. The thought made Naya's stomach clench.

She'd wanted to become a doctor to help people. Now she wasn't so sure that's how she should go about it. She'd seen enough death and didn't want to witness more. With the Yates fortune came the opportunity to give back and help the world in ways she'd never imagined.

Étienne emerged from the pool house across from the garden, two glasses of lemonade in one hand, and waved to Naya and Seraphina with the other.

"Go. Be with your friends," Seraphina said, patting Naya's arm. "Don't let an old woman hold you back."

Naya left Seraphina in the grand sitting room that surveyed the French villa's backyard. Being here was so much different from being at home. Everything involving the Yates was sterile and calculated and . . . smothering. She wouldn't have been able to stand this trip if not for her family, friends, and Yana. As long as she had her best friend—her sister—she was never too far from home.

Naya descended the limestone stairs, her bathing suit

cover-up twirling around her legs in the breeze drifting off the Mediterranean Sea.

Étienne met her at the bottom of the steps and handed her a cold glass of lemonade. "Beautiful, as always," he said, and pressed a kiss to her temple. He'd started weekly sessions with a psychologist to deal with his kleptomania, and the healing he'd already experienced made him seem lighter . . . taller.

While Yana and Gabe would head off to Northwestern in a few weeks, Naya and Étienne were still making plans. She'd deferred enrollment at Johns Hopkins. She needed to pause and reassess her future. She wasn't ready to map out her whole life, not quite yet, but she also wasn't ready to say goodbye to Étienne.

Yana's phone trilled in the distance, and she and Gabe sat up, motioning for the other couple to join them.

"How are my favorite people?" Amelia squealed on the other end as Naya and Étienne huddled behind Gabe and Yana to fit into the screen. She sported a pixie cut and nose ring that would have made the Amelia of the past gasp in horror but suited her so well, it was difficult to remember what she'd looked like before them.

"Are you boys all healed?"

"Yep. Got a gnarly scar to prove it." Gabe pulled down the collar of his shirt, showing off his battle wound.

"And I have two." Étienne lifted the side of his shirt, revealing a glimpse of his toned core and the pink scar that bloomed like a flower against his side before turning around to show a matching blemish on his back. "Doctor said that if I'd been hit a few centimeters over, I wouldn't be here today."

"I'm so glad you are," Naya said, leaning over to kiss his cheek.

"By the way, Yana . . . Laurie Stewart's arraignment is today," Amelia said, eyes wide with anticipation.

Taylor's mom.

Naya had chosen not to pay attention to the news or follow the case. While they were in France, relaxing and continuing to heal, she and Yana had agreed they would stay off news apps and sites. It seemed like they should have also included video calls on the list.

"I'll draft the article and send it to you," Amelia continued. "I don't want to embarrass either of us in front of your editor."

Naya settled her hands on her hips. "I thought we were staying *away* from the news."

Yana hiked one shoulder, her cheek lifting in a lopsided grin. "Mel's doing me a favor as a freelancer. I can't be at the arraignment, but reporting about it is part of my *Yatesville Sun* intern duties."

"And I'm an excellent notetaker," Amelia chimed in. "This real-life experience is actually better than Harvard would've been."

After all that had occurred, Yana never published her exposé about the cheating ring. But Amelia had come clean to Harvard herself, and the university rescinded her acceptance. It turned out, she hadn't wanted to attend as much as her parents' egos wanted her to and was relieved to take the gap year. If she wasn't happy yet, it was good to see her on her way to peace.

A shout sounded in the background, and Amelia rolled

her eyes. "It's my sister," she groaned. "I have to go. Don't forget to send me pics. Miss you. Miss you. Miss you," she said, and blew a kiss to the camera before ending the call.

"Hey, Étienne." Gabe jumped up from the chaise and twisted his beach towel. "You finally ready to learn how to swim?" he asked, snapping the towel in Étienne's direction.

Étienne pulled off his shirt and dropped it next to Naya. "I can float. I think that is enough."

The two took off, joining Adisorn and Blake in the shallow end of the pool.

"Now that they're gone . . ." Yana lifted her sunglasses and placed them on top of her head. "How's it been sleeping under the same roof as Étienne?"

Naya's face flamed as she sat down next to her friend. "There hasn't actually been that much sleeping."

Yana squealed, and the two of them burst into laughter when the four boys turned to stare.

They both relaxed against the chaise, Yana's gaze softening. "And how's everything else? How are you?"

Naya shrugged. "Finally clawing my way out of all these secrets," she said, her attention settling on the journal.

"You think Seraphina feels any kind of guilt for keeping her family so under wraps and setting off the trip from hell?"

"I don't know if she's truly capable of feeling bad for anyone except herself. And I'm sure her estrangement with my father isn't her only secret." Naya set her lemonade on the side table and trailed her fingers along the lines of condensation sliding down the glass. "But that ends with me. From here on out, no more secrets."

"Oh, good," Yana said, pulling her towel up over her legs. "I wouldn't want to have to fight you again."

"Because you know you would lose." Naya flexed and mimed kissing each of her biceps.

"Hey, kids!" Her mom and Auntie Ae waved from the balcony that looked out over the pool. "We just got back."

Auntie Ae adjusted the floppy sun hat that matched Rose's. "We're going to get changed, then get something to eat. Want to come?"

Their moms had gone everywhere together and had been super cute ever since arriving in Antibes. It seemed that Naya and Yana's falling out had affected other people too.

Marcus and Yana's dad, Uncle Seng, came out of the house, flanking their wives in their jewel-toned sarongs.

Marcus held out his hands and did a little spin, modeling the only button-down Naya had seen him wear since he'd married her mom.

Yana laughed and pointed to her dad as he dramatically brushed his shoulders off and smoothed down the front of his equally fancy shirt.

"Looking dapper!" Yana called.

"Your dad and I saw a flyer for a sunset cruise," Marcus said, his brows lifting with excitement. "We should all go!"

Naya and Yana shared a glance that screamed, *Hard pass!* But before they could share the sentiment out loud, their moms erupted with their own arguments.

Rose took off her hat and swatted Marcus in the chest. "They don't want to go on a boat!"

Auntie Ae threw her hands in the air. "The point of this vacation is to *heal* from their trauma, not relive it."

"We're leaving for dinner in half an hour," Rose called, as she and Auntie Ae pushed their partners back inside and closed the sliding glass door behind them.

Naya and Yana glanced at each other and, for the second time, exploded into giggles.

"To be honest," Yana said, wiping tears from the corners of her eyes. "I would be okay never touching the ocean ever again."

Gabe lifted himself out of the pool and tore Yana's towel off her lap. "What about pool water?"

She shrieked in mock protest as he scooped her up, threw her into the pool, and jumped in after her.

Naya set aside her father's journal and slipped out of her cover-up. She waded into the water and smiled at Étienne as she joined him on the back of a giant inflatable swan. It rocked wildly under the uneven weight. She held on to Étienne and squealed with laughter. After all, Naya had proved she and Yana could handle getting a little seasick.

AUTHORS' NOTE

As a biracial Black author and a Thai American author, we are excited to share this story of two teenage girls of color who grew up in the Midwest. Our own childhood experiences in Oklahoma and Kansas have shaped us as writers and individuals. Without them, we would not have been able to write *Seasick*.

For Kristin, being biracial—identifying as both Black and white—has been a constant struggle of being ostracized for not being fully one race and not knowing where she fits in. Growing up in Oklahoma, which is not known for its diversity, she dealt with questions of belonging and acceptance. In *Seasick*, Naya's internal conflicts and triumphs echo Kristin's own journey as she and Pintip explore the strength that comes from embracing all parts of oneself.

Pintip's experience as a Thai American in Kansas offered similar, but distinct challenges. Mocked for her name, embarrassed by her uncommon features, she never forgot for a moment that she was *other*. Now, Pintip draws from her rich cultural background in order to create her stories. In *Seasick*, she weaves glimpses of her Thai heritage into the action-packed narrative. Through Yana, she and Kristin seek to encourage readers to be proud of their roots.

Seasick is a story that celebrates the power of friendship, the importance of diverse voices, and the need for unity. Together, we have poured our hearts into crafting this thrilling tale, drawing on our personal experiences to bring truth and depth to our characters' emotions.

Thanks for sailing with us on this gripping cruise at sea, and we hope that Naya's and Yana's voyages mirror the voyages of our readers—one of self-discovery, acceptance, and, ultimately, joy. May we all live our authentic selves!

With love and gratitude,
Kristin & Pintip

ACKNOWLEDGMENTS

First and foremost, we'd love to thank our editor, Bria Ragin, who was passionate about *Seasick* from the very beginning. We appreciate your guidance, your excitement, your time, and the lengths you go to, to raise the voices of other POC.

Writing a book takes an entire team, and we're fortunate to work with some of the most talented humans in publishing. A huge thanks to Liz Dresner, Ken Crossland, Lydia Gregovic, Alison Kolani, Colleen Fellingham, Shameiza Ally, Wendy Loggia, Beverly Horowitz, and Barbara Marcus.

Much gratitude to our amazing agents, Kate Schafer Testerman and Steven Salpeter, for always believing in us. We look forward to the years ahead!

Sending so much love to Brooke, our first reader and biggest cheerleader. Our best writing retreats are yet to come!

Kristin: Douglas, there aren't enough words to thank you for all you do. I love you.

Thank you to Emily, Dawn, Gretchen, and Cheroka. It's so weird to have this many friends. I love, admire, and am grateful for each of you.

Thank you, Phyllis, mostly because I don't want you to

whine at me about being omitted from my acknowledgments.

And, finally, to my coauthor, Pintip. Thank you for teaching me how to write a thriller.

Pintip: To the Hompluems, the Dunns, and P. Noi, I still stand by my claim that I have the best family on the planet.

Thank you to my four A's—Antoine, Aksara, Atikan, Adisai. You are the breath and joy of my life.

My gratitude is always to my writing sisters—Darcy, Brenda, Denny, Vanessa, and Meg—who are unequivocally on my side.

Last but never least, to Kristin. Who knew that we share the same brain? I've never had so much fun writing a novel!

ABOUT THE AUTHORS

Kristin Cast is a neurodivergent author who was born on an air force base in Japan and grew up in Oklahoma, where she explored everything from tattoo modeling to broadcast journalism. After battling addiction, Kristin made her way to the Pacific Northwest and landed in Portland. In the PNW, she rediscovered her passion for storytelling in the stacks at dusty bookstores and in the rickety chairs in old coffee shops.

kcastauthor.com

Pintip Dunn, a first-generation Thai American, grew up in a tiny town in Kansas, before she went on to graduate with a BA from Harvard University, magna cum laude, and to receive her JD at Yale Law School. She is obsessed with penguins, and her childhood dream was to marry someone whose last name is Gwynn—so that her name could be "Pin Gwynn." Alas, she got stuck with Dunn instead, but her husband and three children are worth the sacrifice.

pintipdunn.com